DANIELLE,

HOPE YOU ENJOY!

THANKS FOR BUYING!

Kate Sander

KATE SANDER

Force
Book Two of the Zoya Chronicles

Kate Sander

KATE SANDER

ISBN-13: 978-0994968036
ISBN-10: 0994968035

PRAISE FOR THE ZOYA CHRONICLES

"Overall, Pulse is a well-written story that deserves praise. It is full of seemingly-real characters, intrigue and back stabbing. Sander has written a great novel that is comparable to the action and strength of the Game of Thrones and Hunger Games series but stands on its own for its creativity and execution."

- Originally critiqued by a member of the Authors Talk About It team

"Kate Sander's PULSE, the first in a series called The Zoya Chronicles, is quite an interesting experiment, a book in which characters from several different worlds interconnect, and the results are surprising... Sander is doing something rather risky here in having so many characters and timeframes, etc., and she wisely chooses to structure the novel into chapters bearing the primary character's name, just to help us keep track—otherwise, I think we might very well be lost. For the most part, the novel is nicely written, and there's a strong visual quality to her writing—so much so that the book might work quite well as a screenplay... It's to her credit that the book, complex as it is, moves as smoothly as it does, and it's evident that she has a great deal of talent. I imagine the series having a lot of appeal to readers of science fiction."

- Judge, 24th Annual Writer's Digest Self-Published Book Awards

OTHER BOOKS BY KATE SANDER

THE ZOYA CHRONICLES

BOOK ONE: *Pulse*

BOOK TWO: *Force*

KATE SANDER

DEDICATION

This one is for my husband, Aaron.

He may never read my books, but he knows the plot for all of them.

KATE SANDER

CONTENTS

PROLOGUE - TORY

Tory watched her best friend die.

Before Tory could say anything, Senka rushed past her and launched herself off the cliff. Tory could only shake her head. Only Senka would take a fifty-foot dive head first and smile. Senka's swords found a gap in the nearest Sun God's armour and she tore his throat out of the back of his neck, breaking her fall. She leapt up and cut and weaved through the stunned Sun Gods, dancing and killing.

Tory wrenched her eyes away. She wanted to protect Senka but she had a job to do.

"ATTACK!" she yelled, voice carrying to the Melanthios, her people, lining the cliffs around her. They were ready to spring the trap on the unsuspecting Sun Gods in the valley below. "FIRE!" the archers listened without hesitation. The Melanthios were outnumbered ten to one but the trap Senka had devised gave them a slim chance at victory.

Ladders were thrown down from the cliffs to the valley.

The archers let loose a volley of arrows. The Sun Gods gave a cry of their own. The Melanthios with swords and warhammers slid down the ladders and attacked. The Sun Gods unsheathed their swords and responded.

The war had begun in a cacophony of cries and blood spatter.

Tory fired arrows into the crowd of Sun Gods, taking time to aim at the gap between the armour and the helmet. Tory wasn't as fast as Senka, but she never missed.

Tory took a break from firing into the crowd to search for Senka. It took Tory a second, but her keen eyes soon found her. Senka's swords were glowing blue. She was the only one of the Melanthios fighting with Pulse weapons and it was all intended to kill the King. Tory knew those weapons were slowly poisoning Senka, but Senka carried them anyway. Senka struck a man in the chest with the electrified sword. He went down in a fit of convulsions. Senka stood there, panting.

A Sun God was approaching Senka from behind. She must have sensed him, because she turned just in time. Tory breathed a sigh of relief as Senka killed him quickly. Tory continued to fire into the enemy. The Melanthios in the valley were beginning to be overrun. There were Sun Gods who had reached the bottom of the ladders and they were starting to climb.

"Archers!" Tory yelled, voice of a hardened general finding its way to her people. "Clear the ladders!"

Her archers listened and began to focus their arrows at the bottom of the ladders. Tory soon realized that it wouldn't be enough. There were too many Sun Gods. They just kept coming, stepping on the bodies of their dead comrades, desperate to climb and kill.

Tory scanned the battle again. Senka's mission was to kill the King. The False King had taken power so fast and so violently that this was the Melanthios' first and last stand. If Senka failed and the King remained alive then the Melanthios would all be killed. Senka was their only hope.

Tory found Senka ducking, weaving; killing in her violent dance. She was making her way towards the rear of the Sun Gods to where the King sat astride a horse, crown sitting crookedly on his traitorous head. Senka was covered in gore. She stopped to wipe the blood out of her eyes. Tory saw a Sun God approach quietly behind her.

"Senka!" Tory yelled. She was way too far away to hear her.

The Sun God raised his sword.

Out of pure desperation, Tory drew and fired an arrow. The shot was out of her range, but she needed to try. The arrow was guided by fear and love. It hit the Sun God in the back of the neck and exploded through his throat.

Senka turned quickly and locked eyes with Tory, giving her a swift nod. Tory nodded back. Tory was forced away from watching Senka. Sun Gods had made it up the ladders further down the valley and were charging through the forest. She could hear their armour crashing through the underbrush behind her.

An arrow flew over her shoulder, grazing her neck. Surprised, Tory turned and fired in a fluid motion, acting out of pure instinct.

She saw it in slow motion.

Her arrow was released from the bow before she locked eyes on her target. It flew through the air. Tory gasped, unable to do anything as her arrow hit a Melanthios archer in the chest.

The archer looked down slowly, shock on her face. Tory's arrow was sticking out of the center of her chest, still vibrating.

Tory froze. She could feel her heartbeat in her chest. She could hear the rush of it in her ears.

The woman dropped her bow. It clattered to the ground beside her. She looked at Tory, confusion and terror on her face. She dropped to her knees. She coughed and blood spurted out of her mouth and dripped down her chin.

The world around Tory stopped. There was no war. There was no Senka. There was only this Melanthios woman on her knees, Tory's arrow in her chest.

The world came crashing back and Tory ran to the woman. The woman looked at her confused. Tory dropped to her knees as the woman fell over into her arms.

"I'm sorry!" Tory sobbed. She was cradling the woman on the ground.

The woman looked like she was trying to say something. Blood bubbled out of her mouth. No words were uttered.

"No, no, no!" Tory cried desperately. She brushed the archer's hair out of her face. The Melanthios woman had dark eyes, almost black. Tory was drawn to them. They were beautiful.

The woman coughed blood one more time. Tory was pressing on her chest but she couldn't stop the blood.

"I'm sorry!" Tory said desperately.

The woman's beautiful black eyes went dark as she died in Tory's arms.

Tory sobbed into the woman's chest. She had killed before, countless times. She'd lost warriors in battle before. But this was different.

"I'm sorry," Tory said quietly into her hair. "I'm so, so sorry."

Tory didn't recognize the woman. She was from a different town than Tory was and had just come to fight in the war. But she was a Melanthios. She was one of her own.

The dead, black eyes stared at Tory accusingly.

"I didn't mean to," Tory sobbed. "I'm sorry. I didn't mean to."

"I'm still dead though," the black eyes said back.

"It's war. Your arrow almost hit me. I thought you were one of them."

"They are people too," the dead, black eyes replied. "You're killing husbands, brothers, sisters, daughters. You're killing them all."

"It's them or us!' Tory yelled at the dead woman. "It's war!"

The black eyes said nothing, they stared ahead, accusing.

Dead.

Tory heard someone scream from behind her. She wrenched her eyes away from the woman she had killed. The Sun Gods were swarming the ridge. They were killing the archers. Her people were breaking rank and running. They were dying.

Tory needed to shut down this overwhelming guilt. She couldn't let more of her people die. She lowered the woman to the ground and flipped her quickly to her stomach. Tory told herself that it was to get the woman's arrows but she knew it was because she couldn't stare at the cold, dead, accusing black eyes.

Tory stood and started firing into the approaching Sun Gods. She stabbed one through the neck with an arrow then drew and fired, killing a Sun God who was hovering over an archer.

The archer turned to smile appreciatively to her when a sword exploded through his chest. Tory yelled something incoherent and shot the offending Sun God in the face.

"Archers!" she yelled through the chaos. Her archers were scrambling away into the forest, leaving the Melanthios to die in the valley below. "To me!" she yelled. "Come to me!"

The fleeing archers nearest to her heard her and turned. They started to work together, firing in unison at the approaching enemy, gathering together in a group. Other archers started to join them. They rallied around Tory and began to regain their line. They needed to keep control of the cliff.

Tory knew that she should have felt pride in her people. But she only felt a crushing sense of guilt. She killed and fired with the rest of them, but her head was with the cold, dead eyes.

"I would have helped," the black eyes whispered in her ear as she killed.

Tory ignored them.

She led the rallied archers to the edge of the valley and looked desperately to the rear of the Sun Gods. She watched the scene unfold. Senka was standing face to face with the King.

Tory watched her best friend die.

Senka attacked the King with a fury and a speed that Tory hadn't known was possible. Senka's electrified Pulse powered short swords flickered out and died one at a time as the King landed devastating blows to Senka's forearms.

Senka stepped back after the onslaught. She was gasping. Tory could tell that she was in pain.

Senka steeled herself and launched another attack. This time, though, she was slower. Tory could tell that the King was inhumanely strong. He landed a blow to her stomach that folded Senka in half. Senka flew back and landed hard.

"Get up!" Tory yelled.

The battle was still raging around her but Tory didn't care. She was completely absorbed in the scene in the valley below. She didn't realize her archers were gathering around her, protecting her. She could only watch her friend.

Senka stayed down. Tory saw that her breath was coming in short gasps. Before Senka could get up, the King attacked again. This time he stomped on her chest. Senka tried to block but the King was too strong. She took the blow directly to the chest.

Tory couldn't believe it. Senka wasn't getting up. The King tried to stomp on her again but Senka aimed a kick to his knee.

It wasn't enough.

Senka tried to crawl away from the King. The King grabbed her and flipped her over.

Tory could feel her heartbeat in her chest as she stood there, powerless.

The King raised his sword over his head.

The world around Tory stopped.

She watched as the King started the killing blow.

Suddenly, Senka sprang up. She thrust a sword through the bottom of the King's jaw and out the top of his head in an explosion of blood.

Tory's heart leapt. Senka had done it! It must have all been an act!

When Senka fell back down, Tory's heart fell with her. It wasn't an act. She watched her ever strong, ever loyal, best friend's chest stop moving. Tory stood a hundred meters away as Senka died alone.

Tory dropped to her knees again. She was stunned.

"I died alone," Black Eyes tittered in her ear. "I died alone and you didn't care. I died alone because of you."

The King's death had an almost instantaneous effect on the battlefield. The Sun God's closest to him started to look around nervously and break rank, fleeing the battle. They weren't sure what they were fighting for in the first place and with no leader they were aimless. Word travelled fast and, to the cheers of the remaining Melanthios, the rest of the Sun Gods fled.

Tory didn't care. She could only watch her dead friend lying motionless on the battlefield.

"You killed me," Black Eyes laughed in her ear. "You let her die. You killed me. You let her die. You killed me. You let her die." Black Eyes chanted it, over and over. A bodiless voice yelling in her ear.

Grief and guilt ripped through her.

Tory put her hands over her ears and screamed.

PART 1

"The true soldier fights not because he hates what is in front of him, but because he loves what is behind him." – G. K. Chesterton

1 SENKA

October 19, 2023, 05:07
Location: Somewhere near Vanavara, Russia.

Senka was in prison.

Senka hated being in prison. It wasn't the first time. She doubted it would be the last. This time, however, she had put herself there. It was technically more of a private dungeon than a prison but that was just splitting hairs. It certainly looked like a prison. Four stone walls with a metal door inlaid, metal bed in the back corner. This prison was luxury compared to her last time incarcerated, back in The Other Place. This one had an old, torn and stained mattress on the metal bed frame and a working toilet instead of a hole.

Sighing, she stood up from the ratty mattress and nimbly hopped onto the bed. She took careful note of her surroundings from the new vantage point, being careful to check the corners of the cell for any inconsistencies. She wasn't very tall, only five foot six, so her head was still a few inches from the ceiling. She was very lean and muscular. She kept her exceptional form hidden under jeans and a plain grey sweater with YALE written across the front in bold lettering. She wore her medium length hair in a pony-tail, with one piece tucked behind her ear. She wasn't beautiful, nor was she ugly. She fit in anywhere, making her perfect for her current employment.

Satisfied there were no cameras or bugs in the cell, she hopped back down off the bed. She could chat in private. Amanda was probably going crazy, Senka hadn't checked in in over a week. Senka sighed and dug a hand into a liner of her jeans, finding a small ear-piece hidden within the fabric. It was discrete and couldn't be seen when lodged deep in her ear canal. She pulled a small, skin-toned sticker out of her jeans as well and stuck it onto her neck. The tiny microphone would allow her to speak normally to Amanda without distortion.

She turned the ear piece on, popped it in her ear and was immediately assaulted, "Senka what the hell! You haven't checked in in a week. You could have been dead! You could have been captured! You could have…" Senka stopped paying attention to Amanda's voice, she let her rant and rave and continued looking around the room. She couldn't see any weaknesses, so she'd have to do this the old-fashioned way.

"Senka! Are you even listening to me?" Amanda Nguyen's squawk brought her back into focus.

"Nope, not at all," Senka replied, still scanning the room. "You were droning on and I lost focus. What were you saying?"

"Why haven't you checked in? I was about to send a unit in to find you," Amanda's voice was tense. Senka smiled, she knew Amanda was probably grating her teeth. Call her petty, but Senka thoroughly enjoyed pissing Amanda off whenever she could. Added a little joy to her day.

"I was busy. You sent me to this frigid nation to track down drugs. I tracked down drugs. I just do it my own way," Senka started bouncing on the balls of her feet and cracking her neck. "Sidenote: Russia is colder than Canada any day. I don't care what we think. Russia wins."

"I sent you to report on Viktor Sidorov's activities. That's it."

"So the fact that I'm currently in the dungeon of his high tech, previously impenetrable fortress in Siberia means nothing?"

Amanda stopped talking. Senka pressed the button on her jeans. The tiny GPS tracker would now give Amanda her location.

"So do you want me to escape and download his files to the hard-drive I snuck in? Or does that not…"

"Shut up," Amanda said sharply, not letting her finish. "We will need to have a meeting. A very. Long. Meeting. I expect a full report, with every. Single. Detail."

Senka rolled her eyes. Her boss, Amanda, had no sense of humor. "Yes, yes. Just like every mission. So have you tracked my location yet? Or do you need to get Carter in to turn on the computer for you?" Carter was Senka's handler, usually on the other end of her ear-piece. She liked him better.

"By the way," Senka added as she checked her watch, stirring the pot even more, "why are you still at work? Isn't it like ten at night there?"

"I will have a chopper there to extract you from the roof in forty-three minutes," Amanda replied, completely ignoring her. "You better be there."

Senka rolled her eyes, "I'm just saying, you need to find balance in your life. It can't always be about work."

"Oh by the way," Amanda snipped, "your brother called." Senka winced. Amanda knew how to exact revenge in the pettiest of ways. "He was wondering if you were going to be in Winnipeg on Sunday for your mother's birthday. I told him I would get you to call him as soon as you were done your shift at Starbucks."

Senka put her head back and sighed. Cracking her neck again she let out a long shriek, followed by, "Help! Oh God help me! My stomach! Why am I here? Oh God it hurts so bad somebody help me!" in her loudest, whiniest, sniveling co-ed voice.

"Really?" Amanda piped up in her ear, "the sick prisoner gig? Should I be sending that chopper for two days from now?"

"Hundred bucks says it works," Senka whispered, laying down in the center of the cell in the fetal position, back towards the door. She made sure she was within sight of the peep-hole.

"You're on," Amanda said. "Carter should be back from dinner soon. He might want in on this too."

Senka shrugged. Carter would be on her side. He always was. He was the brains, she was the brawn. Senka shrieked again, a high-pitched, cutting scream. "I'm dying! I don't know where I am! Why am I here, oh god help me please! Help me! Please, someone, help me! Why am I here?"

"They have probably heard that a million times. What makes

you think…"

"Shut up," Senka whispered, "they're coming."

Senka had indeed heard boots coming down the hallway. Two sets, marching slightly out of time.

"Oh God help me! What am I doing here? I think I was drugged. Oh God my stomach! Somebody help me!"

"Shut up!" A man's voice yelled, distinctly American accent. *So Viktor hired mercenaries*, Senka thought, *that is interesting. This is bigger than I thought.*

"Help! Are you American? I don't know why I'm here! I think someone drugged me! My stomach, oh God my stomach!"

She heard the peep-hole slide open. Senka tensed her muscles. With a pleading sob she wracked her body like she was crying or vomiting. She heard the American on the other side of the metal door sigh and say, "We have to shut her up before the boss gets here. He likes his bitches quiet."

"Doesn't like them hurt or drugged," the second man replied in English thick with a Russian accent. Senka heard the peep-hole slide closed. The last time she broke out of prison she had spared the Queen's, Jules' and Vigo's lives because she needed their help. These men wouldn't be as lucky.

"Look she's quiet, maybe she's dead. I don't want to be the guy to tell the boss," the American said. The Russian must have acquiesced because Senka heard the heavy bolt on the outside of the door slide open. She loosened up her shoulders and let the men come into the room. She kept still as they crossed towards her and circled to see her face. One nudged her with a boot, the other bent down to get a better look. They were dressed in cargo pants and black military grade jackets. They had toques on. One had an M16 draped across his shoulders, the other a Glock 19 on his hip. These men were well armed. *Not very smart though*, she thought when they came in without their guns raised, *definitely didn't take me as a threat.*

They would die for that mistake.

They didn't even have time to register that they had been duped. Senka was fast, faster than anyone. A remnant of her time in The Other Place. She struck out with her foot to the carotid artery of the bending man. She assumed he was the Russian, he was hulking, at least six foot six, with hair so blond it was almost white. The shot to the throat dropped him to his knees, eyes wide. Senka used his body as leverage and launched herself off the ground and, grabbing on to his shoulder, kicked the other man, a brunet, in the center of the throat. The kick crushed his windpipe, causing his tall frame to fall backwards, his head making a loud crack as it hit the concrete floor. He gasped for air a few times, but air couldn't get to his lungs and he died. She turned back to the blonde man and sunk in a chokehold. He gasped and scratched at her and she held on until he passed out. She lowered him quietly to the ground.

She closed the door behind them. The lock was an old-fashioned bolt system and she wasn't concerned about locking herself in. She quickly stole the Glock from the blond Russian man, all of his ammo, and his knife. She left the dead brunet his M16. He was laying directly on top of it and she didn't want to spend the time untangling it from his body. Armed, she felt more like herself. She hated when a mission needed her to abandon her own weapons such as this one had. She always felt naked without them. The Glock felt awkward in her hands, she preferred her Sig Sauer P226. The last three years, ever since she woken up from her coma, her Sig had been by her side.

"So," she said out loud, "one dead, one alive but passed out. Door's open. You owe me a hundred bucks."

She heard Amanda sigh on the other end and laughed, "Put Carter on the line. You must be out two-hundred to sigh like that."

Carter's voice came into her ear next, his gravelly baritone a welcome reprieve from Amanda's nagging, "She was dumb enough to go double with me."

"Cause you're smart enough to trust me," Senka said. "Good thing you're smarter than you look."

"Well we can't all be all brawn with no brains," Carter said with a laugh in his voice. Senka smiled. Carter was a six foot five black man in his mid-thirties. His biceps were bigger than her head. He played college football in the States and was signed to four NFL camps when he decided that football wasn't for him. He had a four-point-oh grade point average in a double masters of

Physics and Computer Science. All impressive, however his high IQ was the reason he was recruited into the Zoya Task Force in the Canadian Security Intelligence Agency. He was all brawn and all brains, but had no stomach for violence, making him a perfect fit as a handler.

"How was dinner?" Senka asked, puffing a little as she dragged the massive blond man to the metal bed frame.

"Pad Thai, delicious," Carter replied. "From the place down the street."

"Damn. I'm jealous. I've had enough vodka and Shchi to last me a life time," she found some zip ties in the dead brunet's pocket and bound the blond man's hands behind his back to the metal bed.

"What's Shchi?"

"Some cabbage soup stuff," Senka replied, slapping the man across the face. He started to blink groggily.

"Hey there bud," Senka said, straddling his one leg, knee in his groin. She pushed her knee down harder and the man's eyes snapped open. "That's better. What's your name?"

He glanced around, scared and confused, and said, "Floyd Taylor."

"Ha!" Senka laughed. "You're the American? Sure fooled me."

"You should know better than to judge a book by its cover," Carter piped up in her ear. "You need him to tell you where the main servers are. Best chance of downloading the most information to that hard-drive in your shoe."

"Why does Amanda give me shit about not checking in? See? You know that everything is going to plan," Senka asked lightly. Floyd's eyes started to dart around again, and Senka put more pressure on to his groin and held his own knife up to him, raising her eyebrows. The man stopped moving and looked at her, wide-eyed.

"Amanda doesn't know you like I do. Also, if you recall, you left a few key details out when you were getting the go-ahead for the mission. Anyways, not a rocket science plan."

"Thanks Carter, I was pretty proud of it."

"You're simple minded and like to bust doors in before

28

knocking. It's your style. This has a lot of finesse for you, so I can see why you'd be impressed with yourself."

"Oh ha-ha," Senka said. She turned to Floyd, "So, how long you been out of the Marine Corp for?"

"How did you…" Floyd drifted off when Senka took the tip of the knife and slid his jacket up his arm, exposing a United States Marine Corp tattoo on his wrist. "Six months," he said shakily.

"I'm assuming a dishonorable discharge. Drank on the job, didn't yah bud."

He stared at her, shocked.

Senka shrugged, "A good marine doesn't get taken down by a five-foot six freshman unless he didn't give a shit while he was on the job. I'm surprised you actually passed training. Pegged you as a quitter, especially if you're working for an ass-hat like Viktor Sidorov. I only thought he was distributing drugs, but I think he's distributing people too," Senka reared back and punched Floyd squarely in the face. "And working for an ass-hat that sells people makes me really not like you."

Floyd blinked stupidly a few times, blood leaking out of his nose.

"You're thinking a human trafficking ring?" Carter said in her ear.

"I'm thinking that we need to have a meeting about the extent of this when I get home," Senka said. Carter's silence meant he agreed.

"You're no freshmen," Floyd said thickly through the blood rushing out of his nose.

"Read the sweater," Senka said, "says Yale so it must be true. Where are the servers?"

"Please! They will kill me if they find out I told you," Floyd pleaded. "And I only took this job cause the job market sucked in the States. The crash of 2019 really put a damper on my options."

Senka nodded sympathetically, then punched him in the face again. "You're selling people. Go home and sell burgers. And it's either they kill you, or I cut your dick off and you bleed out slowly on the floor."

The look on his face told her she'd won.

2 ISAAC

October 18, 2023, 22:07
Location: Toronto, Canada.

Isaac was fuming.

He had the clothes on his back, his phone, and his wallet in his pocket. That's all he had grabbed as he stormed off after his fight with his father.

'Step-father," he muttered to himself. He didn't know where that came from. Chris had always been his father; he was the only father he knew. Isaac was ashamed as soon as he thought it. The shame didn't subdue his anger. His phone vibrated in his pocket. His father's face filled the screen as he received a call. Isaac quickly pressed ignore.

His buddy Jeff lived a few blocks down, that's where Isaac was headed. It was Jeff's fault that he was in this mess to begin with. Isaac had told him last night that he wanted to go home before he was late for curfew. Jeff hadn't listened. So Isaac had been forced to stay at the party. His dad had brought up that Isaac could have phoned him for a ride home, but he would rather *die* than have his dad pick him up from a party.

Isaac walked up the steps of the large house and hammered on the door. The windows were lit but the shades were drawn. He checked his phone and noticed that it was pretty late, past ten.

Jeff's mom was not going to be impressed.

The outside light flicked on and the inside wooden door swung open, revealing an insecure Jeff standing in the doorway.

"Hey," Jeff said. He kept the screen door closed. Isaac felt uneasy.

"Hey," Isaac said. He was trying to be cool and not desperate. He and Jeff had been friends for a long time, but image was always important. They recently moved to the biggest high school in the area and Isaac needed to keep his friends. Meaning he needed to keep up the appearance of being calm and collected all the time.

"Ummm," Jeff said, looking behind him. Isaac had the sense that Jeff's mom was standing behind him out of view. "I'm grounded, Zac. For a while. I can't hang out tonight."

"Yeah, that's cool," Isaac said, coughing a bit to hide the crack in his voice. "I was just wondering if I could crash on your couch tonight. Not feeling the vibe at home."

Isaac stood awkwardly on the step. The screen door stayed closed between them.

"My mom says that you need to go home. Your dad called and talked to her." He gave him a long stare and looked down. "Sorry buddy," he mumbled and he closed the door.

"Screw you," Isaac muttered under his breath as he walked away, heading the opposite direction of home. This was so stupid. This wasn't his fault and he sure wasn't going to be punished for some stupid *shit* that Jeff got him in to.

Isaac walked quickly to the train station. The night was chilly and he only had on a thin wind-breaker. It was new and bright orange. He liked how it stood out against his dark skin. His mom had bought it for him a couple of weeks ago. He had pretended not to like it, then instantly saw how her face had fallen. He then regretted it and wore it every day. His mom said he looked handsome in it.

He was making his way through the doors of the Richmond Hill train station. It would take him from his neighborhood in North York to downtown Toronto. He lived close to the train station so the walk hadn't taken him long. He would run away, get a job and live in Toronto. Hell, maybe he would even leave the country, start his life in Detroit.

He didn't need his mom and *step-dad*. He was black, his parents were white. They didn't have to tell him that Chris wasn't his real father, he was smart enough to figure it out.

Isaac was angry at the world. At how unfair everything that had happened the last few days was. None of this was his fault. And he would make sure that they missed him when he was gone.

The train creaked to a stop and Isaac hopped on. He had his train pass in his wallet, as well as a few hundred dollars he got from his grandma on his birthday. He had saved it for the past month, not really knowing what to spend it on. He would stay the night in a hotel in Toronto, then go and find a job tomorrow.

There were quite a few people already on the train and Isaac had to look for a seat. The train lurched to a start and he collided with another guy in the aisle.

"Sorry!" Isaac said, barely keeping his feet. The man gave him a half smile and quickly hurried down the train.

Isaac found a seat near the back of the lurching train and sat down in a huff. He wished he had brought a sweater with him. *That'll be the first thing you buy with your first paycheque*, he thought to himself. The thought cheered him and he looked out the window, watching his old life fade into darkness. He put his headphones in and began listening to his electronic play list. His dad called it "fake music" because it didn't use instruments. His dad didn't know anything.

He was in high spirits when he got off the train. He checked his phone and found a hotel within walking distance. This was it, his new life. He could live however he wanted without his stupid father telling him what to do. He almost felt bad for leaving his mother without telling her where he was going, but he would call her in a couple of weeks. *Once everyone cools off*, he thought. He strode up the stairs of the brightly lit, *fancy* hotel. He earned a hotel like this for the night. He smiled at the door man and, remembering his manners, took his headphones out of his ears.

Isaac walked through the brightly lit lobby to the front desk. His sneakers made a weird sound against the marble floors. *This is living*, he thought proudly to himself.

The man working at the front desk looked at him. "How can I help you, sir?" he asked. Isaac detected a sneer in his voice. He was blond and had a pointed face. Isaac disliked him, he looked like a mouse.

"Hi," Isaac said hesitantly. He looked at the name prominently displayed on the concierge's chest. "Hi, Nolan, I want to book a hotel for the night."

Nolan, the Ass, as Isaac was starting to call him in his head, looked him up and down.

"I will need a credit card to put on file, *sir*. And our rooms start at two hundred and sixty dollars a night."

"That's fine," Isaac said, reaching for his wallet in his thin jacket pocket. His heart dropped. It wasn't there. He looked around nervously, checking and re-checking all of his pockets. Panic set in. His wallet was gone.

"Sorry, I lost my wallet," he mumbled and, head down, rushed out of the hotel. His face was burning with embarrassment. He knew he grabbed his wallet when he left. It was sentimental, his grandma on his dad's side had given it to him for Christmas last year. It was leather and had his favorite Canadian Football League team logo embossed on the front. It was also filled with cash. Cash that he had gotten for his birthday. He flashed back to the man who had fallen into him on the subway. That asshole had stolen his wallet!

Isaac looked around frantically. There were people milling about, lots of drunk ones. He didn't like the look of anyone. He wanted to go home but he knew he would be in so much trouble if he went back. He needed to let his parents cool off for a little bit.

He made his way down the steps and his phone vibrated again. This time his mother's face filled the screen. Isaac stared at his phone. He desperately wanted to answer. His wallet was gone, his phone was dying. He wanted to go home. But he was fifteen. This was his chance to get out on his own. Considering it the bravest thing he'd ever done, he shoved the phone back into his pocket and let it go to voicemail.

He huddled deeper into his jacket and made his way down the street, making sure to keep his hand on his phone as he walked. A long, black limo pulled up next to him and stopped. The window rolled down, and Isaac saw a white man with red hair and a moustache poke his head out. He started walking faster, the old adage "Don't talk to strangers," going through his head.

"Hello there!" the man yelled. He had an accent that Isaac couldn't place. He thought it sounded European.

Isaac ignored him and sped up, turning down a side street. The limousine slowly followed. Isaac didn't notice there were no longer any people around.

"Hello there, young man!" the accented man yelled again. "I need your help!" Isaac stopped and let the limo catch up to him. He knew not to get into the limo, but helping a man out in need was in his nature. Isaac made sure he kept a few feet between the curb and himself.

"Yes?" He asked. "What do you need?"

"I'm sorry young man, my name is Dr. Freudman and I am visiting your fine country from Germany for a conference. Unfortunately I am not familiar with your customs."

Isaac was still hesitant but the man had a very trusting face and was a doctor. He knew he should be able to trust him.

"I was wondering if you would, by chance, come with me and visit at a coffee shop? I have to give a big presentation and I would like to know more of your language. It won't take long, and I can pay you handsomely for your trouble."

Isaac knew he shouldn't, but he was cold and hungry. This man was promising money just to spend some time. Isaac thought that sounded like good work for him. Who knows, maybe this German man needed an assistant. He started thinking about it more. The promise of easy money was tempting, but Isaac was still uncomfortable. He decided he wanted to make his money the hard way and earn it.

"I'm sorry," Isaac said, "but my mother is waiting for me. I need to get home."

Freudman smiled broadly, "Of course, of course. Thank you for your trouble young man." He held out his hand through the open window. Isaac took it and shook it, smiling back at the German doctor. He barely felt the needle prick his palm.

His vision suddenly blurred. Isaac tried to shake his head to clear it. The man in the limo was still smiling, but his face was swimming. It looked warped. Isaac tried to step away but he felt himself being lifted off his feet and pushed into the dark limo. He wanted to yell but his tongue was thick. The last thing he felt was the German man taking his phone out of his jacket and throwing it out the window. The limo lurched ahead and everything went black.

3 SENKA

October 19, 2023, 05:34
Location: Somewhere near Vanavara, Russia.

"I'm just saying that you don't have to kill everyone. He gave you the information that you asked for."

"Carter, that's why you're over there in the cushy office and I'm over here, pulling the trigger. He would have given me up, and right now I would be fighting a shit-ton of mercenaries instead of running by myself down a dark hallway." Senka was, in fact, jogging down a dark hallway by herself, somewhere in the bowels of the Siberian fortress. She kept her stride light so she wouldn't give her position away. Floyd had said there might be a few other mercenaries guarding the basement, but if she listened she should be able to avoid them.

"Knock him out!" Carter yelled so loud that Senka was sure it could be heard in the hallway around her.

Senka sighed as she came up to a corner in the hallway. Floyd had said two lefts and then a right. So it was on to a right.

"Carter, they would have killed him. And not a quick death, like a knife to the temple he didn't see coming. A shitty, prolonged, torturous death. Even if I would have knocked him out."

She heard Carter start to argue. She also heard someone

coming down the hallway. "Shhh," she said quietly and pressed herself into the darkness of a doorway. Carter immediately shut up. He may not always agree with her, but he would never put her in danger. They were a team. They lived together. They were partners.

Senka waited patiently and quietly in the doorway until the guard had passed and was long gone before continuing on her journey.

"Carter, I know you don't agree, but I've been given permission to do this job by the Prime Minister of Canada, the Queen and the whole of the United Nations. It's messy, it sucks. There's a reason why I do it and you sit over there. And we both know that I've never killed anyone that we needed alive or didn't deserve it."

Carter stayed silent on the other end. She knew he was still there. Carter was always there. But sometimes she pissed him off.

Finally, after a torturous silence, "Tom didn't kill everyone."

Senka sighed and rubbed her eyes, "Yah, Tom did. I was the one who didn't want to kill everyone. Don't try to twist that shit just 'cause Tom's dead now. I talked Tom into keeping them alive."

Carter stayed silent.

"If we would have killed everyone that day, Tom would have lived."

With that, Senka continued down the hall and left Carter to his brooding. *I don't have time for this shit*, she thought to herself. *If Carter doesn't shut up, I'm going to be distracted enough that he will be burying me too.* Senka immediately regretted the thought. It wasn't Carter's fault that Tom had died, it was hers. They were a trio and she was supposed to get Tom out of there with her. Instead, they had placed a tombstone.

Senka didn't meet anyone for the rest of the jog, which was good. She couldn't cause a ruckus until she had filled the hard drive in her shoe. And right now she was so pissed off that she wouldn't kill anyone quietly. There would be a ruckus.

She jogged the rest of the way to an unmarked door on the left, exactly as Floyd had said. Senka didn't regret killing him, he was selling human beings for a living, but she was glad she gave him a quick death. He was greedy and stupid but at least he was honest. The door was locked by a keypad with a red glowing LED light above. Senka punched the six digit code Floyd had given her, 0-6-1-9-2-8. She heard the click as the mechanised lock opened and the keypad light flicked to green.

Senka stood beside the door and pushed it inward. It opened without a sound. She waited for a full thirty seconds, muscles tense, finger on the trigger. Carter knew to stay silent as well. Nothing stirred. Senka walked into the dark room, heart pounding in her chest. She found the light switch and flicked it on, the buzz of the florescent bulbs breaking the deafening silence. She made sure to close the door behind her.

The illumination showed rows and rows of servers. Humming blue lights glowed in each tower. She quickly counted ten rows in total, the door directly in the middle of the rectangular room. She scanned the room, and seeing no hint of movement, made her way to the left, scanning each row as she passed.

"Looks like servers," she mumbled to Carter. She moved slowly through the middle row of towers, gun outstretched in front of her. The safety was off.

"You know that hard drive in your shoe?" Carter asked.

"You bet," she said quietly. She slowly made her way down the last row and made her way along the back wall, clearing the room. She lowered her gun, but kept the safety off. "It's like a backup drive so I can put data from these servers on it and bring it to you," she said confidently. Senka was beyond technologically inept. She could hunt with a bow and skin a deer no problem, but she had no idea how to use the smart phone Carter bought her for Christmas last year. It had taken Carter a week to teach her.

"See I told you I was listening at the mission brief."

"Yah, I lied, it's not a hard drive," Carter said.

The blue lights of the rows of servers highlighted Senka's unimpressed face. "This is why I don't listen to you."

"Ok, so it's a remote access device that will allow me to, from my cushy office, access all the information on these servers, track who uses them and hack into any other servers the person uses as well. These guys are probably global so it will allow me to access all the worldwide servers on the network. It also implants a malware that blocks anyone from knowing I have accessed the information…" Carter trailed off. "See? You're not listening."

"Hard drive," Senka said blankly.

"Exactly. But you need to leave this hard drive plugged in for three minutes, until the little light glows green. Then, if you'd rather the ZTF wasn't discovered, you need to unplug it and take it with you."

"Let me guess," Senka said as she took off her tennis shoe and removed a small black device from beneath the sole that looked like a USB drive. "This will most likely trigger an alarm. They will know where I am and you want me to defend this little black thing? Really? From multiple mercenaries in a room with one door." She hopped on one foot as she put her shoe back on. "Oh, with a gun that's not mine and…" She checked the magazine, "Ten bullets."

"Look, Sen, we can bail. I told you this was crazy in the brief—"

"Sounds like my favorite way to spend a Friday," she interrupted as she slammed the magazine back into the gun.

"It's Wednesday."

"Thursday in Russia," she chirped, "close enough." Senka heard worry in Carter's voice and was doing her best to lighten the situation. She never wanted to die. She'd done that in The Other Place. It wasn't fun. But she did feel an extra push to stay alive since Tom had died. Carter wouldn't handle it if she died on a mission too. "Ok, where am I supposed to plug this bitch in?"

"There's going to be a place on the front of the servers. Any one of the servers will work."

Senka looked and found it. A small, rectangular slot that would fit the USB.

"Ready?" she asked, hand hovering.

"Yes. I'll be able to start accessing the information almost immediately. I'll let you know the building schematic and your route to evac when I find it. Evac is eleven minutes out."

Senka cracked her neck to the side, "Let's do this." She plugged the device in and a small red LED lit up. She started her watch. If Carter said three minutes, he meant it. She took a few steps to the door and slammed the butt of the gun into the key pad. It shattered and she heard the lock engage.

"Alarm's been triggered," Carter said in her ear. She could hear him typing away at the computer. "Already accessing tons of information and saving it over here."

Senka switched the lights off. It killed all the lights in the room except for the small red light emanating from the "hard drive". She ran to the back corner. She didn't need to see, she had memorised the layout and number of steps when she had done her sweep.

"Elite team has been dispatched," Carter said. "I have the security system and floor schematic. I didn't get to the alarm in time, sorry."

Senka didn't say anything. She knelt and closed her eyes, meditating. Air in through her nose, out through her mouth. Just as Master Apollyon had taught her in The Other Place. Two minutes and thirty-five seconds until she could unplug the device.

She heard the heavy tread of five sets of boots running down the hallway. Something else was with them.

"Shit," she muttered.

"What's up?"

"They have a dog with them."

Carter stayed silent. Dogs were a complicated issue with Senka. She wouldn't hesitate to kill a human who had done wrong or to complete a mission, but she'd never killed a dog.

"Sen, you're willing to die so you don't have to kill a dog?"

"Not the dog's fault its been trained to be an asshole. That's the asshole owner's fault. Can't kill a dog for doing its job."

"Seriously, this could jeopardize the mission and your life."

"Not killing it. End of statement. I will just have to choke it out," she heard Carter sigh in her earpiece. She ignored him. The men and the dog arrived at the door. She heard it growling and lunging at its leash. Sounded big.

Two minutes five seconds.

She heard them yelling in Russian from the hallway, "They're blowing the door. Going to send the dog in after to flush me out or kill me." They were planting the explosives on the other side of the door. She could hear the one man riling his dog up into a growling, snarling frenzy.

One minute forty-five seconds.

She heard the boots run away. She braced herself, staying on her knees, and covered her ears with her hands.

The explosion blasted the door off its hinges, leaving a ruined mess of steel. It shook the towers of servers. Senka's ears rang. Dust filled the small room and emergency lights flickered on with an eerie, yellow glow. She hoped none of the servers were damaged. That would ensure that all this work and time were useless.

The server towers rocked dangerously and settled. She didn't think there was any damage to them, which was a relief. The door was mangled on the ground, leaving an open hole to the hallway. A man yelled from the hall, "Leo, kill!" in Russian. The dog rocketed into the room. He knew exactly where she was, following his keen nose.

She kept calm, breathing slowly to keep the dust out of her lungs. She heard the snarling as the dog turned the corner, smashing into the wall. He spotted her, legs pumping hard, and bared his teeth. Senka saw that it was a giant German Shepard with brown and black matted fur with a distinct white line of fur running diagonally across his face. He was foaming at the mouth, barking and growling, running full tilt at her.

Senka checked his aura, a trick she only ever needed to use on animals in this world. People were too predictable. She focused on his aura and her eyes opened wide. Her breath caught in her chest and her mouth hung open in shock.

The dog skidded to a stop mere inches in front of her.

She looked at him, he looked at her. He cocked his head to the side, panting. She held her hand out in front of her. Her distinctive purple and navy swirling aura drifted lazily around her hand. She looked at his aura. It was exactly the same. The same shade of purple and navy, the same swirling pattern, lazily making loops and curves.

She had seen hundreds of thousands of auras and no two had ever been the same.

The dog nuzzled into her hand. She relished the feel of his fur on her hand.

"Sen, what's going on? Talk to me!" Carter's worried voice in her ear, breaking the moment.

"Carter… This dog. He's me."

4 SENKA

October 19, 2023, 05:41
Location: Somewhere near Vanavara, Russia.

"Did you hit your head or something? What are you talking about?"

The dog, who Senka heard was called Leo, nuzzled deeper into her hand and looked at her, wagging his tail. She scratched his ears. He was too skinny, but his dark chocolate eyes looked at her with trust. Senka looked at him and said, "Cover left. Stay low. Wait for my mark."

Senka marvelled when Leo calmly padded away to the other side of the room and crouched low onto his stomach. He's understood her commands. She knew as soon as she looked at him that he would. They were one. They were the same.

He had on a military vest that was old and ratty. His fur was matted and dirty. Senka felt bad for him. She would clean him up when she got him home.

Leo crouched forward on his haunches and stared straight ahead at the wall in front of him. The servers were blocking his view of the door.

"Leo, come!" a man yelled from the door in Russian. Leo didn't move. He stayed, crouched, watching the wall from the other side of the room. Exactly what she told him to do.

"Senka what is going on?" Carter yelled.

She realized that she had been completely ignoring him. She checked her watch. She had forty-seven seconds left until she could unplug the device.

"Sorry, we're adding one to that evac. Still able to upload after the blast?"

"Yes, I can still access the servers. Who is coming with you?"

"Dog named Leo. What if they destroy this room?" she asked as she raised her gun and made her way quickly toward the door.

"If it's before the malware is uploaded it will have all been for nothing. If it's after then I'm in the system and can access the backup information and any other server on the network," Carter answered, and not to be deterred asked, "and why are you bringing a dog home? It probably won't even listen to you! It's someone else's dog!" Carter was incensed.

"Don't worry about it." Senka said sharply. Carter knew that Senka could see auras after she had woken up from The Other Place. It was part of the Zoya Task Force training. Handlers had to know everything about their agents. That meant going through together every gruesome detail of her time in Langundo. He may know what she could see, but he could never understand. She trusted auras as he trusted her sense of touch or her sense of smell.

Senka and Leo had the same aura, a phenomenon she had yet to see. They were one. They were meant to be. The fact that she found him on a trip to Russia was, in her opinion, a lucky accident.

Senka made it to the corner by the mangled door. She whistled softly and Leo crept up still hiding behind the row of servers but closer to the door.

A man holding a leash stepped hesitantly over the fallen steel door, "Leo, come!" It was the last thing he said before Senka shot him between the eyes. The sound reverberated off the walls in the room, causing ringing in her ears. He slumped backward, eyes dead, small hole in the middle of his forehead, a single drop of blood running towards his nose. She was glad Leo had stayed where he was, she didn't want him to see. Leo's fur was matted and un-kept, he looked way too skinny for his size, but that was his old owner and she didn't need him to be traumatized.

She heard the yelling and the rest of the men stormed the door.

She shot them in the head one by one as they entered. Two died in the doorway. The other two wisely retreated from her line of fire. She heard them yelling at each other in Russian as they ducked for cover.

"How long do you need?" she asked Carter, realizing their plan.

"Twelve seconds."

"Shit. Leo!" she yelled, hearing the men fumbling for something outside the door. "Leo, get him! Go for the arm!"

Leo, ever vigilant, jumped over the three dead men without even a second glance at his old owner. Senka followed him through the opening over the mangled door, hard and fast. She had been right. One man was going for a grenade. They would rather kill her and lose the servers then allow her to escape.

Eight seconds.

Leo recognized which of the two had the grenade and launched himself at his hand.

Seven seconds.

Senka shot the other man in the head. He was diving and she missed the forehead, hitting him in the jaw. His jaw shattered, leaving his face contorted in a sadistic smile.

Six seconds.

The grenade fell to the ground, bouncing towards the man she had shot in the jaw. Both men were screaming. Leo had his man's arm in his mouth and was shaking it violently.

Five seconds.

The man she shot rolled over and pulled the pin of the grenade.

Four seconds.

"Leo, come!" Senka yelled. The man with the jaw hanging from his face was laughing maniacally. The other stared wide eyed at the tendons and bone exposed in his arm.

Three seconds.

Leo ran past her through the mangled doorframe and launched himself over the fallen door.

Two seconds.

Senka followed fast and grabbed his jumping form right around the middle. They crashed to the ground together and Senka grabbed for the fallen door.

One second.

The grenade exploded in a fireball. Senka pulled Leo into her chest and cowered under the steel door. The explosion pushed them into the server room, passing the bodies of the dead men. Senka held on to Leo and the door tightly, head ringing, eyes closed. She could feel him breathing rapidly as he cuddled into her chest.

The explosion ended as rapidly as it occurred, bits of debris falling from the roof. She waited an extra few seconds, just holding on to Leo, feeling his chest rise and fall. She pushed the door off them and let go of Leo. He scrambled to his feet. She did a rapid assessment of herself. Nothing broken, a couple of small lacerations here and there, bit of a burn on her lower back. She would live. With deft hands she felt Leo over as well. He stood still as a statue, letting her feel his joints and fur. No damage to him.

She breathed a sigh of relief and patted him on the head. He wagged his tail and scratched himself, unfazed.

"Carter, still there?"

Her ears were ringing but she heard the faint reply through her *thank god* undamaged earpiece, "Yes. You guys ok?"

"All good. You get it?"

"Yes, we got in right before the explosion."

Senka breathed a sigh of relief, "Server room is destroyed. I won't be able to find that nifty little device you gave me."

"No worries," Carter replied, she could hear relief in his voice. "If they find it they find it. We can deal with that. Hopefully it's so destroyed that they can't figure anything out." Always on task, Carter continued, "Evac is eight out. They will come to the west side of the roof. I have the security feed and a map. I'll get you up there."

Senka nodded. She quickly searched the least charred of the bodies while Leo laid down and yawned.

"Lazy shit," she mumbled at him. He rolled his eyes and huffed at her, resting his head on his front paws, bored with it all.

She managed to find another Glock and a magazine with nine more bullets. That put her at fifteen bullets total.

"How many?" Carter asked.

"See me?" she asked, looking around the drifting smoke for a security camera.

"No camera is busted. I just know you. How many bullets do

you have?"

"Fifteen total, two guns."

"Ok, the explosion triggered every alarm known to man in that building. They are coming for you. Go right out the door, back the way you came."

"Let's go, Fatass," she mumbled at Leo. He leapt up, tail wagging. They went right, Leo taking the lead by about three feet. Senka didn't have time to marvel at how fast she and the dog had fallen into step with each other. It just came as naturally as breathing. They ran quickly.

"Right here, four down the hallway," Carter said.

Senka knew she was in the basement. "Leo, right," she said. Leo listened and she saw his hackles raise at the same time that she heard the men coming down the hall.

"Stay."

Leo obeyed and crouched at the corner, hidden.

Senka made the turn fast and shot four rounds. Four men dropped, bullets in their heads. They didn't even have time to raise their guns.

"Let's go," she said. Leo jumped up and took the lead again. As they jogged by the mercenaries Senka stole one of their M16's. It felt heavy in her hands but it would do the job.

"Up the ladder. It will take you to the first floor. There should only be seven men covering all of upstairs, the rest went downstairs the other way to check out the server room. One is waiting by the hatch as guard."

Senka nodded. She squatted and said, "Leo, up!" Leo ran and jumped on her back. She positioned him so he was draped over her shoulders and started to climb the ladder. Leo panted happily in her ear.

"Good thing I don't skip leg day," she said, puffing slightly. Her two weeks of touring around Russia on this mission had taken its toll. Leo licked her cheek.

"Blah," she said. He panted happily.

She made it to the top of the ladder.

"Hold," Carter said. Senka waited patiently. Carter would be watching the guard at the top of the ladder on the security camera footage.

"Go!"

Senka pulled hard on the ladder and sprang both feet to the top rung. She opened the hatch with one hand and muscled it open.

"Hey!" a man yelled.

"Go Leo," she said. The man was across the room, she had rudely interrupted him as he lit a cigarette. Carter had waited for the perfect moment. Leo was off her shoulders before the command, running and weaving towards the mercenary. The man managed to get his gun up at the charging dog and pull the trigger. A shot rang out as she pulled herself off the ladder and Leo launched himself at the mercenary. Her heart dropped with worry. The man screamed and fell under the weight of the attacking German Shepard. Senka swung the M16 off her back to the ready. Leo had a man by the arm and was violently shaking his head. The man was yelling and trying to punch Leo with his free hand.

She aimed swiftly and said, "Leo, drop!" The dog dropped the arm and collapsed onto his stomach, giving Senka an open head shot. One that she took and didn't miss. Leo padded back towards her. She quickly checked him out, again he was unscathed. They were in a non-descript concrete room with three doors and a window showing snow and mountains. She saw a grey-blue sky outside. Sunrise was approaching.

"Go left. Up the stairs. No one in the next room."

Senka nodded and she and Leo ran. She could hear men coming from the other two directions following the yells. The next room looked exactly the same, except it had a large metal staircase that ran all the way up to the top of the compound. They pushed hard to the stairs. Halfway up, she stopped, turned and settled her heart, aiming at the door.

Men burst through and she picked them off with well-aimed shots. There were too many of them. Bullets started to rain around them. "Come!" she yelled and she and Leo bolted farther up the stairs. A grenade was thrown but they were well clear by the time it exploded.

"Nice," Carter said. "Roof should be empty. Evac is thirty seconds out."

Senka smiled to herself as they continued to pound up the stairs. Hopefully those men had blocked off their own path. There were ten flights total and they burst out a metal door. She breathed in the beautiful cold air, staring at the morning sky above and mountains all around. Senka saw the helicopter burst over a nearby hill, snow swirling and dancing below. This fortress was in the middle of nowhere, ice and snow sparkled on the surrounding mountains. She wasn't sure what Viktor used it for, she hadn't found much out on this expedition.

She quickly got her bearings and ran to the west side. The chopper hovered as they lowered a rope down to her. She hooked the back of Leo's vest to the rope. They quickly hoisted him up, his tail happily wagging. She turned her back, trusting the Joint Task Force 2 members in the helicopter to protect her dog. She crouched and covered their exit.

The Joint Task Force 2 Division of the Canadian Military were a group of special-forces used for a myriad of different tasks. The Zoya Task Force worked closely with the JTF2 to accomplish missions. The JTF2 soldiers were the toughest of the tough, they could handle anything and they were smart. Senka trusted them fully when they were used on missions together.

Men burst through the door to the roof. Senka started shooting. She heard, "Engaged! Cover fire!" coming from a man above. A machine gun was fired up and bullets were concentrated on the men by the door.

Carter knew his job and transferred her earpiece to the crew in the chopper.

"Package is secure," she heard in her ear. She was relieved, Leo was fine.

"He's pretty cute. Lowering rope for package two."

They lowered another rope to her.

"Cover fire," they concentrated bullets towards the door again, making the mercenaries dive for cover.

Senka turned and grabbed the lowered rope. The chopper immediately rose and Senka hung on to the rope with both hands as they raised her up. They weren't worried about her falling. The JTF2 men didn't know about her mission, but they knew she was a ZTF agent and they didn't have to worry about her. They hoisted her to the chopper door. She looked down. They were forty feet above the ground and she wasn't hooked to anything. Lovely.

Two JTF2 men pulled her in, patting her roughly on the back. She turned to smile at them and thank them, looking for Leo when something caught her eye glinting off a hill.

"Sniper! Pull up!" she yelled.

The shot rang out as the pilot banked hard. The bullet ricocheted off the top of the door. A searing pain ripped through Senka's face and she fell back into the men's arms. She could only see red as the blood poured down her face.

"She's hit! She's hit! The package is down!" it sounded far away. Everything seemed like it was pulsating. She could barely feel the chopper rising and speeding away. She felt Leo lick her face. He let out a high pitched whine and everything faded to black.

5 ISAAC

October 19, 2023, 14:32
Location: Unknown.

The whirling of a fan woke him.

"Mom, turn that fan off," he mumbled. The fan continued to rumble overhead. Isaac buried his head farther into his elbow. He was sore all over and sleeping on a hard surface that didn't feel at all like his bed.

"Mom! Can you turn that fan off please?" he said louder. He realized that he didn't have a pillow and had a searing headache.

"It's not a fan," a girl's voice answered him.

Isaac opened his eyes and was confused when it was darker than his room at home. He didn't recognize the girl's voice. He noticed that he was on a metal floor. He pushed himself up to sitting. A wave of nausea took hold and he closed his eyes, waiting for it to pass. He opened them and took notice of his surroundings. He was in a metal box with a single, sick yellow light on the roof, swinging away with the motion of the box. He then realized that the box was in motion. He noticed a girl sitting cross-legged against the wall opposite of him, about five feet away. She was staring at him with brown eyes, leaning her head against the back wall. Isaac noticed that one of her eyes was black.

"Where are we?" he asked. He was trying to recall how he had come here but he couldn't put it together.

"I think we're on a plane," she answered. She didn't move. She was sitting quietly in her black tank top and jeans staring at him. "I'm not sure, I've never been on a plane. But it sounds like a plane and my ears popped a while ago. My buddy said that can happen when you fly."

She talked slowly, deliberately, still staring at Isaac. His headache was starting to subside and the drowsiness was fading. He really tried to look at her. She looked as young as he was, maybe fifteen years old. She was pretty, with long brown hair and brown eyes. She looked tired.

"How'd we get here?" he asked.

"I'm not sure how you got here. You were already here when they tossed me in. I got here 'cause some red-headed dude with a weird accent tricked me." Her eyes darted away from his face. She wouldn't meet his eye. Isaac stared at her for a bit then lowered his eyes. She made him uncomfortable, he didn't know why.

The fog in his brain was starting to lift.

"I think the same guy tricked me too. How come you woke up sooner?"

"He didn't dose me with anything," she answered, still looking anywhere but his face.

"So you must know where they took us before the plane?" Isaac started patting his jeans. He needed his phone. He needed to call his parents. He was in trouble, he had made a terrible mistake. They would get him out of this. The fear that had been growing started to ebb as he thought about his parents.

"No. They had a bag over my head," she nodded to the corner of the box. Isaac looked and saw a brown bag in the corner. He started to fervently dig through his jeans and his coat pocket. It wasn't there. It had to be there, he always had his phone. "They would have taken it," the girl said. "They wouldn't forget to get rid of your phone. If you have people to call that means that someone would be looking for you. They wouldn't take that much of a risk."

Tears welled and Isaac angrily wiped them away. The girl graciously looked away giving him some time to compose himself. He wrapped his thin jacket around himself, now grateful for it. He missed his mom and the smell of her shampoo when she woke him up for school. He missed his dad and throwing the football around. They needed to know where he was so they could come and help him.

The girl let him cry for a bit. Once Isaac pulled it together, he looked at her. Ashamed he asked, "What's your name?"

She cocked her head, "Kelly. You?"

"Isaac. My friends call me Zac though."

She nodded curtly. The plane lurched slightly in the air. She looked around scared and tried to grab the sides of the metal container. Isaac closed his eyes and rode the turbulence out.

"I always hate flying," he said.

"That's normal?" Kelly asked and her voice hitched. In the yellow light Isaac noticed her eyes were darting around.

"Yea," he said. "It's called turbulence. It happens when the plane hits air pockets or something when it's flying." He saw that she still looked scared when the plane lurched again so he decided to change the subject to take her mind off of it. His mom used to do that when he was little and scared of thunderstorms. His heart skipped again when he thought of his mother. He needed to change the subject as fast as possible.

"Where you from?" he asked her.

She was pale, looking around, terrified. "Toronto," she answered vacantly. Isaac noticed her hands shaking.

"Cool, me too. What high school do you go to?"

She looked at him, "I don't go to school."

Isaac was surprised, "Oh, cool. You like, home-schooled or something?"

She stared at him, stone-faced. Isaac started to blush. He must have hit a nerve, "Sorry," he mumbled, "I didn't mean to pry."

They were spared from more awkward conversation when the plane pitched forward slightly. Isaac felt the pressure in his ears and knew they were on the descent.

"Where have you been on a plane to before?" Kelly asked him.

"My parents have taken me to Disney World a few times," he answered, "and we went to New York last summer. You've never been on a plane?"

She looked uncomfortable and started rubbing her ears.

"Do this," Isaac offered. He showed her how to plug her nose and blow gently to get her ears to pop.

She copied him and smiled, "Thanks. Wish you were here on the way up."

"How'd you get that shiner? That asshole give you that?" he asked. The stark violence of the black eye made him uncomfortable and was emphasized by her pale, sweaty skin. He realized in an instant how cushy his home life really was. Kelly had such a hard edge to her. It was something he couldn't place.

"No, I had this from before."

"Are you ok?"

"Nothing I can't deal with."

Isaac stared at her for a long time. Finally, "My parents will get us out of here. They will get us home. My dad's never let me down. Then you can go home too. Plus your parents would have reported you missing too so that's twice as much information for the police to go on. They will find us." He was trying to convince them both and he thought he was doing a pretty good job.

"I don't have any parents," she said flatly.

The plane bounced and lurched. They were thrown and jostled in their small metal box. Kelly managed to stay sitting up but Isaac ended up lying on the ground. The loud whirling of the engine slowed down and Isaac figured they were coasting down the runway. The road was bumpy and rough. They came to a lurching halt and Isaac, who had just pulled himself up to sitting, was bucked to his side again.

Isaac managed to get himself up to sitting again. Kelly looked at him and smiled. He smiled sheepishly back. He heard people above him start to leave the airplane, their steps echoing above.

"Holy crap!" he exclaimed when they heard the footsteps echoing above. "We're in a commercial flight! I thought we would be on a cargo plane or something. Those people don't even know we're here!" Isaac starting banging against the side of the metal container.

"Help!" Isaac screamed. "Help! We're down here!" he banged on the side of the container with everything he had, but the footsteps upstairs didn't stop walking.

"I tried that," Kelly piped up after Isaac's voice starting going dry and cracking. "Before you woke up. Didn't work. They can't hear us."

Isaac sat down heavily again. They waited in silence. A door to the side of the plane opened and Isaac could hear men chatting and laughing in a different language. It sounded like German but he couldn't be sure. Isaac exchanged a sidelong glance with Kelly and they both sprang up at the same time and started pounding and yelling on the side of the metal container. The cool metal hurt his hands but Isaac didn't care. He needed someone, anyone, to hear him.

Isaac heard laughing and someone banged back on the other side. They both jumped back as the sound reverberated around the container, hurting their ears.

"Shut up!" a man yelled at them in a thick accent. Isaac could hear the men laughing and joking on the other side.

"They must have known we were coming," Isaac said. Kelly sat down again and rubbed her hand through her hair. She tilted her head back again and looked at him, hurt in her eyes. He noticed that her face was white and she was still sweating. The container lurched upwards and Isaac wisely sat beside Kelly before he fell down.

The container jerked as it was set down and Isaac could hear a truck starting. The container pitched forward and they bounced down a road. Isaac was scared, but he knew his dad would find him before anything bad happened to him.

They sat in silence for a long time. Isaac started feeling uncomfortable so he said, "Kelly, when we get out of here you should come stay with us. I don't have any siblings. I bet my parents would love to have you."

He looked over at her. She had her head against the wall but her face was white. She was sweating and shaking.

"Kelly, are you ok?" he was getting worried. She looked sick, and he realized it must be more than the fear of flying.

"I'm f-f-fine," she stuttered. She wrapped her arms closer around herself. Isaac took off his jacket and gave it to her.

"What's going on?" he asked her.

She wrapped the jacket around herself and leaned into him, putting her head on his shoulder. Isaac's heart gave a lurch and he wrapped his arm around her.

"It will pass in a couple days," she said. "It will get bad, I've seen it happen to my friends. But then it will get better. Will you help me until it gets better?" she asked. Her voice was fading. She suddenly doubled over in pain.

Isaac jumped up and started banging on the side of the container, "She's sick!" he yelled over and over until his voice was raw.

"Zac," Kelly said weakly. She had vomited all over the container floor. Isaac stopped yelling and went over to her. He gathered her away from the puke so she didn't get dirty. "Zac, I'm not going to die. I will be O.K. It will take a couple days but it will go away."

Isaac sniffled and wiped a tear, "How do you know?"

"I just haven't had my fix for a while. In a few days I'll get better. Just stay with me for a few days."

Isaac fought the shock. He had never met anyone addicted to anything. He wanted to ask her to what but he bit his tongue. She didn't need him prying into her life.

"My parents will find us," he reassured her. His hope was starting to fade. "And then you can stay with us and you can get better. It'll be all better."

Kelly let him ramble, she didn't have the energy to argue with him. Isaac held her until the bumping stopped. He realized that she had fallen asleep.

The container was unloaded again and the wall away from them was opened. The light hurt his eyes after the dull yellow lamp. He shielded his face and Kelly stirred beside him. His eyes took a long time to adjust. Once they did, he noticed two large men standing in view of the open door. They had crew-cuts and were wearing black cargo pants and black t-shirts, showing large muscular arms. Isaac noticed guns on each of their hips. Another man, a tall and skinny man in a blue suit and slicked back hair was standing in between them. He was holding a tablet in front of him.

"Two, one male one female," he said, ticking something off on his tablet. He had a thick French accent. He walked into the container and, wrinkling his nose, said, "Who vomited? Smells like shit in here."

Isaac rose, leaving Kelly sitting on the ground looking up at them.

"She's sick," Isaac said, pointing at her. "This is your fault, you need to fix it."

"What's your name?" the man said, looking Isaac up and down for a very long time. The predatory look in his eyes made Isaac uncomfortable.

"Isaac," he replied, jutting out his chin.

"Isaac," the French man said. "Well, Isaac, my name is François. I am in charge of this little operation. My employer has sent you here and my job is to keep you alive. There are no rules on how alive I need to keep you. Is that understood?"

Isaac kept his chin out. When François tried to get past him to get to Kelly he stepped sideways to block his way. "Don't touch us!" Isaac yelled.

François smiled at him and back-handed him across the face. Isaac was surprised by the blow and didn't get his hands up to block. His skinny form fell heavily onto the ground, just inches from Kelly's vomit. His face stung and there was blood leaking from his mouth. He was too shocked to move, no one had ever hit him before. François yelled something and Isaac was pulled to his feet and was halfdragged half walked out of the container.

"Kelly!" he yelled, trying to turn his head to see where she was. They were in a large garage with military trucks and other men dressed the same milling about. No one looked up or was even surprised that a fifteen year-old was being forced through the garage against his will. Isaac struggled but the man was too strong. He dragged Isaac through the garage and to a back door. It opened and Isaac was greeted with what looked like an old prison. It was carved out of stone and there were doors made of old steel bars. Isaac looked through the bars and saw children of all ages, two to a cell, looking at him with sad eyes. Some looked sick and unhealthy, others had blackened eyes and broken teeth. Isaac stopped struggling and stared at them. The children stared back. The only thing in common was the fear in all of their eyes.

The man tossed Isaac into one of the cells. Kelly was tossed in shortly after. Isaac made a run at the door and the man slammed it in his face. François came to the door, "Now," he said, "you would do best not to talk to any of the others. My guards don't like noise. This may or may not be your final destination. I'm not sure."

Isaac was breathing heavily, anger running through him. "Where have you taken us?" he asked.

François smiled at him, showing a row of perfect teeth, "I won't tell you that. Just be encouraged by the thought that you will never ever see your family again. I specialize in pairing children with buyers. I suppose you can figure out what that means."

Isaac blanched. "You're not selling us. You're not touching us."

François' eyes darkened. "An annoyance of mine," he said, leaning closer to the bars, "is being told what to do by a snivelling little rat like yourself."

Isaac spat in his face.

François straightened. Carefully and deliberately he pulled a handkerchief out of the top pocket of his jacket and wiped his face. He looked Isaac in the eyes and Isaac took a step back. There was an evil there he had never encountered before. François snapped his fingers twice and the two large men returned, jogging.

"Her," he said, pointing at Kelly's huddled body.

"No!" Isaac yelled.

The men rushed in and Isaac tried to fight. One punched him in the face again and he dropped to the concrete as pain exploded. One man put a knee into his back, keeping him pinned against the ground. Isaac struggled as the cold concrete pushed against his face. He was having trouble breathing, the weight of the man's knee pushing into his chest.

"I'll go, just stop hitting him," Kelly said softly. She stood shakily, wiping the sweat off her face.

"No," Isaac moaned as Kelly walked out the door. She didn't look back. François took her by the hand and led her away. The guard holding him down released him. Isaac had a head rush as oxygen returned to his brain. He stayed on the ground, gasping for air. The two guards locked the door and followed Kelly and François.

Isaac paced the cell for a long time. Guilt was rising. He didn't know what they were going to do to her. He didn't know what to think. He had made terrible mistakes.

Kelly was led back to the cell later. He felt relief when he saw her followed by intense guilt. A guard was supporting her and she was limping slowly, head down, her hair over her face. The guard opened the door and she collapsed inside the cell.

Isaac ran to her and collapsed on the ground beside her. He

gathered her into his arms. "I'm so so sorry," he muttered into her ear. "What did they do to you? I'm so sorry Kelly."

She looked up at him. Her face looked the same, there was no damage and Isaac was relieved. But her eyes made his stomach boil. They were dark and dead.

"Don't worry about it Zac," she said weakly. "Nothing I haven't handled before." She leaned into him and closed her eyes, "I just need to sleep. It will be better in the morning."

Isaac wrapped her closer and cried quietly into her hair. He had a crushing feeling that his parents would never find them.

6 DR. CHARLIE PENNER

October 19, 2023, 15:48
Location: Dorfen, Germany.

She watched the white lab rat run around its enclosure and sighed. The rat was oblivious to the chemical compound she had just added to its water. It scurried around its cage acting as natural as it had this morning.

Charlie sighed and looked at her watch. It had been a full ten minutes with no results. She marked it down on her tablet and returned to her station, sitting heavily in the plush work chair. She had access to all the resources she needed, no limit on budget and the best equipment that money could buy but she still couldn't get results.

She stared at her reflection in the darkened screen of her computer. She had long, flowing red hair that was pulled meticulously back into a bun. A pale face highlighted the bags under her eyes, despite the makeup she had applied that morning. She sighed and looked at her own bright green eyes. She was stressed and tired. She rubbed her neck and put her tablet onto the dock at her desk, instantly transferring all the data to her computer and the onsite servers. She moved the mouse and turned on the screen of her computer. She absent-mindedly rubbed the empty spot on her left ring finger where her wedding ring used to sit.

The 3D rendering of the molecule she designed popped up on the screen. It was a cross between ketamine and *gamma*-Hydrobutyric acid. She had, in a last ditch effort, thrown a GHB molecule onto a Ketamine and tried it out. Clearly it hadn't worked. She needed to figure this out. She took the stylus out of the top left pocket in her crisp white lab coat. She missed paper sometimes.

She was thirty-two and had grown up with technology. She was a doctor in biochemistry with a smattering of other minors and specializations. All lending themselves to her expertise. She took the stylus out and started to rotate the 3D model on her screen. No result was worse than the molecule just killing the host. At least if it killed the rat it was proof the molecule was interacting with something in its body. She didn't know where to start. She had been given this ridiculous task more than a year ago. She needed to produce results.

"Dr. Penner!" she heard in a thick French accent from behind her. Her lab assistant, Luc, was staring at the cage of the white rat they had brought out for testing this morning.

"Yes, Luc," she replied harshly. She did not like to be interrupted.

"You might want to come and look at this," he said, not noticing her tone. Or he noticed and didn't care. Charlie had a string of international assistants come through her doors. She usually never even bothered to learn their names, she was always so lost in her research. She knew Luc because he had stuck with her the longest, a full six months.

Charlie heaved herself out of her chair and walked towards the cage in the center of the lab. Her mind was still with the molecule, rotating it, manipulating it. She stopped beside Luc, her tall six-foot form (taller in her bright red heels) making him look small in comparison. He was staring at the cage. She followed his eyes and saw the white rat in the middle of the cage. It was having a seizure, foam and vomit coming from its mouth.

Charlie sprang into action. "Luc! Stop standing there, get the EEG set up immediately."

Luc moved quickly, moving a large white machine to the cage. It was a portable, wireless electroencephalogram. It read the brainwaves of any animal that was in its beam.

"You!" she yelled at a timid assistant staring glassy-eyed into a microscope. "Stop that, get the video camera and record this. Now!" the glassy-eyed assistant looked terrified at being singled out, but to her credit scrambled to get the video camera ready.

Luc had the EEG machine set up. Charlie went and watched the screen. There was a feed of the regular Alpha, Beta, Theta and Delta waves across the screen. They were showing what would be expected in a seizure. Charlie also had the feed set to capture Infra-Low waves as well, the least studied but most useful of the five. Especially for what she was researching.

Her eyes focused on the screen and on the waves. The rat stopped seizing and the waves went flat-line. Instant disappointment rushed into her heart.

"I'm sorry," Luc said dryly. He was standing beside her watching the screen and the rat in the cage. It was dead. The glassy-eyed assistant kept the camera pointed at the dead rat.

Charlie didn't say anything. She refused to acknowledge Luc. Her mind was racing. It was back to square one. She kept watching the flat waves go across the screen, mocking her failure.

A huge wave appeared in all five wavelengths. It was completely different from the normal pattern of any type of consciousness. The waves danced and weaved across the screen, no pattern detectable. It lasted approximately five seconds before they began to fade to flat-line.

"Putain de merde," she heard Luc whisper beside her.

She couldn't help but smile and repeat in English, "Holy shit." Shaking off her disbelief, she said to him, "Bring up the EEG we have on file for Z207."

They moved to her station. Charlie sat down in her chair, Luc and the other assistant joined her. Charlie turned on her station, lighting up the five large computer screens mounted on the wall. Charlie brought up the recorded pattern for the dead rat on the left. Luc brought up the file she had asked for on the right screen. The EEG danced and weaved in the exact same pattern that the rat had shown, all five waves moving in a weird cross between jagged edges and flowing waves.

Charlie couldn't help but smile. "Now Z209."

Luc replaced the current EEG with a new one. The same pattern twirled on the screen. The rat's EEG was shorter than the others but it showed the exact same characteristics. One that was rarely seen.

"I did it!" Charlie exclaimed in disbelief, sitting heavily in her plush chair. She couldn't stop staring at the computer screens.

She heard a slow clap coming from the door of her laboratory. Charlie winced and turned slowly, staring her boss, Alejandra Jimenez, in the face. She was dressed in a tailored suit, blue heels with her loose brown hair falling around her mocha pointed face. She walked towards them, heels clicking sharply on the ground.

"Congratulations!" Alejandra said, voice singing in her Columbian accent. She clapped Charlie on the shoulder and bent down to join them looking at the screens.

"Yes," Alejandra said with a smile, digging her nails painfully into Charlie's shoulder, "I do believe you have done it."

"Well, we need much more research to make sure…"

"Our employer will be most pleased," Alejandra continued. She was leaning so close that Charlie could smell her perfume. It was floral, but there was a dark sweet undertone that Charlie couldn't place. Both Alejandra and her perfume always made Charlie excessively uncomfortable.

"We need months more to research this! It could just be luck," Charlie rambled.

Alejandra turned slowly and deliberately to stare at Charlie's face, "I will take care of further research. I do believe you've earned the afternoon off." Charlie started to interject. Alejandra held up one finger, stopping her before she could get any words out. "No! I will not have my best scientist staying at work after a discovery like this. You will go and take the afternoon. I insist."

Charlie heard the venomous tone and her heart dropped. "Yes ma'am," she conceded, lowering her eyes.

"Good!" Alejandra said, straightening. "Luc will finish off cleaning and packaging the research for the servers. I do believe they are serving steak this afternoon for our evening meal." She turned and walked away, finishing with, "I will ensure it's up to your impeccable standards. Luc, make sure our dear Doctor doesn't work too hard." Alejandra left the lab through the clean room.

Charlie let out a shudder that she'd been holding in. She reached for the stylus and Luc grabbed her hand roughly, "No!" he said, wrenching her hand away from the computer so hard that it would bruise. Charlie's face flashed burning anger and hate.

"Ms. Jimenez said no more work for you today," Luc said.

Charlie pulled her hand away, "I'm signing my research. I always sign my research."

Luc stared for a long time. Charlie matched his gaze, anger boiling. Luc eventually just shrugged and stepped back from the computer.

She leaned forward and put her classic signature from her Bachelor's degree on the molecule: C.B.Penn.

Luc looked at her quizzically, "Used to be my nickname in University. I sign everything with that until I publish. Old habits." She smiled at him. She quickly copied the file to the server.

"Go to supper. I will finish this up," Luc said flatly.

Charlie obliged and left her lab through the clean room. She stripped and pulled on her sweats and a clean t-shirt. She didn't care about the cameras in the room, she'd done this every day for the last year. Sometimes you became immune to being self-conscious. She used her key card to get out of her laboratory, nodding to the guards standing armed at either side of the door.

"Jergen, Kurt," she said. They both nodded towards her and then stared straight ahead.

She used her key card to get out of the hallway and went to the gym. Her key card only worked on less than a quarter of the compound. She wasn't allowed access to anywhere her employer didn't want her to be. She had time for a run before dinner and she definitely needed to take her mind off things. She ran hard on the treadmill, trying to relieve herself of the stress of the day. She showed no emotion on her face. She knew the entire compound, both inside and out, was recorded by cameras. She finished, puffing, and went to have a shower.

She went to dinner, which was indeed steak. She ate silently in the empty mess hall and noticed Alejandra come and check on her to ensure that she was where she was supposed to be. Alejandra watched her from the door for a while then left her with her lonely meal.

After her dinner, she walked to her bedroom and locked the

door. She turned off the lights and allowed herself to think. The cameras in her room wouldn't be able to see her face in the dark. She let out a tear and a sob, disgusted at what she had become. She pitied herself more than ever before and her shoulders heaved in silent grief. She wrapped her hand around a necklace under her night shirt. It was a gold dragon wrapped around a ruby. It was her only possession from her life before and she clung to it dearly, pouring emotions into it.

She gradually relaxed and came to a conclusion. One that she had thought of before but never had the incentive to pull off.

She needed to break into her lab and steal her research back. She needed to destroy everything. That was the only way to undo what she had done.

7 CARTER

October 21, 2023, 09:55
Location: Toronto, Canada.

Carter sat beside her hospital bed, head in his hands. It had been three days since they had gotten Senka out of Russia. The army crew that had retrieved her had managed to keep her alive and stop the bleeding in the helicopter. They had sped to the nearest Canadian Military base where Senka had gotten stitched up and had been flown home as fast as possible.

The surgeon contracted to the ZTF had done his best to repair the damage to her face. She had then been transferred to the ZTF headquarters in Toronto for recovery. The Zoya Task Force headquarters was located in a normal apartment building in downtown Toronto. They had the middle two floors of the fifteen-storey building to themselves. The walls between the apartments had been removed, state of the art sound proofing added, and access to the floors was blocked by elevator and the stairs. The people living in the building had no idea there was a world-class military organization right under their noses.

The upper floor was archives, the secured server room and the medical recovery ward. They had the best of the best medical equipment and a couple of hand-picked nurses. The two other beds in the recovery ward of ZTF headquarters remained empty. Carter wasn't the only one in the room visiting. Leo was asleep beside Senka's bed and hadn't left her since the ricochet bullet had hit her. It proved difficult to try to move him as he would bare his teeth and growl when anyone tried to get him out of the ward. Finally, Carter had bought him a bed and food from the nearby pet store and Leo had made his home. Leo had even let Carter bathe him and groom him while Senka was in her last surgery. Carter figured they both had needed the distraction.

He heard the door of the ward open and both he and Leo raised their heads. The head of the Zoya Task Force, Amanda Nguyen, stepped into the room. She was medically trained and used to be in charge of recruitment, which had previously led her to the Riverview Medical Clinic to recruit Senka when she woke from her coma three years ago. Amanda had posed as her nurse and thus was privileged to all of her information. When their previous boss had retired, Amanda had taken his position.

She walked in in her power suit and her heels clicking away on the tile. Leo huffed and put his head down. Carter stayed seated.

"Any change?" Amanda asked. She busied herself checking Senka's chart at the foot of the bed.

"No," he answered. He was tired. "Is she…" He was afraid to ask.

"No," Amanda said, putting the chart down and leaning against the bed. "She's not in The Other Place. Not in a coma at all, actually. Just resting. She's had a long couple of days. The doctor said she'd be fine."

Carter was relieved but he still couldn't look at Senka's face. It was covered but he knew she would have a large scar running down it for the rest of her life.

Amanda was watching him, "She had that in The Other Place," Amanda said. "The scar. You of all people know that. She will know what it's like."

"Hasn't she earned not having it?" Carter asked. "Everything she did in The Other Place? Everything she's done here?"

Amanda shrugged, "You know it's not about earning it. Children with cancer never earned it. It just happens. She made choices and this is what happened. And she's killed a lot of people. Maybe she has earned it."

Carter shook his head, "She does what we can't. You wouldn't be able to pull the trigger, nor would I."

"She's not the only Zoya out there. She's not the only one working for us. They all pull the trigger. This has been happening more and more. History is repeating itself. You know how Tomo died? It was the same in The Other Place. I don't know why, but just be thankful she's alive."

Carter flinched when he heard Tomo's full name. His mind was momentarily filled with the view he had from Senka's camera that fateful day. He saw the explosion. Senka's wretched scream filled his ears as they watched the truck Tomo was in burn. He shook his head, trying to put the memory in the past. He and Senka always shortened the name, it was just easier that way. Amanda refused. Carter rubbed his forehead, the echoes of the scream never really leaving him. He figured that Amanda, of all people, was allowed to call Tomo whatever she wanted. Still didn't stop the pain.

"Anyway your lunch is over. It's time to brief."

"Shouldn't we wait for her to wake up?" Carter asked, nodding towards his sleeping partner.

"You can fill her in. My office in five," she walked away.

Leo and Carter watched her walk away. "Well, that was fun," Carter said to the dog. Leo huffed his agreement.

Carter left Senka's side and walked down the stairs to the lower floor, nodding to the two military guards at the door. They had a few highly trained guards on staff for security and for an extra set of guns if they needed them.

The Zoya Task Force was small but effective. His station was one of seven, with each handler having one agent. They each had a series of computer screens at their desks set up how the handler wanted. There was a large screen on one wall for joint efforts or when Amanda wanted to take the lead. It was playing the news, which it always did unless there was something important happening. They had a weapons room on this floor and Amanda had a glass office that doubled as a briefing room that could fit the entire task force.

They were the best of the best. Seven agents, Zoya from all over the world, worked out of here on international affairs. Carter only knew what Senka was doing and her mission. He knew the other handlers and agents, they were all friendly, but they had distinctly different missions. They only knew the details when an agent was killed or when a mission was a success. Many of these missions were years in the making, but all were absolutely influential in world events.

Carter stopped at his station to pick up his tablet and a folder with papers readied for Amanda. The Zoya Task Force symbol was embossed on the front of the folder. A globe surrounded by a shield with a sword and a Z over the hilt. Simple, yet effective; same as the ZTF.

He focused on the large screen. He shook his head. Another tsunami in Japan. It was the third this year. The number of environmental disasters all over the world was exponentially on the rise. The major scientific consensus was global warming. However nobody knew why, despite global green efforts, there had been a sudden increase of natural disasters over the last three years.

Carter pulled himself away from the screen and entered the briefing room. It was glass-walled but one hundred percent sound proof and bullet proof. It had a large monitor, one which he could control from his tablet. Amanda was sitting behind her sparse metal desk, hands folded in front of her, all business. She could see and observe her entire floor from behind that desk.

Avoiding formalities, Carter sent the data he wanted to share to the computer in the room. He walked to her desk and gave her the paper folder.

Amanda flipped the hard copy open, "What am I looking at?" Amanda asked.

"Well, we're going to start with the more important information I've been able to unlock." He paused, looked up and smiled.

Senka walked into the briefing room with Leo by her side. She was leaning on an IV pole and her hospital gown was flapping open behind her. He could tell by the looks of the handlers at their desks that she wasn't wearing any underwear.

Carter took three big strides towards her and wrapped her in a bear hug. He stepped back to look at her. She had removed her dressing and her face looked sore, a cleanly stitched cut running from her hairline down past her chin. It actually looked better than he thought it would.

"Thanks for waiting, team," Senka said sarcastically as she sat in a chair. Leo circled and sniffed a few times and lay down heavily beside her.

"We figured you would be up and at it soon," Amanda offered.

"Good seeing you up and about," Carter said, smiling at her warmly. "You look just as ugly as ever."

Senka tried to smile but Carter could tell it hurt her face to do so. Her eyes smiled, though, "Look better than you any day. Besides, the scar makes me distinguished."

Carter laughed, "We were just getting started." He was visibly more comfortable now that Senka was in the room. "So I've been trying to unlock the server data that you gave me access to. The servers that were destroyed in Russia were just the tip of the iceberg. You gave me access to a whole worldwide network of servers. There are multiple firewalls and the passwords change for each folder every hour so it's been slower going than I expected."

"Seems like pretty extreme levels of security, even for a drug ring," Senka said, all business. Amanda wouldn't say much during the brief. It was more her style to listen and watch her handlers and agents then ask her questions later.

"Exactly," Carter replied. "Why the security? We were just going in thinking it was an international drug ring. I think it's more."

"I think it's people," Senka offered.

"I think you're right, but it feels even high security for that."

"What have you found?" Amanda asked, keeping them on task.

"I've managed to access a few folders, mostly just locations across the world. I've also been able to access the list of folders." Carter brought it up on screen. There was a list of folders with their symbols that popped up on the screen.

"What's that?" Senka asked, pointing towards the top-most folder. It was a golden symbol of a tribal insect with an A in its body, surrounded by a purple background. The title beside read Ampulex.

"I honestly have no idea," Carter replied, "that has the most information but it will be the hardest to access. They have firewalls on their firewalls on that folder."

Senka squinted her eyes at the picture, "Is it just me or does that look like a wasp?"

Carter squinted, "I guess if you look hard and tilt your head. I think it looks like a bee."

Senka rolled her eyes. "Ok, let's agree it's a flying, stinging bug. Folder obviously has the best shit," Senka said, changing the subject. "If it has the highest security."

"Right, but I wanted to find out some more stuff before I tackled that."

"Fair enough," Senka said.

"Anyway. I found a very interesting folder and I was able to access most of it. Actually, that was by mistake. I was online getting my bearings in the server and this data was uploaded." Carter brought up a folder and opened it. Inside were research notes.

"Drug design?" Senka offered. Carter was scrolling through the data fast, "Stop!" Senka said when Carter scrolled by a 3D model of a molecule.

"What is that?" Amanda asked, being drawn in with both of them.

"As far as I can tell it's a new molecule. Looks like a Ketamine molecule with a GHB molecule added," Carter said looking closely.

Senka wasn't even remotely surprised that Carter knew that off the top of his head. Carter knew everything.

"I don't know what that means," Senka said.

"Ask the nurse," Carter said smiling at Amanda and taking a drink of water.

"Ketamine is used as a sedative. GHB is the same but it's mostly used as a date rape drug. Ketamine can also cause hallucinations," Amanda offered, brow furrowed. "Carter, can you zoom in on the bottom right?"

Carter obliged. As he did, a signature appeared beside the molecule.

"Good eyes, boss," Senka said, "What does it say?"

"C.B.Penn," Carter offered and shrugged, "Old school practice, researchers signing their stuff. This must be the guy who made the molecule."

Amanda was squinting at the name. Senka saw a look of shock pass over her face, disappearing as quickly as it appeared.

"What did you see?" Senka asked, cocking her head.

"Nothing. I've never heard of him," Amanda answered. "Continue Carter."

Carter nodded, oblivious. "This is really the only thing I've been able to access, this and a couple of emails," Carter said, scrolling quickly through the research. He paused at a brainwave pattern labeled Z207, looking at his own notes.

"Stop!" Amanda barked when she saw it. "That I recognize. Those are the same brainwave patterns as people who are Zoya."

"No…" Senka said in disbelief.

"That's a Zoya?" Carter asked.

"Yes," Amanda said, "that's the brainwave pattern of a Zoya while they are in a coma."

"Why do they care about Zoya?" Senka asked.

Carter was focused, quickly skipping through all the information he had accessed.

"No idea," Carter replied. "I was hoping the other thing I was able to infer helps with that. No one uses names in the server, it's all numbers."

"So if the server was hacked, no one would be able to find anything," Senka offered.

"Exactly. But the easiest thing to access was a string of emails going back a couple of weeks. Seems to me the boss was coming to a facility to visit. It was all pretty vague. Anyway, in a flurry of emails there was a slip and a name was used," Carter brought the information up. "Someone calls him Freudman."

"Find him," Amanda said, staring at the screen intently.

Carter obliged. They waited in silence, all three lost in thought. A profile popped up showing a man with well cropped red hair and a moustache. This time Amanda really did gasp.

"Dr. Wolfrick Freudman," Carter said, staring at Amanda intently, "says here he's a notable neurosurgeon in Germany. Why the gasp?"

Amanda returned to her desk, staring at Senka.

"When you were in your coma, a man came. Dr. Freeman. I caught him performing unauthorized research on you. It actually almost killed you."

Senka stared at her.

"That's him," Amanda said, pointing at the screen. "This is way bigger than drugs or human trafficking. Carter, you will pick a team of three of the best hackers available to the Canadian Government.

You will unlock everything in these servers, including that folder labeled Ampulex. We need to know everything yesterday, understood?"

Carter nodded.

"Senka, you have a new, low-profile mission in the interim," Amanda reached into her desk and pulled out a folder. She walked to Senka's side and put the folder and a smartphone on the table in front of her.

Senka leaned over and read the title of the dossier. She paled.

"No," Senka said, pushing the folder away. "I've refused before, I'm refusing now. I'm not doing it."

"Yes, you will," Amanda said. "I have no use for you here. Your mother's birthday is tomorrow evening. You leave tomorrow morning."

"No, I'm not," Senka said flatly.

Amanda ignored her, "I've also taken the liberty of running your civilian Facebook page for you while you were away in Russia."

Senka's eyes went wide as she scrambled to unlock her phone. "No, no, no, no, no!" she exclaimed as she looked through her phone. Carter caught Amanda hiding a smile. Senka's face went even whiter as she read hastily through her phone. "You put me in a relationship!" Senka groaned.

"Yes," Amanda said, "It was about time that you were."

"Who am I supposed to be in a relationship with?" Senka exclaimed.

"That's in your mission dossier. You should probably review it before you get to Winnipeg."

"All she's going to do is ask me about my relationship. God, she even liked it! What did I ever do to you?" Senka whined.

"It's part of your contract that you maintain a semblance of civilian life," Amanda said, stone faced. "And your psychiatrist thinks that you need a trip home. I happen to agree."

"I'm taking Leo and we get the private jet," Senka said, a full blown pout on her damaged face.

Amanda stared at her for a long time. Senka stared back. "Fine," Amanda acquiesced, "but there is a Honda Civic waiting for you at the airport. Your family thinks you still live in Brandon."

"A Civic?" Senka said, slouching lower in her chair. Grasping at her last rope of freedom, she said, "How do you explain this?" as she pointed to her face.

"Bike accident," Amanda said, beginning to busy herself with her computer.

Senka seemed to perk up slightly, "Well, least I own a motorcycle."

"A pedal bike accident," Amanda said firmly.

Senka's face fell. Carter tried to smother his laugh and he patted Senka sympathetically on the shoulder. She rose, mumbling incoherently and left with Leo contently padding behind.

"You had to give her a Civic hey?" he asked Amanda once Senka left.

"Consider it payback for bringing an unauthorized animal into this office," Amanda answered coldly, and without looking up from her computer said, "make sure she doesn't forget her dossier."

8 SENKA

October 22, 2023, 16:05
Location: Winnipeg, Canada.

They were fighting for their lives.

The mission was doomed from the start. The American Senator's daughter was most likely dead anyway, even before they launched into Brazil. They were both surrounded by men. Senka was out of bullets and was panting. Tomo was on her knees, having taken a vicious blow to the stomach. Her bright green eyes were angry and glaring at the leader.

"Now," said the leader, stepping towards Tomo, "how much money do you think the United Nations will pay to get their golden girls back?"

"The United Nations doesn't negotiate with terrorists," Tomo replied. She wiped her face. Blood was seeping from her eyebrow and running down her cheek. It was almost the same colour as her hair.

"But I think they will negotiate for you," the leader said. Tomo was grabbed around her middle and dragged towards an army truck. Her arms were outstretched, reaching for Senka. Her eyes were wide with fear.

The dream shifted, as the dreams always did.

Senka was suddenly on a dirt bike, chasing the truck Tomo was in through the Brazilian jungle. Trees were ripping by, cutting her face and arms. She was so focused on Tomo and the army truck racing away through the jungle that she ignored the pain. She lost them for a second coming over a ridge. She was yelling at Carter to call off the airstrike but it was too late. The truck was engulfed in flames as it exploded. Senka screamed.

The dream shifted again.

She was in The Other Place, walking through her old town of Ismat. She saw her own body being burned on a pyre. It was surreal, watching herself being burned. She looked so peaceful.

The Shaman was suddenly beside her. She didn't turn, she felt his presence. She watched the flames consume her.

"It's only started," he said.

"I know," she replied.

"You will come back."

"Haven't I earned rest?" she asked. Her body was engulfed in flames on the pyre.

"While the evil lives, no one can rest."

Senka turned towards him. He was just as he always was. White hair, dark crinkled face, carrying his staff with the bright red stone on the top. He smiled at her, knowingly. He had been one of the few who had shown her kindness in The Other Place. He had reached out to a Zoya, a person to be feared. Senka hadn't seen him in three long years. She missed him.

The Shaman's skin started bubbling. He opened his mouth. Flames burst from his mouth and eyes, consuming his body.

"No!" Senka yelled, reaching towards him.

The Shaman exploded outward in a mass of fire and sparks. Senka covered her face with her arm. The heat burned her skin.

Senka sat bolt upright in the plane, panting. She was reaching towards her sidearm that was hidden beneath her leather jacket. Leo was awake and standing. He had his head on her lap and was staring at her, big brown eyes worried. She stared at him and gradually calmed as the dream faded. Her hand left her gun and Leo licked her finger.

"It's ok," she said, taking deep breaths trying to relax, "it'll be ok." She was on the private ZTF plane, heading to Winnipeg. She had fallen asleep. She gradually returned to the present.

Leo stared at her, head on her lap. She rubbed his ears and gradually sank back into her chair. She was used to the dream about Tomo. That was a nightly event. But the one with the Shaman and pyre was new. Senka was perturbed. She knew in her gut that it was more than just a dream. That was disconcerting. She had died in The Other Place three years ago. Three years in Langundo without the Shaman present meant that it was, and most likely still is, in a state of emergency.

She stopped scratching Leo's ears, lost in thought. Leo nudged her hand and she smiled. Her face hurt but was healing nicely. She restarted scratching Leo's ears preoccupied with worry for The Other Place. It was bigger than Langundo. When she was over there she hadn't realized The Other Place contained anything other than her own little world.

Tomo had been in The Other Place the same time that she was, but on a completely different continent. There were multiple places that Zoya woke up, all over that world. She wouldn't be surprised if the whole world over there had gone to shit.

"Well, it can join this world then," she mumbled at Leo. He was panting happily, having done his job ensuring that Senka didn't accidentally shoot the pilot. Senka needed a drink. Amanda had made sure that the plane was left with only non-alcoholic beverages. *Amanda needs to mind her own business,* she thought grumpily.

The plane lurched as they landed. Senka and Leo left the plane directly on the tarmac, away from the main airport. Senka didn't like people, especially in large groups.

She grabbed her bag and hoisted it over her shoulder. The blue Honda Civic was waiting in a Canadian Military hanger. She dropped her bag in disappointment. It looked like it was from 2002. It had duct tape on one of the bumpers, the mirrors were bent and the back window had so many hail chips she wasn't sure if she'd be able to see through it. She thought she saw pink fuzzy dice hanging from the rear-view mirror. If Senka could cry, she would.

They walked to the Civic and she tossed her bag unceremoniously in the back seat. Leo jumped in the passenger seat, happy as ever, looking out the window. She tried to close the door and it bounced open. She threw her head back and sighed audibly. She held the latch and finally got the door to close. She adjusted the rear-view and tore down the fuzzy dice, tossing them in the back seat. She didn't need pink fuzzy dice in her life right now.

She fired up the car and ripped out of the hanger, pushing the Civic as fast as it could go. Which was a disappointing eighty kilometres an hour. She merged into traffic and prepared herself mentally for the evening. She would make it just in time for her mother's birthday supper. She had to survive the night then she could leave in the morning. This was worse than her mission to Siberia and she was more nervous than during any other mission in memory.

She limped her car to her mother's house and parked it. She moved her gun to the holster concealed at the small of her back. She didn't expect to need to use it. "Unless I blow my brains out," she muttered. Leo looked at her and growled lowly. "Yah I get it. Not a funny joke," she muttered to him. She grabbed her bag and opened it, seeing a handsome leather collar with a tag on it. Carter sure knew how to take care of her.

"Yah, see? Not as fun when you have to join me in embarrassment," she told Leo as she attached his collar. He actually seemed happy, moving his neck to jingle the tag and wagging his tail.

"Of course you like it," she muttered. She took out a leash. Leo's ears went back and his tail stopped.

"Don't pout at me," she said, attaching the leash. "Bylaws are bylaws."

She grabbed her bag and exited the car with Leo. The door bounced open and she kicked it viciously. It finally latched closed. "Fucking Civic," she muttered under her breath.

Her mom was at the door, waving excitedly. Senka took a big breath in and smiled as wide as her healing face would let her.

"Hey mom!" she called. Leo was having trouble staying by her side, he always took point. He kept pulling at the leash then looking at her with sad brown eyes when the leather leash stopped his progress.

"Elizabeth!" her mother yelled, running out of the house. Her mom seemed pretty put together, wearing clean jeans and a nice cardigan. Her mother wrapped her in a hug. Senka let her, and actually felt herself going soft in her mom's arms.

Her mom held her at arm's length, taking her in.

"Oh, honey I'm so sorry about your face!" she said, raising her hand to brush Senka's hair out of her face and get a better look at the cut. "I would have come to see you in the hospital in Brandon but I didn't know you were there."

"It's ok, mom," Senka said awkwardly, "it looks worse than it is. Just had a run in with a parked car when I was biking to work." Her stomach lurched when she said it. She hated lying to her mom. Plus this lie was embarrassing.

"And this handsome fellow must be Leo!" her mother said, crouching and giving Leo pets on the ears and neck. Leo was loving it and rolled on his back panting happily for a belly rub. Her mother obliged. "Your Facebook said you got him from a shelter! He's a handsome boy! I think you'll be good for each other."

Senka felt the rising guilt. Her mother loved her so much and Senka gave her nothing in return. Her mother was so desperate for information about her that she clung to the fake messages Amanda posted in her name, desperate for information about her reckless and lost daughter.

Her mother rose from giving Leo attention and said, "Gang's all here! James arrived a couple hours ago. We can have supper!"

Senka followed her into the house, it had been a full year since she had been here, but it hadn't changed. She noticed a bouquet of yellow daisies on the dining room table and felt guilty. Her dad had always brought home daisies for her mom on her birthday. James must have brought them. Senka had been so self-absorbed she hadn't even brought her mom a gift.

"Go put your bag down and say hi to the boys," her mom said. "They sure are excited to meet Leo."

Senka took off Leo's leash and followed him to the basement. Leo's tail wagged excitedly as he followed his ears to the chaos below. The boys had out the old gaming system and were playing a hunting game. James was yelling at sixteen year old Kenny. Billy and John were playing on another team. She watched them for a second, noticing how bad their shots were and smiled. Leo ran up to them and James immediately paused the game.

"Liz!" he yelled and ran up to her, wrapping her in a giant hug. She could hear Billy laughing as Leo jumped up and licked his face.

"Hey big brother," she said, looking at James' green eyes.

"Good to see you sis," he said, squeezing her tighter.

"Hey boys!" she said awkwardly as James let her go. They all waved and said hi, coming single file to give her a hug. Leo was sticking close to Billy, licking his hands and bouncing excitedly.

"I just have to put my bag in my room," she said. She turned as Billy started wrestling with Leo on the ground and suppressed a smile.

She walked into her basement room and her heart fell again. Her mother had moved to Winnipeg to be closer to her after the accident and had moved her bedroom with her, keeping details as close as possible to the original in The Pas.

She had her camo bedsheets and her bow was hung over her bed, just as it had been when she was growing up. Her mother had even brought all the pictures that were on the desk.

This was why she hated coming home. It was a reminder of who had died in that accident.

She tossed her bag on the bed and opened it to put Leo's leash back. A small silver package that shouldn't have been there caught her eye. She picked it up and saw that the box said Tiffany's in white across the top. She opened it and saw a beautiful silver necklace of a bow and arrow. There was also a card. Senka opened it and the front read, "Happy Birthday Mom!" in bright yellow writing.

She shook her head. Leave it to Carter to make sure that she had a birthday present and a card for her mother when she came home to visit. She felt so inadequate. She exchanged her leather coat for a sweater and slipped the box and card inside the front pocket.

She returned to the boys, leaning on the wall quietly and watching them play their game. They weren't good, missing as many shots as they hit. But their giggles and laughter meant it didn't matter.

James noticed her silent form and yelled, smiling, "Move over, boys. Let the master show you how it's done."

Senka laughed and took the fake gun. She hit every shot, to the applause and laughter of her brothers.

"Kids! Dinner's ready!" her mother yelled from above.

The younger boys launched out of their chairs and off the couch and ran upstairs. Leo looked at her for permission. She gave him a quick nod and he followed. She could hear Billy's laughter as the dog caught up with them.

"Billy really likes him," James said.

"Yah he's a good dog," Senka said.

James was staring at her intently, "Sure does listen to you. You've only had him, what, a week?"

"Five days."

"Wow. You must be a dog whisperer."

Senka shrugged, "Match made in heaven. I saw him and I knew."

James kept staring at her. Finally, he rose and said, "Good to see you, sis."

Senka nodded. She was getting choked up. James understood and patted her on the back and walked past her up the stairs.

"Where's your sister?" her mother asked from above.

"Just going to the bathroom," James replied, giving her a cover.

Senka gathered her courage and went upstairs.

Supper was wonderful. The family laughed and talked like there were no years between meetings. Her mom didn't even bring up the relationship that Senka was supposedly in. She heard all about Billy's drama and Kenny's hockey. John was into soccer. James was a successful engineer in Winnipeg. She looked at them all, her mother listening attentively. They were so happy. No one asked her how her job was going. They allowed her to listen and laugh with the rest of them. She didn't even think about why that was. They just let her be Liz for a while.

Senka was lying in bed downstairs after the fun filled evening, Leo curled up at her feet. She hadn't laughed like that in a long time. She wouldn't sleep that night. She knew it. She heard a scrape of a chair upstairs. Leo's ears twitched and Senka sighed. She rose and they went upstairs. Senka had seen it in her mother's eyes that afternoon. She had hoped she was wrong. Senka was rarely wrong.

Leo beat her to her mom, sniffing and licking her hand. Her mother was sitting at the kitchen table, the lonely oven light casting dark shadows around her face. She tried to hide the bottle when she saw Senka. Senka shook her head and went and grabbed herself a glass. There were bags under her mother's eyes. She couldn't have known how much they looked alike in that moment.

Leo put his head in her mother's lap. She sunk her hand into his fur, much the same as Senka did.

Senka picked up the bottle of Jack Daniel's and poured herself a glass, topping her mother's up as well.

"Elizabeth. You can't sleep either?" her mother asked. She looked so old.

"I don't sleep much. Looks like you don't either."

"I used to drink too much, right after the accident. I shouldn't be drinking at all. If the boys found out–"

"Mom, stop. I'm not going to tell the boys."

Her mother looked at her gratefully. Senka drank, relishing the burning feeling in her throat. Her mother wiped her eyes.

"I miss him. It's been over seven years and I still miss him. Isn't that silly?"

"I miss dad too, mom. But... it's different for me."

"You died," her mother said suddenly. "You woke up, but it wasn't you. I don't know how to deal with that. You died and I grieved. You woke up and I grieved. It's hard, seeing you."

Senka wasn't hurt. This was honesty. This was more honest than the laughter at the supper table that night. Time for her to be honest, "I hate coming here," she admitted. "It reminds me that I died. It reminds me that I'm not the same. It reminds me of everything I put you through."

Her mother grasped her hand across the table. They both finished their drinks. Senka filled their glasses.

"You don't work at Starbucks, do you?" her mother asked tentatively. "I missed you and I couldn't get a hold of you so I went to Brandon. I sat at every Starbucks there for hours every day. I never saw you."

Senka thought to argue then didn't. She just shook her head.

"Plus, you know, I can tell that you have a gun in your lower back," her mother added with a smile. "I felt it through your leather coat when I hugged you this afternoon. Your dad used to keep it in the same place when he took you hunting and didn't want me to know he was taking the handgun."

"Damn. Not used to getting hugged," Senka admitted. "Thought I was being sneaky."

Her mother looked at her and smiled, "You never were good at being sneaky with me." She held her hands up in front of her. "I don't want to know," her mother said. "If you haven't told me then I don't think you want to or you can't. That's fine honey."

Senka appreciated the sentiment more than her mother knew. She filled their glasses again.

"If I go, mom, you're going to hear a lot of things. Don't believe them, ok? I'm doing the best I can. I'm doing the right thing. It's hard, but it's the right thing."

Tears filled her mother's eyes and she gripped her hand tighter. But she nodded. Senka felt the heaviness in her sweater and realized that she hadn't given her mother her necklace.

"My partner got you this," Senka said. She couldn't take credit for Carter. "He knew I'd fuck it up and forget. He slipped it into my bag."

She slid the box over the table. Her mother opened it and her eyes welled up again. She took out the silver necklace and played with it in her hands, "Tell him it's beautiful. It's something you would buy."

Senka smiled at her. Her hand went inadvertently to her own necklace that she wore under her clothes. The ring Jules gave her was always with her, just out of sight, on a chain around her neck.

They sat in silence and finished the bottle. Her mother took another bottle out of her hiding space in the kitchen and they finished that bottle as well. She helped her mother to her bed and left a garbage can beside her head in case she puked. She weaved her way downstairs and fell face down on her bed. She grasped her necklace in her hand and went to sleep.

It was the same as every night. She dreamed terrible things.

9 CARTER

October 23, 2023, 12:03
Location: Toronto, Canada.

Carter was bundled up. It was chilly for October. He was taking a much needed break from the server problem that had him working overtime at the ZTF headquarters. It wasn't going very fast and there was an algorithm that he couldn't break for the server's password manufacture. Senka was due back that afternoon and Carter really needed a breakthrough. He realized that sometimes you needed to take a step back to take a step forward, so he was headed to meet an old friend at a pub for lunch.

He stepped inside and relished the warmth. He looked around him and saw his old buddy, Chris Hayes, sitting at a booth. Carter took his jacket off and walked up to the table.

"Hey, Chris."

"Hey! Carter," Chris stood and shook his hand. His hands were as big as Carter's were. Carter took a good long look at him and could tell that this lunch would be for business.

They sat across from each other, sizing each other up. The waiter came and Carter ordered a water and a burger. Chris stuck with his beer and some French fries.

Carter hadn't called for this meeting so he was waiting for Chris to speak first. When he didn't and looked around himself nervously,

Carter decided to take initiative.

"I was surprised to hear from you," Carter said. "It's been almost sixteen years. How have you been?"

Chris looked a bit surprised that Carter was talking. He was most definitely distracted. "Good. I've been good. Moved to Canada with family more than ten years ago. Sorry I've never been in touch."

"Not a problem. Just nice to hear from you," he paused for a minute. "Chris, you seem distracted. Is everything alright?"

"You always were good at reading people," Chris said. They waited as the waiter set their food down.

Chris sighed, "I heard you were a cop."

"Something like that," Carter said. "I work for the Canadian Military in a role much like a cop," Carter always kept his lies as close to the truth as he could. Easier to remember that way.

"You have any kids?" Chris asked. The sudden change in topic caught Carter off guard.

"No," he said, "me and an old girlfriend were talking about it once. Never got the chance." Carter's honesty shocked himself. He usually didn't talk about Melanie like that. Chris' behavior had put him on edge.

"I have a son," Chris' eyes welled up. "He's missing Carter. We can't find him."

The sentence hung in the air.

"Why did you come to me with this? Go to the cops."

"I have. They aren't doing enough."

Carter sighed, "How long has he been missing?"

"Five days," Chris answered.

"Listen, Chris. I know this must be excruciating, having a child go missing. But five days hasn't even given the police enough time to investigate properly."

"No!" Chris said fervently. "I need to do something. I need to do more. There's been no sign of him. He vanished without a trace."

"Tell me what happened."

"We fought," Chris said, tearing up, "he ran off. I can't even remember what we fought about. It seems so stupid now. He went to a friend's house down the street. His friend was grounded too and his mother told him to go home."

"Is that the last time he was seen?" Carter asked.

"No, he hopped on the train to downtown Toronto. He tried to get a hotel there. I guess he didn't have his wallet, the cops talked to the guy who was working the front desk. He left the hotel. That's the last time anyone saw him."

"Chris, if they've gotten that far already that's not bad. At least they are looking for him."

Chris dug around in his pocket and took out a family photo. It showed him, his wife and their son, all hugging in the grass. The boy was about fifteen years old. Carter was drawn to his eyes. They were brown with copper flecks running throughout. Carter sat back, shocked. He knew those eyes. He looked at Chris, surprised.

Chris misread Carter's surprise, "Shelly was already pregnant when we met. Like only six weeks along. She wouldn't tell me who the father was. I never cared. He's mine, Carter. I raised him. I was in the birthing room. I don't care that he looks different than us. That's my son."

Carter nodded. He couldn't say anything. He was choked up. He looked at the kid's eyes. He couldn't look away.

"What's his name?" Carter asked, finally finding his voice.

"Isaac. Isaac Hayes. He's fifteen. He just had his birthday," Chris started tearing up again. "Find him. Find my son."

Carter looked at the boy's eyes for a long time.

"I'll try."

10 SENKA

October 23, 2023, 03:02
Location: Toronto, Canada.

Senka's eyes fired open, fully awake. She always woke like this. It was a mix of ZTF training and Master Appollyon. She waited a moment, eyes adjusting to the dark, and tried to figure out what had awoken her at this hour. She figured it was around 03:00 AM and was confused why she could hear Carter on the stairs approaching the loft. He should be in bed by now.

She rolled over and saw the lump next to her and sighed.

"Get up," she said gruffly, slapping the man on the shoulder. He was naked and tangled in her sheets. She sat up and got out of bed and found a tank top and sweats on the ground. The lump of a man still hadn't moved.

Senka gathered his jeans and collared shirt, pulled off in a hurry when they got home from the bar last night. *Not the only thing that was fast*, Senka thought to herself gloomily. She made her way to the wall and flicked on the light. The lump in her bed finally groaned and covered his head with his arm. Leo was curled up on the floor. The dog groaned and flipped on his back, paws waving lazily in the air. *Lazy shit*, Senka thought.

"Get up!" Senka said louder, throwing the man's clothes at him. He was pretty, blond hair with a well-kept and gym-honed body.

She remembered through the drunken haze that he was a doctor or something. The perfect specimen for anyone but her. The clothes hit him in his face and she saw that the alcohol was starting to wear off of him too. The lump, or Surfer Doc as she dubbed him, looked at her hurt and confused.

"Don't give me that shit," she snapped. "I told you to get your ass out after we were done. You're the one who decided to make yourself comfortable."

Surfer Doc didn't say anything, he clutched his clothes to his chest and stared.

"Five minutes and you're out of my house."

Senka pulled the door open and left her room, the man wide-eyed and confused behind her, her lazy dog asleep on the floor. *Being no help*, she thought as she walked through the kitchen and grabbed her half empty bottle of Jack Daniels off the dirty counter, flipping on the lights in the loft on her way. She realized it was her turn to do the dishes and frowned. She grabbed the last clean shot glass from the cupboard and was sitting at the kitchen table by the door by the time Carter walked in.

"You're home late," Senka said, filling the shot glass with a clink and drinking the burning liquor. It did its job, chasing the dregs of the copious amounts of alcohol of the evening before and focusing her. She looked at her watch, Surfer Doc had three minutes before shit started to hit the fan.

Carter sighed, "You're home early."

"Went as well with my family as you'd expect. And I was always supposed to come back this afternoon. You're never home late," Senka said and poured herself another shot. When Carter turned from her to put his keys and wallet down on the table by the door she knew there was trouble. Carter had never turned away from her before.

"I was out," he offered, a short reply.

"You haven't been out in damn near a year."

Surfer Doc had a minute and Senka couldn't hear him moving in her room.

"Over a year, actually," Carter said, "and what? Your newest conquest won't leave?"

"Nope," she said, "can't remember what I told him I did for a living, but I'm almost entirely sure that it wasn't the truth."

"You're not that dumb, even when you drink."

Senka flashed him a smile, healing wound glinting in the light. It was almost the exact injury she had suffered in the dungeons of Solias, but with modern medicine it was healing already. She had also noticed that it matched Leo's white fur running down his face.

"Car salesman?" Carter offered, pulling up a chair.

"I don't think so," Senka said shrugging, pouring another shot, "used that one on the guy a couple nights ago. Oh and here we are, only thirty-five seconds late."

The door to her room opened and a sleepy Surfer Doc shuffled his way through rubbing his eyes.

"Hey," Surfer Doc said as he made his way to the kitchen. Carter passed him his wallet that he grabbed off the side table by the door. He glanced at Carter and looked troubled by his presence.

"Roommate," Carter offered.

Surfer Doc nodded and looked at Senka, blue eyes glinting under his flowing blond hair, "I had a really great time last night. I was hoping to take you to dinner or something. I left my card on the nightstand. Call me, my conference runs all week." He waited awkwardly, and when Senka didn't offer him any reply, turned to the door.

Carter gave Senka a pointed stare. She rolled her eyes.

"Wait," she said. Surfer Doc turned with a half-smile on his face, looking at her expectantly. "You have enough money for a cab?"

His face fell and he nodded. "Call me," he said and slipped out the door.

Senka shook her head and poured herself another shot.

"You could be nicer to them," Carter offered, watching her throw back the shot.

"I told him last night that it was a one night thing, no strings. Not my fault men don't listen."

Carter left it.

"So," Senka said, looking at him pointedly, "you gonna tell me what's going on or are you gonna make me guess? 'Cause I don't like to guess."

Carter sighed and rubbed his face. He felt old, older than his thirty-six years. He was so tired.

"A friend of mine texted me today, asked me to go for lunch. I haven't heard from him in years so I agreed." Carter paused, collecting his thoughts. Senka let him. She knew not to push him and she had plenty of whiskey left.

"We used to play football together at MIT, back in the day. Better university than football team, but we had fun. He was on the defense with me. Anyways, we were close. He moved up here a few years back. I didn't know he was in town, let alone in Canada. I'm off topic. I'm rambling."

Senka sat and stared, fiddling with the glass in front of her. She had gone years without a voice and she appreciated having one. She knew when to use it. Now was not the time. She took another shot of burning liquor. It would take a lot more to get her near drunk.

"Well, back in the day I was quite the wild man. Had one night stands with any girl who would let me. My buddy, Chris, was more the stay at home fatherly type, even when we were twenty." Carter looked around. He looked lost. Senka was disconcerted. This was going to be a big deal. Emotional trials weren't her forte.

"Chris settled with a woman and quit the team around the same time. He said it was so he could focus and he cut himself off from the party life which included me. I just assumed it was his woman taking control, and I was pretty jealous. Always wanted to have a woman care about me that much." It was distant. Senka didn't need to say *you did*. They both knew it.

"Chris had a son shortly after, raised him as his own." Carter pulled a photograph out of his inner pocket and slid it across the table towards her.

Senka looked. She saw a smiling man and a pretty woman, around thirty-five, arms draped around her son. He looked to be around fifteen, laughing and smiling at the person holding the camera. He was clutching her arm around him, bright gold flecked brown eyes crinkled at the sides.

Senka looked up at Carter, shocked. She recognized the eyes in the man sitting across from her.

"Chris said he didn't know who the sperm donor was. She was already pregnant when they met and he raised the kid like his own. I didn't tell him."

"Did you know?" Senka asked. She stared at the broken man in front of her. Her Carter was a good man, but everyone had a past. She hoped he didn't know.

"I didn't. I was partying and having fun. She never told me, she never approached me. I don't know why." Tears formed in his eyes.

"You didn't know. She didn't tell you. You're not a bad guy, Carter."

He shook his head, "It's not that. I always wanted kids. We wanted kids so bad."

Senka heard the slip. This was going to be bad. She knew it in her heart. It was the same feeling she got the day Tom died.

"Anyway. Chris didn't see the resemblance. He was more just reaching out to a buddy. He thinks I'm a police officer and was coming to me as a last ditch effort. The boy's name is Isaac and he's missing."

Senka nodded, somewhat relieved. This was a mission. This was good for both of them. Gave them a focus. She felt guilty for her relief but she would get over that.

"How long?" Senka asked, returning the picture to Carter.

"Five days. No one has seen him. Chris said they had a fight and Isaac stormed off. He's fifteen so he left it, thinking the kid went to a friend's. When Isaac didn't show up for breakfast he was worried. No leads."

Senka could tell by the tone of Carter's voice that the mission wouldn't be enough. This was going to be bad.

"We'll find him. Five day's isn't a huge head start," she said, rising. She reached for the bottle.

"Leave it," Carter's voice was gruff with fatigue. Senka looked at him for a long time. She finally nodded and started back to her room.

"Sen?" Carter said behind her, barely audible.

She knew it was coming. The question. The one that hadn't been asked.

"Why did you get to come back? Why didn't she?"

Senka didn't turn. "She was dead. She didn't have the chance. We went to the funeral together. It was right before Tom's funeral. Tom was there with us." Not the question, but one so close. New grief so often dredged up old grief. One of the worst parts of remembering the past. She almost missed only having three years of memories to live with. She started for her door again.

"Do you ever stop seeing them?"

She didn't turn. She waited.

"Sen, when you've killed someone, do you ever stop seeing their eyes? All I see is her eyes."

"No." She replied. "You'll see Mel's eyes forever, Carter."

She heard the sob and escaped to her room. She lay down and heard the sounds from the kitchen. The one-year Alcohol Anonymous coin heavily hit the table. The unmistakable sound of the glass neck of a bottle of Jack hitting the side of a shot glass.

Leo jumped on to the bed with her and snuggled in. She sighed and closed her eyes burying a hand in his fur. *This is going to be bad*, she thought and drifted into an uneasy, nightmare-fueled sleep.

11 DR. CHARLIE PENNER

October 24, 2023, 18:30
Location: Dorfen, Germany.

Charlie had a plan.

She had been locked in the living quarters, her key card only allowing access to her room, the gym and the mess hall. They had blocked her key card from accessing all other areas of the compound, including her lab. No one had spoken to her in five days, even at meal times. She ate alone. She was a ghost in the compound.

That was all fine by her. She didn't want to speak to anyone anyway and usually didn't. She was busy watching people, something that she didn't generally do. She'd been wrapped up in her research for over a year. Time to change that. They had given her a challenge, one she had been reluctant to accept but accept she had. Now that she had completed the challenge and taken a step back, she realized she had made a terrible mistake. She needed to eliminate her research, every single shred.

She knew that she had to act soon, or she wouldn't be able to act at all.

She was at supper, sitting alone in the corner, like she always did. The research team came in at the end of the day, Luc leading the way. The woman who was the lab assistant followed behind.

Alejandra brought up the rear, heels clicking away on the tiles. They didn't even look at her. She was forgotten.

They walked up to the line-up for food. There were a few security guards there as well as others from the compound. Charlie didn't talk to anyone, she never did. Hers was a lonely existence. She had been so absorbed in her research that she hadn't noticed.

Charlie waited and watched. Luc got to the front of the line. She knew that he kept his key card clipped to the front of his pants. She needed to steal it. A long time ago she'd had quick fingers. Now was the ultimate test.

Charlie rose and took her tray full of garbage and a half empty drink. The garbage can was conveniently located near the condiments. The pasta dish had been bland today and she was hoping Luc would go for the hot sauce like she had. She wasn't disappointed.

She put her head down and walked straight into Luc with her tray. The result was as chaotic as she was hoping. Luc ended up with half her drink on his clothes. His meal was all over the place. He swore at her loudly in French, hate and resentment all over his face.

"Oh my God," Charlie said, blushing. "I'm so sorry!" she grabbed some napkins and tried to wipe him off. The entire kitchen staff and everyone in the mess hall was looking at the scene.

"It's fine," Luc said angrily, pushing her away.

"No, I insist!" she replied, trying again to rub the soda off of his clothes. Luc pushed her away again.

"I said its fine!" he said angrily. Kitchen staff came and started to clean up the mess around them.

Charlie hung her head and mumbled another weak apology and hurried herself out of the dining hall, stares and angry mutterings chasing her. The stolen key card weighed heavily in her pocket. She went straight for the hallway that led to her lab and used the card. The light glowed green and the door unlatched. Her stomach unknotted in her victory. She needed to get to her lab and destroy everything before they discovered that Luc's key card was gone.

She hurried her way down the dark hallway toward her lab. Her old habits were starting to return and her footsteps were light and quick. She got to her lab and noticed that the two usual guards weren't there. She took it as a bit of good fortune and unlocked the door. She did an internal victory dance as she accessed the lab. The dance was cut short when she saw the state of the room.

Five days had really taken a toll. All her equipment was pushed to the sides of the lab out of the way. The rats had been moved away, their cages cleaned out. In the center of the room was a large fume hood attached to a ceiling discharge. Charlie saw that there were about ten pink pills, candy coated, in a bag in the fume hood. She couldn't understand how they had gone from her molecule to pill form in less than a week.

She moved her slack-jawed form to her computer station. That, thankfully, had been untouched. She went toward her station and now was full of questions. They couldn't have gone to human trials. That would be disastrous. She needed to figure out how far they had taken the molecule. They should have tested thousands of dosages and variations with thousands of different animals to figure out what to put in the pill. Even then she didn't know why the molecule worked or even if it did. Thousands more hours of research should have gone into this molecule before reaching this point.

She unlocked her computer. They hadn't changed her password. She figured that they didn't expect her to get this far. She didn't think much of it and logged into the servers. She didn't have access to the entire server. She knew that. But if she could delete her research and anything new that they had done then maybe it would slow them down.

She busied herself with trying to find any new information she could. She was confused by how they had advanced so quickly. She was getting wrapped up in the question instead of deleting her research. She was bent over the computer, lost in thought.

A hand with a steel grip grabbed her shoulder and turned her roughly. Charlie almost jumped out of her chair except the hand was putting so much pressure on her she could barely move. She was turned and she was staring directly into the face of Alejandra. Her pointed manicured nails were digging into Charlie's shoulder so hard they were drawing blood.

"Well," Alejandra said, Columbian accent thick. "Isn't this interesting?"

Charlie began to say something when Alejandra slapped her

across the face, hard. Charlie was thrown from her chair and hit the ground. She immediately grabbed her bleeding face. Alejandra's nails had raked lines across her face so deep that they were bleeding freely. Charlie lay in a heap on the ground.

"We have an experiment this evening for the director of this facility," Alejandra said deliberately, slowly. "I would hate for you to miss it, considering that your research made all of this happen." She dragged Charlie to her feet. Charlie was still dazed and couldn't bring herself to fight back.

"First, we will need to go and pick out a suitable candidate for this monumental research," Alejandra twisted Charlie's arm behind her back and pulled her so close that Charlie could smell her sickly sweet perfume. Charlie tried to struggle but Alejandra pulled out a knife and held it to her throat. Charlie immediately stopped moving. "Better," Alejandra whispered in her ear, "I have no inclination to keep you alive."

Alejandra moved them through the lab, out the door where two security guards were waiting. Charlie was shoved roughly towards them. They caught her by the arms as she stumbled and held her upright.

"Make sure she doesn't do anything stupid," Alejandra said. "She's coming with us."

The guards nodded silently and Charlie was marched between them in Alejandra's wake. Her face burned, but she didn't think of it. She needed to get out of here. But she couldn't. Not in good conscience.

They walked her through doors and hallways she'd never seen. She had been confined to a tiny area of this compound. She hadn't realized how big this place was. They brought her to a door with guards guarding both sides. Alejandra didn't swipe her key card. A camera overhead was watching them and the door opened automatically.

Charlie was marched through behind Alejandra. She walked up to a man with slicked back hair and a tailored suit.

"François, my dear," Alejandra said, holding out her hand. François took it and kissed the top.

"You look as ravishing as ever," he said with a French accent. He completely ignored Charlie's presence. That told Charlie that he had been expecting her.

"Do you have what we are looking for?" Alejandra asked him.

"Of course, my dear. It's my job to find the perfect fit," François led them down the hallway of cells.

Charlie had never felt real guilt. She thought she'd had, but what she felt before had nothing on what she was feeling now. The cells were filled with children. She guessed that they ranged from ages ten through seventeen. There were two per cell. They were dirty and looked famished. Many of them had a dead look in their eyes.

Charlie looked around frantically. She hadn't known that there were children in here. She was trying to make herself feel better but it wasn't working.

These people were monsters.

She had no idea how right she was.

She was marched to a cell in the middle the row. Inside were two of the older children. They were huddled in the back of the cell together, a boy and a girl. The girl had a bright jacket wrapped around her shoulders. When François stopped in front of their cell the boy looked up, fire in his eyes. Charlie was shocked. She'd seen his eyes before. She knew those eyes. They were brown with flecks of copper. Her world was reeling and she couldn't keep up.

"The girl," François said. Two more guards came up and unlocked the door. The boy tried to put up a fight but it was no use. He was quickly overpowered. The girl was ushered out.

"Kelly!" the boy yelled.

Charlie tried to say something but her guard punched her in the stomach, doubling her over. All breath was knocked out of her. She would have collapsed but the guard held her upright. The boy stared at them with burning hatred in his copper flecked eyes.

"Is she what we need?" Alejandra asked. The girl named Kelly stood upright, eyes downcast, arms crossed. Alejandra walked around her, looking her up and down.

"Yes," François said, "she'd be a tough sell for me. Morphine addiction as well as a history of prostitution are hard sells."

Alejandra nodded in agreement, "No morphine recently? We don't want anything that could interact."

François shook his head, "No. She hasn't had anything for at least five days. As you can tell she's even stopped withdrawing."

Charlie was disgusted. They were talking about this human being, this girl, as if she were a piece of livestock.

"She'll do," Alejandra decided with finality.

François nodded, delighted. Charlie was shuffled from in between the two guards. One guard twisted her arm behind her back. The other went and grabbed Kelly in the same way.

"Are you coming to the demonstration?" Alejandra asked François as they left the cells.

Children with dead eyes were following their progress.

"I wouldn't miss it," François said.

François and Alejandra led the way out of the cells and back through the hallway. Charlie could hear the girl's breaths coming beside her in gasps. She was scared. Charlie's free hand was the one closest to the girl's and she reached out and grabbed the girl's hand. She was trying to comfort her as best as she could. Charlie could guess what was in store for the girl. Maybe for both of them. She needed it to be both of them.

They were marched somewhere in the building. Charlie didn't know at this point where they were in the compound. She gripped the girl's hand as long as possible. They were paraded into a room that looked like an office. It had a large oak desk to one side. The floors were concrete but a thick gold and purple rug covered the center of the room. There was a door on the other side of the room.

They were wrenched apart. "No!" Charlie gasped. The guard twisted her arm so hard behind her back that she thought it would break.

"Shut up," he said quietly in her ear.

Tears formed and Charlie nodded.

Alejandra grabbed the girl's hand and led her to the center of the room. François stepped to the side.

A man entered. He had red hair, much lighter than Charlie's own. Where hers was rich and dark, his was light and orange. He had a red moustache. Charlie knew exactly who he was. He had met her when she had first been brought to the compound.

"Hello, Dr. Freudman," Alejandra said.

He nodded and smiled. He had a face that anyone would trust.

Charlie knew better. He was pure, unadulterated evil.

The doctor nodded to them all, smiling. His eyes didn't even blink when he saw how Charlie was being held. He looked at them like they were all out for an enjoyable lunch with friends.

"Hello, all," he said in his German accent, "I understand that you have made a breakthrough."

"We have," Alejandra agreed. Kelly just stood in the center of the room, looking around, deathly white with fear, shaking uncontrollably.

"Congratulations to all!" Dr. Freudman exclaimed, then looking pointedly at Charlie. "A special congratulations to yourself! I understand you were instrumental. I knew you would be a useful acquisition."

Kelly turned towards her and stared. Her face was stricken with hate and misunderstanding. Charlie mouthed, "I'm sorry," to her but Kelly just shook her head in disbelief.

"Now, let us begin!" Dr. Freudman said.

"No!" Charlie yelled, the guard pulled tighter on her arm but she didn't care. "Take me. I invented it. Let me."

Freudman walked towards her, smiling, "My dear. She is expendable, you are not."

"You have what you want from me, make me test it instead. You don't need me anymore."

"She is a hooker. A drug addict. Her life is expendable," Freudman said calmly.

"She's a person!" Charlie yelled, then deciding to switch tactics said, "she is a child," Charlie pleaded. "She's of no use over there. I am."

Freudman nodded sympathetically, "I understand. But I have reasons for keeping you here. Unfortunately, it is her cross to bear." He walked back over to Alejandra.

One of the guards brought in a chair with an EEG attached. It looked like an old electric chair. Alejandra sat Kelly down and strapped in her arms and her legs. Then Alejandra shaved Kelly's head. Tears fell from her face as she watched her brown hair litter the carpet but she didn't move. Charlie was crying freely and the whole scene was blurry. She told herself that she couldn't look away. She had done this, she couldn't look away.

Alejandra attached the electrodes to Kelly's head, carefully, almost gently. Silent tears fell down the girl's face. Alejandra took the pink pills out of her suit pocket.

"What is the dosage?" Dr. Freudman asked, holding out his hand. Alejandra put a pill in his hand. He inspected it closely then gave it back to her.

"We have run an algorithm for weight to drug ratio. As you know, we haven't had a lot of time to test but it has worked in one hundred percent of the cases. Or so we think. I don't believe there can be a dose too high."

Dr. Freudman nodded, "I will be the judge on whether or not it works. What dose are you using?"

"5000 milligrams," Alexandra answered, picking out five pills.

Dr. Freudman nodded, "Proceed," he said. He went around the desk and sat in a plush chair.

Alejandra nodded. Kelly was crying and shaking, eyes wide. Alejandra grabbed Kelly violently around the chin and forced her mouth open. She shoved the pills in and held her mouth closed until she was sure that she swallowed.

"No!" Charlie yelled. Her guard pulled upward on her arm again so hard that she heard her shoulder pop. Pain exploded in her back and shoulder. She wanted to fall to the ground, but the guard held her upright by her now useless arm. She told herself she needed to watch.

Kelly went flush from head to toe, a stark contrast from her pale white. Her eyes rolled back into her head and she started shaking violently.

Charlie couldn't stop crying. She weakly tried to pull away from the guard but her hurt arm had left her with no energy. He didn't let go.

Finally, after what felt like an eternity, Kelly stopped. Her head fell forward and she remained motionless.

Alejandra was watching the EEG on a screen behind her head. Freudman was watching her intently. Alejandra held up one finger as she watched the screen.

"Now," she said. The EEG showed the pattern of brainwaves that they had seen in the rat. It slowly faded into nothing.

Freudman nodded and leaned back in the chair, breathing slowly. Charlie was confused. It looked as though he was meditating. They waited, silently. Charlie's arm throbbed but she barely felt it. She just stared at Kelly's dead face.

Suddenly, Freudman sat up and smiled.

"It worked!" he exclaimed happily. "Ladies and gentlemen, it worked! We have created a Zoya! One who cannot be killed from this world. She's dead here, she's alive in The Other Place! Great success!"

Alejandra smiled broadly. Freudman went and embraced her.

Charlie's heart sank. She had been so preoccupied with the task at hand she had never actually thought of the consequences.

"Now," Freudman said, staring pointedly at Charlie, "I was told to keep her alive. I never agreed to a state." He looked at Alejandra, "I believe that the cells are a good place for her."

Alejandra smiled and nodded.

They dragged her to a cell in the same hallway as the children. She was lost in thought, shut down to the world.

She'd created the ultimate weapon for The Other Place. Zoya were only kept in check by dying in this world or waking up from their coma. There could now be an army of Zoya in The Other Place with no way to stop them from here. Her invention would lead to mass death and destruction.

And if The Other Place was destroyed, what would happen here?

PART 2

"Better to die fighting for freedom then be a prisoner all the days of your life." — Bob Marley

"Those who make peaceful revolution impossible will make violent revolution inevitable." – John F. Kennedy

KATE SANDER

12 TORY

October 23, 210, 15:05
Location: North Langundo.

Tory was struggling. The snow was deep, almost past her knees. The wind whipped over her covered face. She was heading north, just like she always was.

"Just always north," she muttered, trying to lift her knees as high as possible.

"You're the one who listened to the old man," Black Eyes answered from somewhere beside her. "I still have no idea why you listened to the Shaman."

Tory still couldn't see her. She didn't even remember what Black Eyes looked like. But she was there, ever present, always by her side. And her voice was grating as hell.

"Ever present and annoying," Tory muttered. A gust of wind rose from over the tundra and Tory took cover behind her arm. She had a seal skin balaclava covering her face, given to her in the last village, but the wind still cut her to her core.

"You can't call me annoying," Black Eyes said tersely, "you killed me, remember? And evidently I'm stuck with you. None of this seems like my fault."

Tory shrugged and huddled into her coat, trying to block the biting wind that was whipping around her. It was cold. Colder than she had ever experienced. She had been trekking north for over three years now. Making her way north east to north west, finding villages and people along the way. She worked for food and water and allowed herself a respite from the cold in each village. But she still hadn't found her father.

"Someday," Tory mumbled, "you're going to have to forgive me for that."

"Forgive you for killing me?" Black Eyes scoffed. "Not a chance. I had a good life before I was sucked into that war."

"We all had a good life before the war," Tory snapped. "You may be dead but I lost my family. Senka died. Jules, her boyfriend, the one who led the Sun Gods into the trap in the first place is most likely dead. In case you didn't notice he took a knife to the back."

Black Eyes tried to interrupt but Tory was on a roll. They must have had this same conversation a thousand times during their journey and it still pissed Tory off.

"Eli," Tory said, holding a finger up to Black Eye's general direction, "Was injured. Not as bad as Jules was but still. I have no idea where he is. He most likely died in the fire."

Tory's mind snapped to the fire in Ismat three years ago. The Shaman had sent her on this stupid task of finding her father in the north. Ismat was nestled into the foot of a mountain. As Tory climbed, she noticed that Ismat was burning. Instead of retreating down the mountain to help evacuate, she'd continued up the mountain in the direction the Shaman had sent her.

Tory regretted the decision every single day.

"And Ujarak…" Tory drifted off after she mentioned her love. Ujarak was a hulking quiet man, steadfast in his love. They had found each other years ago. Tory's heart hurt just thinking about him. She missed him more than anything.

"Ujarak promised that he would protect them until you got back," Black Eyes said softly, almost kindly.

"That was before he knew Ismat was on fire," Tory snapped. They quieted, Tory lost in thought. She focused on picking up her feet and making her way through the snow. She knew she was so mean to Black Eyes because of the guilt that was slowly eating her away. It was the only constant in her life. Well, the guilt, along with the cold and a pissed off dead woman. Tory couldn't win.

"You ever get the feeling," Tory said after the gust of wind had died down, "that the Shaman sent us here to find nothing?"

"All the time," Black Eyes responded. All was forgiven. For now, anyway.

"You don't even feel the cold," Tory said. She steeled herself and started making her way through the knee high snow again. North. It was always north.

"But I do feel boredom," Black Eyes said. "All I see, every single day, is you struggling to make your way north. Now there aren't even any mountains or trees. Just snow. Flat, boring, cold snow."

Tory couldn't argue.

She had wanted off the mountain ranges for years. But now that she had ventured north of them, she missed them. At least there was a change between the incline and the decline. When you were climbing you missed descending. On the descend you missed the climb.

And now she missed both.

She slept in a shelter made of snow. She made water out of snow. Her bed was snow. Snow, snow, snow. If the cold didn't kill her the monotony would. She could use a rock, or a tree, or a shrub. It would be a break from the flat, white, snow.

She was starting to puff and sweat and the sun was setting over the tundra.

"I think it's time to make a shelter," Tory said through breaths.

"Up to you," Black Eyes said. "I can't die again, remember?"

"You know, someday you're going to have to get over it," Tory said. She heaved her backpack to the ground. It had gotten significantly heavier over the past three years. The people in the villages where she had stayed would gift her with one thing or another to help her achieve her quest. Senka's bow, the one gifted to her by the queen, was unstrung and attached to the outside of the pack. The quiver was covered and strapped to the other side. Tory had taken both the bow and the quiver from Senka on the battlefield after she had confirmed that Senka was dead.

Tory kept her shovel tied to the outside of the pack. She quickly loosened it, now well practiced with her seal skin gloves. She dug down into the snow, making a hole. She burrowed for a little longer and crawled inside, digging all the way. The snow was deep enough that she ended up with a hole about three feet high, tall enough to sit comfortably. She made it big enough to move around in. Taking a stick she poked a bunch of holes through the roof. She had enough room to start a fire. She would keep it small, she didn't want to have it take all her oxygen, but she had learned the importance of having a hot meal every night.

She ate her warmed seal meat greedily.

"Looks good," Black Eyes said quietly.

"Surprisingly not bad," Tory answered, licking fat from her fingers.

Tory warmed some snow from the side of her shelter over the fire in a small metal bowl provided to her by the last village.

"You're going to run out of wood soon," Black Eyes said. "Not only that but food as well."

"Yah, everything but snow," Tory said. She rummaged through her bag and her heart fell even more. It was almost empty. This was the last of the wood. There were two more sinewy strands of dried seal. That was it.

"I told you a week ago that you were past the point of no return," Black Eyes said. "Why didn't you listen to me?"

"Because I'm stubborn," Tory answered. "Ujarak always said that..." Tory drifted off. Thinking of Ujarak hurt. Thinking of anyone from back home hurt. She tried to avoid it, but she had nothing else to think about on these long nights. She couldn't even see the stars, not in a snow shelter.

"You're going to die out here," Black Eyes said.

"No shit."

"But I don't want you to die. If you die, what happens to me?"

"Maybe you actually get to go where you are supposed to go," Tory offered sullenly.

She heard Black Eyes sigh, "Maybe I want to stay around."

"It's the only way..." Tory began but she stopped herself. She didn't believe any of her old excuses either. Why should she? The Shaman had sent her to find her father. A man who had abandoned her when she was five. A man who didn't care enough about her to stick around. Tory wasn't even sure if she wanted to find him. She'd probably punch him in the face. Who abandons a five year-old girl just weeks after her mother died?

"An asshole," Black Eyes offered. Her voice pulled Tory out of her reverie.

"Don't do that," Tory said.

"Do what?"

"Go into my head. I don't like that."

"I'm always in your head," Black Eyes said. "Your thoughts are loud. They shout at me. I couldn't ignore them if I tried."

"Topic shift," Tory said. She was too exhausted to be angry. "Ira from the last village said he saw my father come this way over six months ago. He disappeared into the snow and was never heard from again."

"Right. And that was the village farthest north. They don't even know what's out here. They go south to hunt seal."

"Right," Tory said.

"No one comes back from out here," Black Eyes continued. "That's why this is where people are exiled. Everyone dies. What makes you think your father is alive?"

"He was transient for twenty years," Tory said, "hopping from place to place. He came from the north the first time five years ago. At least that's what they said in the last village."

"No, they said he appeared one day out of nowhere. He had such bad frostbite on his face his nose was black, so they assumed that he had come from the north."

"He came from the north," Tory said, determined.

"Sure, whatever you say then," Black Eyes offered. Tory could tell by her tone that she was getting frustrated with her. The two of them had this conversation every night. And every night it was the same.

"Except every night you weren't on the verge of dying," Black Eyes said angrily.

"That's a tomorrow problem," Tory said.

"You should have turned back."

"Can't now!" Tory said. If she was honest she was tired. Bone tired. The last thing she had seen from her old home was the fire. She had turned away from everyone she loved to find her father. Three years she had been out here, alone, with a dead woman who hated her. She wanted it to end, one way or another. So she would travel north as far as she could. And that was the end of it.

"End of it for who?" Black Eyes asked.

"Both of us, hopefully," Tory snapped.

She left the small fire burning. It was the last of her wood and there would be no need for a fire tomorrow. And if she was honest with herself, the crackling of the small fire and the smell of burning wood kept her company. Reminded her of sitting around the fire with Ujarak and Eli on their hunts. Before Senka and Jules had shown up and her life had been changed forever. The snow insulated the room from the elements and it was actually quite warm. She stripped out of her seal hide coat and mitts. She needed them to dry out as much as possible. She put a small hide down on the ground to lie on. That would insulate her from the ice underneath her.

She didn't sleep. But mercifully Black Eyes kept silent and let her rest. The night lasted an eternity.

"It's morning," Black Eyes said quietly.

Tory rose silently and repacked. The snow had blown over the doorway of her little shelter. She dug her way out and used the tip of the shovel to chip away at the ice covering the doorway.

The day was the opposite of the day before. It was calm. Not even a breeze. The sun was out and, though still cold outside, it was manageable. She could even leave her balaclava in her pack. The morning sun reflected off the snow. A few years ago she would have marvelled at the beauty of the light dancing off the snow. Now she sighed and grumbled. A few years was a long time to feel alone.

She heaved on her backpack and started forward. The sun was out but it wasn't warm enough to melt any of the snow. She waited until her stomach was growling audibly to eat one of her remaining two strips of seal meat.

Black Eyes hadn't been lying.

Today would be her last day.

"You knew it all along, didn't you?" Black Eyes said after her long and sullen silence.

"You know everything I know," Tory said.

"I don't know why. You've kept that secret, even from yourself."

Tory waited a long time to answer. She focused her little remaining energy on just picking one foot up and then the other. One step at a time. The tundra was just snow in every direction.

There were no trees or rocks. The people of the nearest village had told her that the snow would eventually break into ice drifts that covered water. Vast amounts of water, just like what was south, east and west of Langundo. There was no sign of anything that lived. She hadn't seen an animal in a week.

"I miss him," Tory said finally. Her exhaustion had led to the realization. She couldn't hide from the truth anymore. And really, why bother?

"He's my father. I don't remember much about him. But he used to pick me up and throw me in the air," she smiled, "I was always asking him to go higher and higher. He always would. He loved us, before mom died."

"He abandoned you, remember?"

"People do shitty things," Tory said. She sat in the snow and opened her pack. She munched on the last of her seal meat. "Apparently it runs in the family. I abandoned my family too. When they needed me the most."

Black Eyes didn't have an answer.

"So I'm out here," Tory said, rising. Time for one final push. "Trying to find him. So that we can be cowards together."

She started walking north again.

Towards nothing.

She could see for miles and miles. She could see there was nothing there. She was walking towards nothing. But she wouldn't give up. Something flashed in her eyes from the north. It looked like sun reflecting off of water.

"You never would have abandoned Ismat if that Shaman hadn't told you to," Black Eyes said.

"Ah, but maybe I would have," Tory said. She was starting to have trouble bringing her knees to her chest.

"No. That Shaman sent you on a wild chase," Black Eyes said.

"I was always the general. The first into battle," Tory said, "But maybe it was just because I knew I'd run away if I was at the back."

"I don't believe that," Black Eyes said.

Tory noticed her voice was fading. It sounded like it was coming from miles away.

"I'm going to rest here," Tory said, "just for a minute." She sat down heavily in the snow. She liked how it made a bit of a seat for her to rest her back.

"Don't stop moving!"

"I'm just…. I'm just…" Her tongue was lead. "I'm just going to rest. Just for a little bit."

She was surprised that she wasn't cold anymore. She had gotten used to being constantly cold. But now she was warm. From the tips of her fingers to the soles of her feet.

The world started to blur around her. Tory leaned her head back. With slow, rhythmic breaths, she gradually descended into a much needed sleep.

13 HEAD OF JUSTICE

October 24, 210, 15:35
Location: Solias, Langundo.

The council meeting was going as it always went. Terribly. Justice was sitting straight upright, trying desperately to maintain some sort of professional integrity in the meeting. Unfortunately, only he and a few others shared this sentiment. The Head of Housing, a woman of sixty who had now served four different Kings, sat beside him. She was sitting up straight as well, trying to focus on the babble that was coming out of the current King. The only other member of the council that had survived the last four years was the Head of Goods. A man of soft character but apparently with enough wits to not be killed.

The old Alchemist Omega had died of natural causes. If falling from twenty feet off of a building and hitting the ground was natural. He ended up going mad and taking his own life soon after King Sebastian had returned from the failed war campaign declaring himself the King. As there was no more Quicksilver, the King had declared the position of Alchemist irrelevant and had not filled the position.

The new Head of Treasury and the new Head of Intelligence were both stupid goonies that did exactly as King Sebastian told them. The King himself had taken over the army, so the Head of

Peace was not replaced.

Justice's heart fell when he looked at the new Head of Intelligence, a short, stupid and fat man named Bamber. Justice refused to think of him as Intelligence. That name was saved for his one love whom he had hung at the gallows three long years ago. He missed her every single day. The way she had run her hands through her short blonde hair. Her strength that had made men quiver in their boots.

Justice was snapped back into focus by the King. He was draped lazily in his chair with his feet hanging over the arm rest. The flickering lights of the fires now used to light chambers highlighted his gaunt face. He wore all black and the crown was crooked on his head. He was drinking ale from a chalice, one that had usually been saved for special dignitaries. This King had no class or sense of tradition and he wasn't scared to show it.

"Pardon?" Justice asked. He had been so lost in reverie he hadn't heard what the King had asked him.

"I said," the King smiled, "when is our next public hanging?"

"Sire, I have suggested before that we stop with the public executions. Stop with executions entirely. We are losing population too fast."

The King sat up straight, swinging his feet around to face Justice, "Are you telling me that we have no more prisoners to hang?"

Bamber, the idiot, piped up, "I can assure you sire that there are plenty of prisoners in *my* dungeons." He sneered in Justice's direction. Justice tried to ignore him. When Bamber talked his fat face bounced up and down. Disgusting.

The way Bamber put emphasis on *my* made Justice want to put his fist through his face. But he was strictly non-violent, *other than putting a noose around a neck*, he thought. "Those people have been arrested for petty crimes," Justice said angrily. Housing nodded beside him. "Most of them for theft because the people are starving!"

"Theft is still a crime, whether you're starving or not," Bamber said, smug look all over his stupid face.

The King stood up suddenly and drained his ale. He slammed the empty mug down on the counter, "I want you to publicly execute five of those in jail for theft."

Justice's blood boiled. "I will not!" he said and he slammed his fist on the table so hard the King's cup bounced. Instantly, six Sun Gods surrounded the table and drew their swords. Their once gold and shiny armor was now dull and tarnished. Even the Sun Gods were suffering under the rule of the mad King.

Historically, there were no weapons or bodyguards allowed in the council room. This made sure that words were used to make decisions instead of violence. But Sol XVIII, rest his soul, had allowed Sebastian into the chamber to accompany the old Head of Peace, Armend. Now King Sebastian was using it to bring his small troop of "bodyguards" to every council meeting. It ensured that no one questioned the King.

King Sebastian stood and walked slowly around the table to Justice. He waved his hand and the Sun Gods sheathed their weapons. He leaned over to Justice, so close that he could feel his hot breath on his face.

"I want," the King said. From this close, Justice could see that the King's eyes were red and bloodshot. His breath was foul. Justice did his best not to recoil. The King smiled crookedly, "A public execution. I want it to be *understood* what happens when you break my laws. Do I make myself clear?"

Justice nodded once.

"Good," the King said, "in a week's time, I will have all the help I need to manage this place. You would do well to remember that your position can be easily terminated." He turned to walk away but didn't see the servant girl scurrying behind him to refill his glass of ale. He ran into her, spilling the tankard of ale all over himself.

"I'm…. I'm… I'm…" She stammered, taking a quick step back. Justice saw terror in her eyes. He honestly couldn't blame her.

The King cocked his head and stared at her, ale dripping down the front of his shirt. He struck her across the face backhand so hard she went sprawling to the ground.

Justice didn't think. He sprang to his feet and pushed past the King, kneeling beside the girl. She was dazed, sprawled on her back. He brushed the hair away from her face. She recoiled slightly at his touch then stopped when she saw who it was.

"Are you ok?" he asked quietly. She nodded slowly and looked past him, fear all over her face.

The King was staring at them, white-faced and shaking, "You will come down to the dinner hall tonight," he said to Justice. Justice stared at him and nodded once again, but he didn't leave the girl's side. The King tried to hold his gaze and, failing, returned quickly to his chair.

Justice knew that he'd been stupid but he was so angry he wasn't afraid at all. He gently helped the girl to her feet and brushed her off.

"My glass is still empty," the King yelled.

The servant girl nodded and scurried away. Justice held his head high and headed back to his chair. Housing softly brushed his hand while he was sitting, but he ignored her and stared at the King. It was subtle, but the small show of support steeled his resolve.

"That is all," the King said suddenly.

The council rose silently and bowed. Justice, Housing and Goods all took their leave quickly. They didn't need to see Bamber and Treasury suck up to the King. They didn't speak and they split up at a hallway. Each taking their own separate route, one that changed after every council meeting.

Justice moved his tall frame through the castle and down to the market, at least what used to be the market. When King Sebastian returned with the crown from the war towing a line of tired and defeated Sun Gods, the people of the market had been hesitantly optimistic. The rule under the Sol lineage hadn't been bad. It had been neutral. But Sol XVIII and the Queen had wanted peace. That was a concept the city of Solias hadn't liked.

And they had all paid for it. The market looked like the slums. No one had money, so no one spent any. Those from Carabesh had returned to their country. The others hadn't been so lucky. Now they lived in poverty. There was no line between the market and the slums, it was all slums outside the castle wall.

Justice picked his way through the decrepit shops. He didn't even pause at the place where he grew up, he walked right by. He was from Carabesh. He moved to Solias with his father when he was twelve to start their spice trade business. They had made a good life together. He had risen in the marketplace as the authority on disputes. This came to the attention of Sol XVIII and he was promoted to Head of Justice for the entire city of Solias.

Thinking of Sol made his stomach lurch. He knew he had been key in the downfall of the long-living monarch. In his defense he hadn't known that was Armend's plan. Justice just thought the Melanthios were dangerous and had been horrified to learn the Queen had been working with the enemy. He had just wanted safety.

He told himself that, over and over, as he picked his way through the crumbling city. He knew it was a lie. He had wanted power. And he had lost his love, Intelligence, in that quest. He had caused countless deaths. He vowed to never make the same mistake. His late father would have been very disappointed. Hell, Justice was disappointed.

He strolled past beggars and made his way to his meeting. The brothel had also fallen on hard times. Mud, the owner, had to drop prices. That, coupled with the overwhelming number of people willing to sell their bodies for a meal had led to a difference in supply and demand. There were too many hookers and not enough buyers. Mud now only kept four women and one man who he considered the best of the best. Justice walked through the door. The fireplace was burning brightly. There were no buyers in the brothel and all five of the workers sat in the main entrance reading books.

"They beat you here," one of the women said, eyes never leaving the page. "They are upstairs." Justice nodded and, saying nothing, made his way up the stairs to their habitual room. The woman wasn't lying. Goods, Housing and Mud were all waiting tensely in the small room, furnished only with a bed and a chair.

"Taking your sweet time," Goods said tersely. He was standing by the window, staring intently outside for anyone who would have followed them.

"Took the long way," Justice said. He looked around the confined room. Mud was a smooth-talking middle-aged man from Carabesh. His dark skin was highlighted by the bright green suit he wore. He was a long-standing member of Solias and had been notorious for staying out of politics. That is, of course, until his business suffered. He was sitting in the chair smoking a pipe, looking as though he didn't have a care in the world.

Housing was sitting on the bed and Justice sat down heavily beside her.

"That was really fucking stupid you know that?" Goods said.

"What was?" Justice asked innocently.

"Making him mad."

Justice rose, subdued anger boiling over, "I helped a servant girl to her feet after a madman struck her. If that's all it takes to make that asshole mad then I do not care!" his hands were in fists beside him. He was shaking he was so angry.

"It's ok," Housing said. She rose fast and placed herself between the two men. "We're all on edge."

"We have been planning this attack on the King for almost two years," Goods said. He pointed angrily at Justice, "And he can't just suck it up for two more weeks. Two weeks. That's one more council meeting. You just blew it! Everything we've been planning!"

"I don't think it's quite as dire as that," Housing said. "We can still go forward as planned."

"Were neither of you listening?" Justice asked. "Use your brains. He knows something is happening. He said he has reinforcements coming within the week! He knows there is a revolution."

Goods shook his head in denial, "No, that can't be what he meant. We've covered our tracks. He'd have no idea."

"Even if he doesn't know," Justice replied, "what could he have meant by reinforcements?"

The question defused the anger in the room.

"He could be lying," Mud said, disinterested. He was puffing on his pipe, watching the show.

"I don't know if we can take that chance," Housing said.

"Mud could be right, you know," Goods said, almost desperately. "He could be lying."

"Do you really want to take that chance?" Justice asked. "I understand your desperation for it to be a lie, but can you imagine the mad King with reinforcements? A new army?"

"It has to be a lie," Goods said with a sigh. "It has to be."

"I don't think it is," Housing said. "He came up with it unsolicited. He just told us about help. I don't think he'd do that unless it was fresh on his mind."

"We have to move the attack up," Justice said suddenly. "Regardless if he's lying or not."

The room stared at him, shocked.

"There's no possible way," Goods said.

"We send a letter to our contact and tell him that we are moving it up. He is supposed to be in the outer parts of the forest by now," Justice said. It was the only thing that made sense to him.

"The whole point of having the attack November seventh is that it is Sol's birthday," Housing said, she was looking at Justice with disbelief. "He turns eighteen. Our contact promised that he'd be present–"

"We have had no confirmation that Sol has even been found," Justice said, not letting her finish. "He is the true King. If Armend was smart when he made a play for the throne he would have eliminated him and hidden the body."

The room went uncomfortably silent. No one knew that Justice had helped Armend obtain the throne of Solias, but Justice had the feeling that they had all guessed. He ignored it and pushed on, "We have to go through with it. In five days."

Goods looked shocked. Housing gasped. Mud laughed quietly, adding more tobacco to his pipe, "A week. We can push it up to a week from now. Not five days."

"It has to be five. It has to be well before anyone gets here. It's the only way."

"What if our contact can't get here?"

"Then I do it," Justice said with resolve. "If the revolution can't get here in time, then I sneak in to his room and do it myself."

"We'd have to hang you," Housing said quietly. "Treason is treason, even if the true King is placed on the throne due to the act."

Justice nodded, "But then it's done. And the council runs the city until we find Sol or Titus."

The others nodded. Mud rose, "I'll send the letter. It's going to be close. They will be tired when they get here. But I agree, it's the only way." Mud looked out the window and his eyes went big. "Shit! They found us!"

Justice and Goods ran out of the room without looking back. Mud let out a sharp whistle and followed. Justice ran to his assigned room and disrobed quickly. He could hear Goods run into the room next to him. There were light feet running up the stairs. Justice hoped they had reacted in time. He hadn't looked out the window, but there would be no reason for Mud to lie.

He heard Mud say downstairs, "Hello, fine gentlemen. What can I help you with this lovely afternoon?"

A prostitute, young, blonde and beautiful slipped into his room. She disrobed quickly and walked towards him.

He was in love with a dead woman. But he was still a man. He felt himself go hard as she rubbed him and blew softly in his ear.

"Well, I might as well die happy," he mumbled into her ear. He grabbed her by the waist and they toppled into the bed. She let out a cute giggle and Justice lost himself in her. He touched her and she moaned. They heard men coming up the stairs and she straddled him quickly. He went blind as she guided him into her.

He barely heard a soldier open the door. His woman let out a small, fake scream.

"Sorry sir," the Sun God sputtered, backing out quickly. "Our mistake!"

Justice smiled at her, "Good job," he whispered in her ear.

She smiled back, "This job makes me a good actor."

"I take that as a challenge," he said and he deftly shifted their positions.

She let out a small scream as his hands got busy. Justice smiled to himself because he knew that this scream was real.

14 HEAD OF JUSTICE

October 24, 210, 19:17
Location: Solias, Langundo.

Justice steeled himself and walked through the dining room door.
He had been followed all the way from the brothel. The Sun Gods
weren't as sneaky as they thought they were. Justice knew that they
wouldn't be able to meet or communicate again. The attack would
go in five days, whether they liked it or not. It was too risky for them
to speak outside the council room ever again.

He opened the door to the chaos that was now the castle. King
Sebastian had always had an affinity towards bare-knuckle boxing.
So, when he named himself King, the dining room had been
changed into a bare-knuckle boxing ring. There was a match going
on right now and a hundred men surrounded a large ring. Money
was being passed around and men were shouting with bets flying
back and forth. The King was sitting draped across his chair beside
the ring. The men inside the ring were bloody and looked tired.

The King saw him enter the room and waved a hand slightly. A
Sun God, armour painted black to show he was one of the King's
personal guards, leaned over the King's shoulder. The King
whispered something to the Sun God and he nodded, looking at
Justice. Justice stopped his immediate reaction to wave. He must
tread softly to get out of this meeting alive. The Sun God walked

towards Justice at the door. The crowd of gamblers parted ways, letting him through. Justice realized that this was all an elaborate show, even if the King didn't know it. The crowd had one eye on the King the whole time and were acting how they thought he wanted them to act.

Justice waited for his escort and had a very uneasy feeling. This entire room was on edge. Reflective of the current vibe in all of Solias. The Sun God made his way to his side. Justice noticed another Sun God bring a chair, noticeably lower than the King's. Justice smiled to himself. The Sun God beside him leaned over and said, "The King is expecting you."

"I can see that," Justice said. He strode across the room towards the King, leaving the Sun God to follow. The crowd parted ways as he passed through. The men wouldn't meet his gaze. Justice held his head high and ignored them. The fight continued in the middle of the ring. The men seemed evenly matched and blood was starting to spurt after every hit.

Justice reached the King. The King didn't rise or even look at him, his eyes were glued to the fight. He held out a hand and Justice, burying his pride and disgust, leaned over and kissed his ring. Justice then sat on the small chair beside the King. He was over six feet tall, the King much shorter than him, but in this chair he had to look up to see his face. Justice understood the message loud and clear.

"You sent for me, my lord?" Justice said tensely.

"Funny thing," the King said, eyes never leaving the fight, "you, Housing and Goods were all fucking at the brothel at the same time this afternoon. Seems like quite the coincidence."

Justice feigned mild surprise, "Not really all that surprising," he said. "Council meetings have been... increasingly stressful over the past year."

"So you didn't know that Goods and Housing were there as well?"

Justice smiled, remembering the girl, "I was busy," was all he said.

The King finally turned towards him.

"I'm on to you," he said. "I'm watching you."

"There's nothing to watch," Justice said, shrugging. "I had no idea at all that Goods and Housing were both at Mud's place at all.

I went straight there after the council meeting, as I do after every council meeting. I went upstairs and was busy throughout my hour. Then a Sun God burst in," Justice smiled, "I was momentarily distracted but I pushed through."

The King didn't smile. A fighter was starting to pull ahead of the other and was landing more punches.

"Do you ever wonder," the King said, watching the losing fighter take shots to the face, "why I keep the council around?"

Justice was surprised by the sudden change in topic. "No. The council has been around for hundreds of years. Council positions are for life. You'd be…" Justice trailed off. He needed to tread softly here. If he was arrested and tortured he would probably crack before the invasion of Solias. He needed to stay alive until the city's rescuers came.

"I'd be insane to get rid of the council," the King finished for him. "Is that what you were going to say?"

Justice glanced down and shook his head, "No, my lord. I was just going to comment that you'd be the first in memory to eliminate the council."

"Not the first," the King said, "there was no council, long ago before the Sol's stole the crown. The King ruled as he saw fit."

"I see, my lord. I did not know."

"Well now you know," the King said. "So, the Sol line was the only reason that there was a council. So knowing this why would I keep you around?"

Justice shook his head, "I don't know," he answered honestly.

"Well if I would have killed you all off then the people would blame me for their suffering," he said. One of the fighters landed a massive blow to the other's jaw and the recipient went down hard. The winner stepped back and raised his arms in victory, turning towards the King.

"No," King Sebastian said. The room went quiet. "Three minute break. The fight is to the death. Either one of you dies in there or both of you do." The room was so quiet that Justice could hear the men inside breathing. The downed boxer's friends were the first to get over their shock and ran to his side and helped him to his feet and back towards his corner. Everyone else stood still. The King looked around, seemingly confused by the silence. "Carry on."

The men in the room started yelling again with gusto but there was a shift in attitude in the room. It was serious. There was now a man's life on the line.

"I keep you alive and on council so they hate you," the King said, gesturing around him. "They have never had a fight to the death before. You walked in, we begin to chat, I tell them to fight to the death. They now hate you instead of me. Quite simple, really."

Justice had never thought about it before. He hadn't any reason to. The council had always been there. As long as there was history there had been a King or Queen and their council.

The King looked at Justice's confused face and laughed. Justice looked at the King's manic eyes and instantly had the feeling that he didn't know much of anything.

"Why did you let me be King?"

Justice was caught off guard again by the shift in conversation. "You said the King had passed the crown to you in his dying breaths," he said quietly. "Tradition says that's how it's passed. On the battlefield. Unless there is a suitable heir. And there's no suitable heir."

The King smiled, "You trusted Armend far too much." He leaned in closely to Justice's ear, "I *stole* the crown on the battlefield. Armend was slain. I picked it up and ran."

Justice's hand balled at his side. The King noticed and laughed.

"Why are you telling me this?" Justice asked, barely supressing the growing rage.

"Maybe I get pleasure from watching you suffer," the King said. A bell rang and the fighters went at it again. This time more hesitantly. Neither wanted to be a killer.

"And there will be a new world order soon," King Sebastian said, "this is our last opportunity to chat."

"That's a mistake," Justice said before he could stop himself. "A lot can happen in a week."

The King laughed, "That's the most honest you've been with me this entire conversation. Now, let me be honest with you," the King said. He leaned in again, "I killed the Queen, not your precious Intelligence. On orders from Armend, the man you helped to eliminate the Sol lineage. All this is because of you."

One fighter was holding the other down and pounding him in

the face, over and over and over again. Justice wasn't paying attention. He was distraught. He had hung his love because she had committed treason and killed his Queen. But Sebastian had killed the Queen. Justice was confused and starting to panic. Truth and lies blurred in his head.

His fist was flying towards King Sebastian's face before he knew what he was doing. King Sebastian smiled and said loudly, "Not another move!" Justice stopped his fist an inch shy of the King's wicked smile. The King nodded towards him and Justice looked down. The King had a small dagger, glowing blue with Pulse, sitting right underneath his chin. One small touch from the dagger and Justice knew that he was dead. He breathed heavily, suddenly very afraid.

"I was in the field, doing Armend's dirty work for a lot of years," the King said. Justice was unnerved by how crazy the King really was. "And I kept a little Quicksilver for myself. Are you going to settle down?"

Justice nodded and slowly sat back into his seat.

The King nodded and turned off the Pulse on his weapon and sheathed the dagger.

"I own you," the King said. "Don't forget."

Justice nodded and sat quietly. He felt a Sun God's heavy arm on his shoulder. His mind was reeling. He steeled himself. He knew he'd be taken down to the dungeons. He just had to outwit the idiot Bamber for five days. That's all.

The King seemed to read his mind. He nodded then turned to watch the fight. Justice followed his gaze. He watched in horror as a man beat another man to death. Justice had the feeling that his fate would be the same.

15 ELI

October 24, 210, 19:30
Location: Melanthios forest, Langundo.

Eli was leaning against a tree at the outer edge of the forest. He was picking his teeth with a small stick. His arms were folded in front of him, hiding a couple of throwing knives. Just in case. Always paid to be prepared.

His group simply called themselves the Revolt and were a mix of ex-Sun Gods and Melanthios. They had surrounded ten Sun Gods in a clearing in the forest, and dispatched them of their weapons quickly and without fuss. They were kneeling in the clearing, eyes shifting around trying to count the Revolt's numbers. Eli was hanging back and watching his group's leader, Vick, work his magic.

"You have been tracking us for a long time," Vick said. He was pacing in front of the Sun Gods. He was strong and broad chested and spoke with confidence. The Sun Gods were kneeling in a line, most of their eyes averted. Eli noticed that they looked tired. "Why?" Vick asked.

"You are a traitor to the crown," the Captain of the Sun Gods replied. "We are hunting traitors."

Vick laughed, "We are no traitors."

"You work with those," the Captain spat, "abominations." He looked directly at Eli when he said it.

Eli smiled and waved at him.

Vick's eyes flashed dark. "That was just plain rude," he said.

"You are traitors to the crown," the Captain said again. "I don't care if I'm rude to traitors. You're working with the enemy."

Vick smiled, "Whose enemy?"

The Captain looked confused. Eli shook his head. They were always so stupid. So noble and subservient. They had no idea why they were fighting anymore.

The Captain seemed to gather himself, "You have been declared an enemy of the King."

"Which King?" Vick asked.

"Our true King, King Sebastian the First," the Captain said. His voice shrank and he averted his gaze.

"My true King is King Sol the Nineteenth," Vick said, "this King Sebastian, the mad King, is not my King. So I haven't betrayed anyone. You're the betrayer to your true ruler."

"*Prince* Sol the Nineteenth is dead," the Captain said.

Vick laughed, along with the fighters in the trees. Eli joined them. The Sun Gods looked around themselves nervously. They had apparently misjudged the number of people surrounding them. Vick had fighters hidden all throughout these trees, they numbered close to one hundred. And Eli knew that these ten would soon be joining them.

"Prince Sol the Nineteenth is dead!" the Captain said again, trying to exude confidence.

"Who told you that?" Vick asked.

The Captain glanced around again. The other soldiers averted their gaze.

"The King," the Captain said nervously. Eli smiled. Vick was starting to get through to him.

"The usurper," Vick said.

The Captain nodded, looking down, embarrassed. Vick switched tactics.

"Since the usurper took power, how has life been for you?"

The Sun Gods stayed silent but started glancing around nervously.

"Well, the rain stopped," Vick said, "and then the dry period. No rain for almost a full year. Famine and chaos ensued. Where was your King?"

The Captain stayed silent.

"Well, from what I can see, he certainly wasn't giving the Sun Gods any money," he leaned down and grabbed one of their swords. He ran a finger over the blade and smiled, "See? Dull. He sends you to lose, to die." Vick turned and talked to the man beside the captain. "You hungry?"

The man nodded vehemently, "We haven't eaten in days, sir."

"Shut up, Petrov," the Captain snapped.

Vick smiled, "You're telling me that members of the Sun Gods, his noblest men, are being allowed to go hungry?"

"The drought–"

Vick interrupted the Captain. "Revolt!" he yelled, "Have you eaten today?"

Eli cheered with the rest of them in the trees. They had learned to scavenge food in this new environment. They all ate or none of them did. It was a way of living for the Melanthios and their newly reformed Sun Gods soon learned and embraced the concept. They were always hungry, but never famished.

The Sun Gods looked around enviously.

"Look," Vick said, waving his hand dismissively, "I will not have any further discussion with you about things you already know. The usurper will not stop until he is the only one alive in this country. My true King is Prince Sol. Or Prince Titus. But that lineage must be returned to the throne. Join us or walk home naked." Vick smiled, "It's up to you."

"He has our families!" the man the Captain called Petrov exclaimed. He jumped to his feet. Eli readied his throwing knives but he didn't think he'd have to use them. The man was scared, not violent.

"If we defect they kill them," Petrov yelled frantically. "They would have killed all your families!" he cried to the woods.

No laughter. Just uncomfortable silence. The men and women in the trees who had defected from the Sun Gods were suddenly sullen. They had no idea if this was true. No one contacted their families in the Revolt. From any background. Their entire life was for the cause.

"How does he know who has defected?" Vick asked, brow

furrowed. "No one contacts. You have no lists. How does he know?"

"He took them all inside the inner walls. If we don't check in they are sent to the prisons. They aren't heard from again."

Vick nodded. The information aligned with what they had been told from their contacts on the inside. "They aren't killed," he said. There was a collective sigh of relief from the Revolt. "They have not had easy lives, but they are alive. Before I continue, will you join us? Will you fight to get the true bloodline back where it belongs?"

Petrov nodded. Vick smiled and clasped his shoulder.

"Get this man some food!" Vick yelled. Petrov smiled and a few of the Revolt rushed forward and ushered him away. The other Sun Gods looked longingly at his back from their knees.

"Last chance," Vick said, "join us or return to the city unarmed and shamed."

Eight of the Sun Gods sprang up to cheers from the Revolt. They rushed into the forest and were directed to a small meal of berries and roots. But to them it was a feast. The only Sun God left kneeling was the Captain.

"I took an oath to serve my King," the Captain said.

Vick crouched and stared at him in the eyes, "That is not a King. That is a peasant in King's clothes. He cares nothing for you or for Solias. He will bring Langundo to the ground."

The Captain nodded.

"You took an oath to serve the Sol family. To serve Sol the Nineteenth and Titus. Therefore we have the same master."

Convinced the Captain nodded. Vick held out his hand and clasped his forearm, helping him to his feet.

"How do you know they are alive?" the Captain asked.

"Titus is. He's being cared for by one of the Revolt, hidden away for the time being. Guarded by the best."

The Captain looked as though he was going to ask another question. Vick held up his hand, stopping him, "Go eat. We will talk tomorrow after your stomach is full and you've had rest." The Captain nodded. And, with cheers, was ushered into the forest to join the rest of the men.

Eli strode quietly and confidently towards Vick.

"Kept a lot back," he said.

"I don't trust him," Vick said, turning towards Eli and rubbing his brow. Eli thought he looked old.

"Never heard Jules described as the best before," Eli said smugly.

Vick smiled and shrugged, "Hey I had to get him to join somehow. And that involved a lie this time."

Vick was worried, Eli could tell. Hell, Eli was worried. The attack would be in two weeks. They were stressed. Two years of planning and it was two weeks away.

"Any news from Ujarak?" Vick asked him.

Eli shook his head, "No. He hasn't found Sol. At least he hasn't told us if he has."

Vick sighed again, "We will have to go ahead without them."

Eli was startled, "All of this is designed to go around Sol's eighteenth nameday. When he legitimately has a claim to the throne. He turns eighteen in two weeks and we attack on the same day. That's what we decided…" He drifted off.

Vick clasped him on the shoulder, "We will have to put all of our hope in Titus. And you. For what you've agreed to do."

Eli nodded slowly. A raven swooped down from the sky and landed on Vick's shoulder. Vick immediately tore at the letter attached to its leg and read hurriedly. Eli saw his face fall and prepared himself for the worst. When Vick finally spoke, Eli wasn't disappointed.

"Our contacts in Solias think we've been discovered. The King has reinforcements coming in a week."

Eli blanched, "We can't attack in a week! Ujarak will have no way to make it!"

Vick shook his head, "No, we attack in five days. Before reinforcements can arrive."

"There's no way!" Eli said. "We will barely make the wall in five days."

"It's prepared. We have to. Send a letter to Jules. Tell him to move, now. We take the city regardless. If Titus isn't there then we hold it until he makes it." Vick strode away.

"That gives us no chance!" Eli yelled.

Vick turned, "You are our chance. And Titus. All our hope lies in him. We leave in six hours. Just after midnight. It gives the soldiers time to rest."

Eli watched his back in the fading light, stunned. All hope lied in Titus. Meaning all hope lied in Jules. His heart fell. He hoped Jules' shoulders were wide enough to carry the weight of an entire nation.

16 JULES

October 24, 210, 16:39
Location: Shamrock, Langundo.

Jules had his feet kicked up on the bow of the small fishing boat. He was leaning back, eyes closed, fingers interlaced behind his head. His tanned skin was soaking up the hot sun. He was completely and utterly relaxed.

A splash of sea water on his face surprised him so much that he almost toppled the small boat in his surprise.

"Hey!" he sputtered. He had salt water in his eyes and he rubbed them with the back of his hand.

"Just making sure you're awake, old man!" Titus yelled from beside the boat. The teenager's head was sticking out of the water, sideways smirk on his face. He had just come up from a dive and his blond hair was plastered to the side of his face.

"You could have just yelled!" Jules said, laughing. He leaned over the side of the boat and splashed at Titus. The boy laughed and swam away quickly. They were on the western coast of Langundo, farther south than Jules had ever been. The bright blue sea was framed by large cliffs behind him. They were in a cove with clear, calm water. The boy was diving for scallops and mussels for dinner.

Jules smiled at himself. He internally referred to Titus as a boy, even though Jules was only eleven years his senior. And Titus was fifteen now. He had grown at least six inches over the past year. His voice had dropped and his shoulders were beginning to fill out. He took after his father. He would be over six feet after he was done this growth spurt, Jules was sure of it.

"Old man!" Titus yelled. He was swimming towards a small beach that lined the cliff. "Shall we continue with our training?"

Jules laughed. "Who are you calling old man!" he yelled back. He grabbed the oars of the boat and rowed after Titus. Jules rowed hard, sweat dripping from his face, but Titus was a strong swimmer. *Especially for a kid who was landlocked his entire life*, Jules thought through gritted teeth. He was rowing hard but he knew he was no match for the teenager. Titus was naturally gifted at anything physical. Jules was now more worried about training Titus' leadership ability. Titus could swing the sword, but he was so hot headed Jules wasn't sure if he knew when he should.

Jules felt the bottom of the small boat grind against the sandy beach and the boat slowed suddenly. He jumped out, cool, clear water pooling around his knees. Keeping his back towards the beach, he pulled the small boat out of the water onto the beach.

He heard Titus' feet shift in the sand and Jules smiled to himself. *Still too predictable*, he thought. He made a show of struggling with the boat with his back turned. He heard the soft footsteps of the boy running at him across the beach. Jules waited until the last second and turned quickly, unsheathing the small dagger at his hip and successfully parrying Titus' attack. Titus had swung hard and the unsuspected parry had sent him off balance and his sword, still a little too heavy for him, pulled him forward. Jules kicked him gently in the stomach and gripped his wrist and twisted, causing Titus' sword to fall into the sand. Jules stepped forward and foot swept Titus sending him on his ass in the sand beside his sword.

"You attack a man with his back turned," Jules said, crouching over the fallen teenager.

"I wanted to win against your old ass," Titus said puffing, trying to smile. He was red-faced and angry, but trying to mask it with humor. Jules could tell. Titus didn't like losing and right now he looked like a fool.

Jules held out his hand. "Was it worth it, to win?"

Titus took it and Jules hauled him up. "No," Titus said.

"Honestly it wasn't."

Jules nodded. "Never attack a man with his back turned."

Titus shrugged, "I was taught differently. In Sun God training it was all about winning. If a man's back is turned to the attack then it's his fault for trusting you to begin with."

Jules smiled and bent down, returning Titus' sword. He then turned his back on the teenager and walked to the center of the beach where they had dumped their swords after the morning session. Jules was happy that Titus didn't charge. The instinct to attack a man with his back turned was proving to be the hardest to break. Titus would soon surpass his limited ability with a sword. Training with Eli, Ujarak, Tory and his beloved Senka had helped him. That move he had just used on Titus was one of Senka's specialties. His heart dropped when he thought of his old family. The memories had an annoying habit of popping up when he least expected them to.

He turned towards Titus. Titus had followed him with a lowered sword. Jules wiped a tear from his eye and he saw Titus frown.

"I'm sorry," Jules said.

"It's allowed," Titus replied, "I miss people too. My family. I'm sorry I attacked you with your back turned. I know you don't like it when I do that. I don't want to disappoint you."

Jules looked at him then sat heavily in the sand. He tapped the sand beside him and Titus, looking confused, sat down.

"You don't disappoint me," Jules said. "You never have. I don't think you could."

"I just... I just want to get Sol's throne back for him," Titus said. "They killed my mom and my dad for it. I want to avenge them. I want to hurt the people who hurt them."

Jules understood completely. "When you were young and in Sun God training, did you honestly want to be there?"

Titus thought about it, "No. I hated it."

"So why are you trying to be like one?"

Titus didn't have an answer, he hung his head and stared into the sand.

"The Sun Gods used to be a noble army, just and fair, only using violence to protect Solias and its royalty. We only got a madman's twisted version of that," Jules said. "Your uncle Armend had been twisting the Sun Gods to his whims and in his image for a lot of years."

Titus nodded and sniffled, "I wish I could kill him."

Jules shrugged and his shoulder screamed. It didn't bother him often anymore but his old injury, suffered in that final battle between the Melanthios and the Sun Gods, acted up once in a while. He had almost died. He used to wish he had. He had passed out and woken and his beloved was dead. The town that he had defected to had burned. Everything had been broken.

"I wish I could too," Jules said. "But my girlfriend took care of that for both of us," he said with a smile. "Your mom started it, Senka finished it."

Titus sniffled again, "They shouldn't have had to. We should have known he was an asshole a long time ago."

"We often overlook the flaws of people we love," Jules said. "Human nature. And your mom and Senka made their choice. I'm sure they would make it again if they were given the chance."

They sat in silence, staring at the beautiful calm blue sea, each lost in his own grief and thoughts. It had been three years and it hadn't gotten any easier. Jules began to doubt it ever would.

"What's that?" Titus said suddenly, pointing out to sea in the distance. Jules squinted his eyes and followed Titus' finger towards the horizon. A ship, larger than he'd ever seen, was starting to form on the horizon.

"Looks like a ship," Jules said quizzically.

"But Hans and the rest of the fleet aren't due back from fishing for a couple of days," Titus said.

"Looks too big to be a fishing boat," Jules said.

"Where would they have come from?" Titus asked. "There's nothing west, just water then the end of the world."

"Don't believe everything you hear," Jules said softly. "We should be getting back to Shamrock anyway. Big Mamma Gertie will be waiting for us for dinner. We can ask her if any ships were due back early."

Titus nodded and hopped up, heading towards their small boat. Jules followed, staring at the vessel looming on the horizon. Jules thought he saw sails, larger than any he'd ever seen, billowing ahead of the ship. They looked purple. There was a gold symbol on the sail, but the ship was too far away for Jules to see what it was. The ship changed course slightly to the north and barrelled away up the coastline.

Jules shook his head. If Titus hadn't pointed it out he would have thought he dreamt it. They each took a side of their boat and pushed it into the sea, hopping in and grabbing an oar. They did so silently, two years of training and living together in the coastal village of Shamrock had them accustomed to the ways of the small boat. They rowed hard south around a small outcrop of rocks to a small dock. They latched the boat to the dock and, grabbing their weapons and small bag of scallops, made their way silently to the village.

The path was steep and rocky to the top of the cliff, but Titus and Jules had made the trek hundreds of times. They were barely puffing when they crested the cliff to see the small village. Its houses were weathered from the salt water of the sea. There were nets being mended outside and the smell of fish was always in the air. Children ran around screaming at each other, their guardians hollering at them to finish their chores.

The village was emptier than usual. With winter quickly on its way and the drought having hit their vegetable gardens, the younger men and woman had taken their fishing vessels for one last trip to sea together. The grandparents were left in charge of keeping the village and raising the children while the adults were gone. Jules and Titus hadn't joined them for this one last fish of the season. They had other things to do.

"Josh, Theo!" a little girl of about eight yelled as they walked into the village. "Big Mamma Gertie is looking for you! You have better brought some scallops!"

Jules smiled at her. "Of course Theo caught scallops!" he yelled back, winking at Titus. Titus held up the bag. The little girl beamed at them. She was going to say something else but her grandfather yelled at her from their house and she scurried away.

Titus smiled, "I'll never get used to our names here," he said lowly to Jules.

Jules shot him a warning look and Titus wisely fell silent.

Titus smiled and they trudged their way to Big Mamma Gertie's house. She was the matriarch, the head of the village. Her house wasn't the largest but it was always the busiest. It was right at the center of town.

She also happened to be Vick's mother. She, along with her husband Hans were the only ones who knew the true identities of Jules and Titus.

They walked down the street and Big Mamma was waiting for them outside the house.

"'Bout time you showed up!" she called with a big smile. Big Mamma Gertie earned her name. She was easily three-hundred pounds, but she held herself with the sturdy grace of a much younger, much smaller woman. She'd had twelve children in her day with Vick being in the middle of the pack. And she was in charge of everything she touched. When Big Mamma spoke everyone listened.

"The kid was slowing me down!" Jules called back. Titus elbowed him with a laugh.

"Bring them scallops in, Theo," Big Mamma called with a wink. Jules couldn't help but smile. Every time Big Mamma called them by their fake names she winked. Jules was sure the entire village had figured that something else was going on by now, but no one said anything for fear of one of Big Mamma's legendary whoopings.

Titus laughed and ran up to her, giving her a peck on the cheek as he went through the door.

"Wash up for dinner!" she yelled at the teenager's back.

Jules followed her and gave her a mandatory peck on the cheek.

"You look troubled," she said. Jules walked through the door and Big Mamma closed it behind them.

"Not ready to leave just yet," Jules said lowly.

"Wash up, dear," Big Mamma said. Jules obliged and made his way to a pot of water beside the table. He washed his hands slowly, watching the household. Jules wasn't usually so sappy and sullen, but he would miss this place.

Big Mamma's youngest son, Stillman, was already cleaning the scallops with Titus. Stillman was small for his age. He was skinny, almost gaunt, with shiny red hair and bright eyes. He knew their secret but as he didn't speak, their secret was safe with him. He had just turned ten, but as Vick had joined the Sun Gods for the family all those years ago, Stillman could live his life in peace.

The Sun Gods and their mandatory enrolment had been ruining

families for a thousand years.

Jules had tried not to sway Titus in the decisions he may make as King one day. But he hoped every day that Titus would see how his decisions would affect families and to go with caution.

"You're lost in deep thoughts, my dear," Big Mamma Gertie said from behind him. Titus and Stillman looked up from the scallops, but a sidelong glance from Big Mamma had them hastily looking back at their work. Titus nudged Stillman and whispered something to him. Stillman smiled sheepishly. The whole exchange made Jules uncomfortable. He shouldn't take Titus away from this place. They had found a semblance of peace over the past two years. Who was he to bring a child into war?

Jules nodded, "Yes, I am. Thinking about what's to come, I suppose."

Big Mamma shook her head. She went and grabbed the clean scallops from the boys, "Go grab the linen off the line." The boys nodded and rushed out. Jules could hear Stillman giggle from behind the house.

"That Titus is good for him," Big Mamma said, taking the scallops and adding them to a pot of stew that was boiling on the stove. "I haven't seen that boy open up like that with anybody."

The comment made Jules even sadder.

"You're worried about taking him away," Big Mamma said. "But really, do you think you could keep him here?"

"No," Jules answered without hesitation, "kid's a fighter. He wouldn't stay. Not if I went."

Big Mamma smiled, "Hun he wouldn't stay even if you didn't go. He's a Prince. He will stop at nothing to return his brother to the throne. As he shouldn't."

Jules was instantly angry. It was a foreign emotion to him, anger didn't often boil over. "He's a child!" he nearly yelled. He maintained a small amount of control. Just enough so his voice didn't carry to outside of the building.

Big Mamma just smiled, stood, and wrapped him in a bear hug between her breasts. Jules almost cried, but he managed to keep it together.

"When do you leave?" she asked him after she let him go.

"Two more sleeps and we will start getting the horses ready,"

Jules said. "I want to arrive a few days early and well rested. It's a six day ride to Solias from here."

Big Mamma nodded, "We will throw a feast for you. Hans and the other sailors are due back tomorrow."

"Hope they caught."

"Oh we will manage," Big Mamma said. "We always do."

Jules suddenly remembered the ship passing on the sea, heading north. He was just about to ask Big Mamma about it when Titus and Stillman burst through the back door.

"What is it?" Big Mamma snapped. Then she noticed the fear on both their faces.

The war horn sounded in the village.

They were under attack.

"Quick, Titus!" Big Mamma said. She heaved open a hidden hatch in the floor underneath the dinner table. Titus quickly jumped down. "You stay quiet, you hear? No heroics."

Titus nodded quickly once, white-faced.

Big Mamma slammed the trap door down over top of him. The basement chamber was dug for Titus when they first arrived. He could hide and watch them through the floorboards. The trap door was seamless in the floor. If Titus kept quiet he'd be safe.

Jules sat at the table with Stillman and Big Mamma started scooping out stew when four Sun Gods burst into the house.

"Everyone!" the Captain yelled. She was a broad shouldered, tall woman of perhaps twenty-five. Her long brown hair was braided down her back. She carried a broadsword and Jules could tell that she knew how to use it. "Everyone! Hands on the table, face down. You!" she said, pointing the sword at Big Mamma. "Put that down and hands on the table."

Big Mamma stared at her, double chin trembling. Jules kept his hands on the table and watched Big Mamma, willing her to put the bowl down.

"I'm dishing out supper," Big Mamma said. She continued spooning stew into Stillman's bowl. Jules could tell the kid was shaking with fear. "You burst in to my house, unannounced. I will finish dishing up my children's dinner."

The Captain stared at her, for a second shocked by the insubordination. Then she laughed. The three other soldiers, all men, turned and looked at each other confused then joined her. The Captain sheathed her sword. "She wants to finish dishing up," she said through laughter. She strode forward and struck Big Mamma across the face, hard, with her armour plated hand. Big Mamma fell backwards with a bang that shook the house. The pot of stew clanged against the floor, spilling the hard earned food.

Before Jules knew what he was doing he was standing and yelling. Two of the soldiers rushed forward and grabbed his shoulders, pulling him down into his chair. They slammed his head down onto the table and one of them held him there with a heavy hand on the back of his head.

He locked eyes with a scared Titus beneath the floor boards. His blue, piercing eyes staring at Jules. Jules knew the kid would be angry and want to protect them, but he couldn't. Jules stared at him and tried to shake his head. He heard Big Mamma drag herself to her feet.

"Who do we have here?" the Captain said. The soldier holding Jules' head down yanked his hair backwards, hard. Jules saw that Stillman was violently shaking holding his spoon, his eyes fixed on the face of his hurt mother. She was bleeding from the mouth, the red blood a stark contrast to her white face.

The Captain walked up to him. He saw it, almost in comical slow motion, as recognition crossed her face. Jules knew her too, from his Sun God trials all those years ago. He smothered the recognition. His only hope now was denial.

"You," the Captain said with a smile. "You! I know you."

The soldiers looked at her with apprehension.

"You have to know me," the Captain said. "You're Jules! The Queen's guard! Traitor to the throne!"

Realization crossed the soldiers' faces and they grabbed on to him tighter. Jules shook his head. "No," he gasped through the searing pain in his shoulder. "No. I've never seen you in my life."

"You think I'd forget you?" the Captain said. "Your face was plastered all over the city after the Queen died. We know you let in those Melanthios scum to kill her."

"I wasn't a Queen's guard," Jules said, gritting his teeth, "I wasn't in the Sun Gods at all. My older brother went for me."

"You have to remember me," the Captain said. "I'm Bestla! You remember your friend, Bestla!" she leaned right in, so close that he could feel her breath on his face. "All through the Sun Gods' training I knew you were a coward. I'm happy I lived long enough to kill you myself."

She stood up straight, standing over him, "Admit it."

"My name is Josh," Jules said. "I don't know what you're talking about."

Captain Bestla rolled her eyes. She gave a sharp whistle and a soldier grabbed Stillman and lifted him right out of his chair. The boy's eyes went wide and he let out a high pitched gasp. The last soldier went around the table and held a knife to the rising Big Mamma.

"If you don't admit who you are," Captain Bestla said, "I will kill both of them."

Jules' insides dropped. He saw no way out of this. *Keep them from finding Titus*, he thought to himself desperately, *Titus needs to live.*

"That's Josh!" Big Mamma said desperately, staring at Stillman. "He's a friend of the family's from a different town over. I swear it!"

"No, he's not," Captain Bestla said, "if that's what he told you, he's lying. This is the Sun God Jules, traitor to the crown. He started a group that calls themselves the Revolt, him along with," she turned to Big Mamma, "your son Vick."

The look of shock on Big Mamma's face said it all.

Captain Bestla laughed, a cold hard laugh, "You think we didn't know?" Jules struggled against the soldiers, straining against the pain in his shoulder. Even Titus was forgotten. Poor silent Stillman, gentle soul, held by a Sun God shattered Jules' resolve.

"Why would I come here? To the south, where these people are as close to the Melanthios scum as can be, if not for you?" Captain Bestla said.

"You're right," Jules said finally, relaxing in the soldiers' grasp. "You're right. I am Jules, the ex-Sun God."

Captain Bestla smiled and whistled. The soldiers holding Big Mamma and Stillman let go. Stillman ran into Big Mamma's arms.

"Take him outside," Captain Bestla said, "we will publicly execute him and bring his head to King Sebastian."

The fight was out of Jules. There would be no future wars for him. Titus knew the plans and Big Mamma would make sure he got to Solias in time. That was his charge, and he figured he'd done his job pretty well for the last two years.

Jules was dragged out of the house. Big Mamma following, leaving a shocked Stillman inside the house. Jules was grateful. At least he could look at Big Mamma when they killed him.

They dragged him into the middle of the street.

"Everyone from this shit-town Shamrock, leave your houses!" Captain Bestla shouted. Jules saw the scared people of the village slowly leave their houses. There were Sun Gods by every door. Bestla had come prepared.

A soldier brought out a large log to the center of the street. The two soldiers flanking Jules kicked his knees out from under him. He landed with a thud. They bent him over so the side of his head was being pressed into the log. He saw Big Mamma and locked eyes. He was breathing quickly. As prepared as he was to give his life for the cause and join Senka, he didn't want to die yet.

"This man is a traitor to the Sun Gods and your king!" Captain Bestla yelled. No one dared move, they were far too outnumbered. The sun was setting and Jules felt the cool air on his face. "He has been sentenced to death," Bestla finished yelling.

She knelt down and whispered in his ear, "You think you've saved them? I will kill everyone in this village after you're dead. Die with their blood on your hands."

Jules found his fight and started struggling against the Sun Gods but it was too late. "No!" he yelled.

Bestla smiled and stepped back. Jules heard her unsheathe her sword.

Run, he thought to Big Mamma with his eyes. She just stood there, wiping tears, being the rock that she always was. Big Mamma wouldn't look away.

Jules prepared himself for the final blow.

He heard the sound of a bow loosing an arrow and a thud, then a gurgle coming from beside him.

The soldiers holding Jules looked around suddenly, relieving the pressure on the back of his head. He looked around and saw Bestla. She was white-faced, gasping and clawing at an arrow sticking out of her neck. She fell to her knees, her sword dropping beside her.

She looked at Jules, lips pursed, gasping for air. She slouched over on her side, dead.

The soldiers didn't know what to do. A yell sounded and more arrows were loosed on the unsuspecting Sun Gods. Both the men holding Jules were killed and Jules struggled to his feet. He was confused by what was happening. He looked towards Big Mamma but she was gone.

He looked around quickly. The Sun Gods were locked in battle. When he focused he saw it was with the sailors. They had returned early from the sea.

Hans, a large white-haired man, husband of Big Mamma, ran up to him.

"Jules!" he said. "You must take the Prince and leave."

"No!" Jules said, "I'm not leaving you!"

"We will win this battle, and the next, and the next. But if you and Titus don't get out of here there will be no end to the battles," he said urgently. A Sun God came behind Jules and Hans stabbed him through the neck with his sword. "Go!" he yelled and launched himself into the fray.

Jules turned and saw Titus on his horse riding hard towards him, Jules' horse in tow. Big Mamma must have saddled them quickly.

"Get on!" Titus yelled.

Jules jumped on his horse and they rode hard out of the village towards the plains. He saw men and women in battle with the Sun Gods and felt shame as he rode away. They rode hard until they were well out of the village. Titus slowed his horse.

"We have to go back!" Titus said, puffing. It was dark by now and they were well out of Shamrock.

"We can't," Jules said. He hadn't had time to process anything. Big Mamma had strapped his sword to his horse along with emergency supplies.

"They are dying for us!" Titus exclaimed. "We never should have left them in the first place. Big Mamma just told me what to do and I panicked!"

"We have to get you to Vick," Jules said. "It's all about you."

"I don't want it to be!" Titus exploded. "I DON'T WANT ANYONE ELSE TO DIE FOR ME!"

Jules stopped and let the kid relax a bit. "You will most likely be

King," he said finally. "That is your birthright. People will always be dying for you. But it's your cross to bear."

Titus looked like he was going to yell again. A raven swooped down from the sky, interrupting him. The raven landed on Jules' outstretched arm. Jules ripped the attached letter open and read greedily by the moonlight.

"We must ride to Solias," Jules said. "We have been discovered. The attack is to begin in five days."

"But we are six days from Solias," Titus said softly.

"Then we better ride hard, kid," Jules said. "We will talk about it later. They aren't dying for you," he said. "They are dying for your parents. Your brother, their families. This is bigger than all of us."

Titus nodded.

They rode north together, taking only short breaks to rest their horses and to nap.

The ship sailing north on the horizon was forgotten.

17 UJARAK

October 25, 210, 12:16
Location: Artesia, Carabesh.

He was hot.

It was always hot here. The sun pierced the sky and baked his skin. He rubbed the back of his neck. It felt like it was burning.

Ujarak sighed. He hated being hot. And Carabesh was always hot. The sun beat down from the sky onto the parched land of sand. *And it was almost winter*, he thought to himself glumly as he made his way through the streets of Artesia, the capital city of Carabesh.

Artesia had been glamorous when he'd first arrived six months ago. The city was comprised of markets overflowing with sweet fruits and spicy peppers, guarded from the sun by colorful awnings. The smells of spices were in the air. The women were beautiful, the houses large and made of sandstone. The flood and drought that had affected Langundo so deeply hadn't crossed the sea to this place. They were thriving here, and Ujarak thought that was the biggest difference of all.

But six months in a place could sure change a person's opinion. Instead of foreign spices in the markets, Ujarak smelled foul body odor. Instead of large houses of sandstone, Ujarak saw wasted space and constant repairs. He was ready to go home, Prince Sol the Nineteenth in tow or not.

He knew that his miserable mood was because he was a failure. He'd volunteered for this. Two long years ago when the Revolt was still young, he'd volunteered to find Prince Sol and bring him back by his eighteenth birthday in November. But he'd followed him here and searched. His efforts had turned up nothing. Every brothel, bar, restaurant, hotel and home had turned up nothing. The Prince had effectively disappeared.

Ujarak made his way to the docks, where large ships creaked and moaned with the incoming waves. It was busy here and Ujarak kept his head up, making sure he didn't bump into any vendors or people on the docks. He was a large man by Melanthios standards, and they were large compared to the people of Carabesh. Ujarak felt like a giant.

He made his way towards a man at the end of the dock. The dock shifted beneath him as he approached.

"Captain?" Ujarak asked. The man was dressed in traditional sea faring clothing, with light chaps and a loose vest.

The man turned from his cargo ship towards him and nodded. Man of few words. Ujarak thought they would get along well.

"I am looking for passage," Ujarak said in his baritone, "to Langundo."

The Captain looked him over and nodded, "You can work for passage," he grunted. "But this is our last trip to Langundo. Trade has slowed and it's no longer worth our while."

Ujarak nodded.

"There are barrels of wine at the end of the dock, bring them over."

Ujarak nodded again. He made his way slowly back across the docks. There was a stack of ten barrels of Carabesh wine. He lumbered over to them when something caught his eye.

He looked sidelong at a fruit vendor at the end of the docks.

There was a raven sitting on the shoulder of a teenage boy with messy brown hair.

Ujarak blinked twice to make sure he hadn't been imagining it.

The raven was there. She had blue eyes. The kid was over six feet tall, light-skinned, dressed in rags. He had disheveled curly hair that reached his shoulders. His face was skinny and gaunt. He looked hungry and Ujarak watched his eyes dart around as he approached the vendor.

After all this time, the Prince was standing right in front of him. Looking at him, Ujarak realized his mistake. The kid had been hiding in the slums. Ujarak had checked the rich areas, suspecting that he would have money and would be trying to use his influence. Instead the kid had hid on the streets, in plain sight. Ujarak had to laugh to himself. At least his future king was smart.

Ujarak watched the kid wait until the vendor wasn't looking and quickly snatched an apple and took off into the crowd. Ujarak shook his head and put a quarter Krit into the vendor's bag while he walked after the boy. He wouldn't lose him again.

Ujarak followed the kid from a safe distance through the crowd. He'd have to find them both another passage to Langundo after he'd convinced the boy to join him. He had no idea how he'd do that. The boy didn't know who Ujarak was. They had never met. Ujarak was going on the information that Titus had passed on after the war. A simple description of a teenage boy and a bird with distinct blue eyes. That's all Ujarak had to go on.

The Prince hadn't shown up with his brother after the war. Titus had found the Melanthios shortly after the fire in Ismat. He'd followed instructions from his mother to find Prisoner 613, who the Melanthios knew was Senka. They had kept watch over Titus while the Revolt formed from the ex-Sun Gods and the Melanthios working together. Sol had never showed up. Two years ago, they had separated. With the Mad King's rule the world was getting more and more dangerous for the two princes. Titus and Jules had gone south to Vick's mother's house for protection. Ujarak had volunteered to find Sol. He was lonely without Tory and needed something to distract himself, especially since he was sure he wouldn't see Tory again.

His woman was on her own path. Ujarak would never stop her. So here he was in Artesia.

Ujarak watched the kid turn into a dark alley. He walked over and peered into the alley. The kid was pacing back and forth, holding a piece of paper in his hand. To Ujarak it looked like he was rehearsing for something. The kid paced and spoke to himself, head down, reading the paper.

Ujarak was confused but curious. He wanted to see what the

kid was doing before he approached him. The kid paced and muttered, clutching his paper, eyes down. The bird was perched on his shoulder, rocking in time of the kid's paces.

After about ten minutes of this, Ujarak watched the kid steel himself and shove the papers into his pockets. Ujarak stepped aside and the kid strode towards the main street. He was focused in his own world and didn't notice the large Melanthios man watching him.

Prince Sol strode down the street towards the capitol building and Ujarak suddenly figured out what was happening.

Carabesh was run under an electoral system. They didn't have a King. There was a council of fifty members, men and women, who spoke for the people of their trade. The council voted for someone called the "President", a man or woman who spoke for the people as a collective.

Ujarak had never understood how they got anything done in this backwards system. It seemed like all they did was argue and campaign for votes, no actual work or change was completed. Every week, the President held an Open Council for the people to share their grievances. The President listened and would either make a decision or take it to the main council for attention.

The kid was going to this council. But Ujarak still didn't know for what.

Prince Sol strode confidently to the majestic white capitol building and spoke with the guard. The guard listened attentively and nodded, stepping aside to let the Prince past.

Ujarak strode up to the guard.

"Hello, good sir," the guard said to Ujarak, "today is the Open Council. Do you wish to put your name on the list for future grievances or to attend as a witness?"

"Witness," Ujarak grunted.

The guard nodded and smiled at him, "Just straight ahead and to the doors on the left, sir. The next hearing will begin shortly."

Ujarak nodded again and walked through the arching doors of the capitol building. He followed the pillars of the hall and entered a chamber on the left, following the guard's instructions.

There were carpets laid on the sandstone ground to sit on. A large white throne rose at the end of the hall. There were a few from

Carabesh already sitting cross-legged on the carpets. Ujarak couldn't understand how you could have nothing to do and be so bored that you listened to other's express trifle disagreements to a President.

Price of luxury, he thought to himself.

He waited, cross-legged on the rug, uncomfortable and so damn hot. *Why was it always hot?* he thought to himself glumly.

A bell rang somewhere in the hall and a man in a white horse-hair wig and black robe walked through a door and sat on the throne.

It took everything in his power not to roll his eyes or sigh audibly.

He couldn't wait to get back to Langundo.

"Presenting to you," a different man said loudly, holding a scroll of parchment in front of him, "Master Semper of Langundo."

The door opened again and Prince Sol walked out. Ujarak was confused as to why the Prince was being dishonest about his name. He should have nothing to fear here. Guards lined the walls to ensure that no violence took place in the council.

The kid had been in hiding for three years. Maybe he was just in the habit of lying.

The kid strode forward, head down reading his paper. The bird perched on his dishevelled shoulder.

"I have come to you..." the Prince said lowly. It was a barely audible mumble and Ujarak had to strain his ears.

C'mon kid, he thought, *you're the future King. Speak up!*

"I cannot hear you," the President said tersely, though not unkindly. "You will have to speak up in order for me to hear you."

The Prince turned red and mumbled something. He shuffled through his papers and dropped them. He hastily bent and picked them up. Ujarak heard the men around him chuckle and was angry for the Prince. He was just a kid after all.

"You have five more minutes to present your case," the President said. "If you do not in that time then we will have to move on."

The kid stood. Ujarak could tell that he was breathing heavily and was clearly upset. The bird on his shoulder nibbled his ear. Prince Sol nodded and took a deep breath.

"My name is Semper of Solias," the kid said loudly. Ujarak

smiled to himself. "I have come to you on behalf of our neighbors to the west, those in the country of Langundo."

The giggling and muttering around him stopped and the observers started listening intently.

"What do you ask of our council?" the President asked. His face remained neutral.

"I come to you on behalf of my people," the kid said strongly. He wasn't looking at his papers anymore. "We have endured undue hardships in Langundo. First the rain, which washed any sort of crop away. Second the drought, which chased all the animals into hiding. Thirdly, and most importantly, the rule of the Mad King Sebastian. He has destroyed our country and has run it into the ground through his villainy."

"Master Semper," the President said, "we have no quarrel with King Sebastian. He does not wish war on us. He has increased the purchasing of our luxuries to Langundo. We have traded with him for more than any other monarch before him–"

"At what cost?" Prince Sol said strongly, interrupting the President. "At the cost of the people he leads! Only he can afford these luxuries you speak. The people are starving, and soon there won't be a Solias left."

"How they choose to run their country is not our concern," the President said. "They have allowed this man to gain control of their country. He is of no threat to us."

"Please, sir!" The Prince said, desperately. "If I could have but one regimen to take with me to Langundo. I would be able to storm Solias and return the proper King to the throne–"

The President slammed his fist and the Prince fell silent. "We have no quarrel with the people of Solias! Not one of my soldiers will step foot across the sea on your venture. And you speak of this proper King. Who do you speak of? As far as I know, both Prince Sol and Prince Titus are dead. The mutiny that your people allowed is not our concern. We have a good relationship with King Sebastian. If your people have an issue with his rule then that is not our problem."

Prince Sol was red-faced and angry, Ujarak could tell. *Tell them who you are. The only way is to tell them who you are.*

Prince Sol stayed silent.

"This meeting is adjourned," the President said. "That was our last appointment for the day." The President rose and everyone joined him. He exited out the side door. The Prince was left alone, head down, raven on his shoulder.

Ujarak sighed. He knew there was really only one course of action now. He was sad to go so early, but not surprised. He joined the crowd exiting the building, keeping his eyes out for the Prince. He assumed the Prince would try to reason with the President alone. That's when he would move.

He thought of Tory. He wished he would have been able to see her again, one last time. Her beautiful copper eyes. He knew they'd be together in the next life and any life after that, but his heart ached. It didn't feel like enough. And to die while he was *so fucking hot* just seemed unfair.

He waited just outside the main doors of the capitol building. He fingered a dagger in his shirt. He had left his warhammer in Langundo and he missed it. That would sure make a splash.

After an eternity the Prince exited the building. He looked agitated and Ujarak smiled to himself. The Prince waited by the door of the Capitol building. Ujarak started to make his way towards him.

The President made his way out of the building with two Carabesh army guards flanking him.

"Sir!" Prince Sol said to him as he walked up to him. "I just need another minute of your time!"

The Guards stepped forward but the President waved them off. They stepped back a few steps to allow the President to speak. "I know this is hard for you to hear because I see that you care about your people," he said to the kid.

Ujarak walked quickly forward and brandished the knife. "Death to the President!" he yelled in his booming voice. He ran forward, towards the shocked men. "King Sebastian sent me!" he yelled and he raised the knife wildly towards the President.

C'mon kid, he thought. He was moving as slow as he could in order to give the prince a free target on the left side of his body. He saw the kid form a fist and he couldn't help but smile. He let the surprised Prince land a soft punch on his jaw and he tumbled forward, pretending that it was enough to stun him.

He landed hard on his face, careful to drop the knife harmlessly away from anyone involved. To his surprise, the kid wound up and kicked him in the face. Ujarak was proud. The kick barely registered but it was harder than the punch was. He faked being knocked unconscious, letting his body relax.

"Arrest him!" the President yelled to the chaos. The stunned guards rushed forward and Ujarak let them haul his hulking arms behind his back. There was a commotion of voices and panic. Carabesh was nonviolent and Ujarak knew that this would be news.

"What did he say, while he was attacking?" he heard the President ask no one in in particular.

"King Sebastian sent me," he heard the Prince reply.

"You, sir, dear master Semper. Your heroics will be in songs! We have much to talk about at our next council meeting. I hope you will join me? We have to investigate this matter further."

Ujarak smiled to himself. He moved his shoulders slightly.

"He's waking up!" a guard yelled.

A heavy sword hilt hit him hard on the temple. This time Ujarak was knocked unconscious, his last thoughts of success and seeing Tory soon.

18 TORY

October 25, 210, 15:28
Location: North Langundo.

"Senka!" she yelled, thrashing around.

"She's dead," Black Eyes tittered in her ear.

"None of that," a man's voice snapped at Black Eyes.

Confused, Tory glanced around and fought with the blankets on her bed. That thought gradually meandered its way through Tory's muddled brain. *My blankets*, she thought, *on my bed. I'm in my home.* The thought solidified her and she gradually took in her surroundings. It was twilight outside and the Shaman was sitting on a chair by her bed.

"Just can't get it through your head she's dead," Black Eyes said in her ear.

"Shut up!" both Tory and the Shaman said it at the same time.

"Humph," Tory grumbled, swinging her legs out of bed to face him. "Thought I was just going crazy. Turns out you're crazy too."

The Shaman bowed his head. Tory was completely naked and he was averting his eyes.

"Wish it was Senka talking in my ear," Tory grumbled and tested out her legs. They were solid. She stood up and busied herself in the kitchen making tea. She was unconcerned with her nakedness.

"Senka is no longer of this world," the Shaman muttered. "She has gone back from where she came."

"Figures. Now I get stuck with this annoying bitch."

"Annoying 'cause you KILLED ME!" Black Eyes yelled in her ear. Tory barely took notice. She needed tea as fast as possible.

"I turned and fired," Tory said. "Caught one of my archers in the chest. I definitely killed one of my own. That's a feeling that I've never felt before."

"Senka is no longer of this world," the Shaman muttered. "She has gone back from where she came."

Tory turned and stared at the Shaman. "You already said that," she said quietly.

He stared back, "Senka is no longer of this world," the Shaman muttered. "She has gone back from where she came."

"What's going on?" Tory asked. She thought she heard Black Eyes yelling at her from a distance but she couldn't focus on the voice. Tory shook her head. She must have taken a head injury in the battle.

"Sorry," she said shaking her head, trying to clear it. "We won so we should be celebrating. Tea?"

The Shaman shook his head.

"I'm assuming I was down for a day?" Tory continued. She steeped some tea leaves and started busying herself finding clothes. Someone had washed the things she had worn to war and folded them on a chair in her house. Tory smiled to herself, despite the rising anxiety in her chest. Ujarak always took care of her.

"Yes, a day. We burned most of the killed Melanthios last night while you were asleep."

Tory nodded. Black Eyes stayed quiet.

"Tonight we will burn Senka and the rest."

Tory nodded again. She was dressed and sat on the chair to put on her boots.

"I need you to miss the funeral," the Shaman was trying to tread softly. It didn't work.

Tory tilted her head back and laughed. "Good one. Really. Senka was my best friend. The least I can do is watch them burn her body."

"Considering you are the one who let her die," Black Eyes chimed in from next to her.

"Exactly! So as I'm the scumbag who couldn't save her, I should probably watch her fucking body burn," Tory took a sip of her tea. When it burned her mouth, she threw the clay cup across the room causing it to shatter against the wall. The pieces tinkled to the ground, small sounds echoing in her ears.

Tory and the Shaman stared at the shattered cup. Tory's chest heaved and she regained her icy calm, "But hey, you asked, so I will follow blindly like everyone else. Sorry if I don't believe you as readily as everyone else. You have tricks, you don't have knowledge."

The Shaman stayed silent for a long time, allowing her to calm herself slightly. Finally, he said, "I need you to go find your father."

Tory stared at him, shocked. Whatever she was expecting, it wasn't that. They stared at each other again for a long time.

"Well," Tory finally said, eyes shooting daggers, "as you're the one who told me he was dead, that seems awfully hard to do."

"I'm going to have to tell you some hard truths. I have lied to you in the past, against my judgment and due to extreme circumstances. I promise nothing but the truth from this point forward."

"Why should I believe you?" Tory asked. Again, she heard Black Eyes from a distance, yelling something at her. She couldn't figure out where she was yelling from, Black Eyes was always beside her.

The Shaman shook his head, "You have no reason to. I've lied in the past, I won't lie now. I have no reason to trick you."

Tory shook her head, "I'll let you speak, but I'm not going to believe you."

The Shaman gave a small nod. "Your mother was a Zoya. She was from another world, across a vast plain of emptiness. The same place Senka was from. Apollyon, Senka's old master, took your mother in and trained her. She made her way to this village and met your father. They had you," the Shaman was talking fast trying to get all the information out. Tory stared at him with her steady gaze. It was hard to focus on his words. Black Eyes was still yelling something. It sounded like she was miles away, Tory could hear her she just couldn't make out the words.

"A common occurrence with Zoya is that they often die without reason. Often as if someone blows out a candle somewhere and the Zoya's soul goes with it. This happened to your mother. Your mother and father were out hunting and she dropped dead. Your father... Your father lost his way. Instead of staying to raise you alone, he asked that I tell you that both your parents died at the same time in a hunting accident. It was easier for him than looking at you. You look remarkably like your mother."

"I was five years old. He needed to man up and raise me. Instead he left me alone."

"He felt that his sister would do a better job than he would in that state. I agreed with him."

Tory saw something flash in the old man's eyes. The same thing that always kept her hesitant when he asked others to follow him blindly.

"Liar," she said venomously. "If you want to lie, get out of my house."

The Shaman blinked a few times then recovered. He was quite adept, due to his position and his skills, at lying and getting away with it. It was second nature. He would have to tread softly to start his plan into motion. He tilted his head in her direction, face wrinkled, eyes downcast, "You're right. I'm sorry that was a lie. I did not agree with him. I thought you needed your father. He didn't agree, and as the Melanthios way is to give final say to the parents, there wasn't much I could do."

"There was a man on the battlefield by the King. He was the man who injured Jules. Did you see him?" asked the Shaman. The change in topic caught her off guard.

Tory shook her head, "Sorry, I was a bit preoccupied."

"He will bring down this nation. All of us will die."

The fervent way the Shaman spoke worried Tory more than the words.

"You need to find your father. He will have a lot of information for you. We have a very slim chance to save the world. This is a crucial part."

"Why can't I leave in the morning?" Tory asked. "Why can't I stay for her funeral?"

"You must leave tonight. Senka's soul is gone, you being around to watch her body burn does not change that."

"You're not going to tell me why, are you?"

"If I tell you why," the Shaman said gravely, "you will not go."

Tory sighed and rubbed her face, "Fine," she said, "I'll go. I don't want to say goodbye to anyone. Eli can't handle and Ujarak.... Well Ujarak will know. Which way do I head in the forest?"

"You're not going into the forest. You're going over the mountain."

Tory snorted and shook her head, then rose to start packing her traveling bag, "You know, for a man of infinite wisdom, you really know how to pile shit on."

"TORY!" Black Eyes yelled in her ear so close that Tory jumped. "TORY WAKE UP!" Black Eyes yelled again.

The world around her went black.

Tory sat straight up, gasping. She wrenched herself violently out of the dream. She had lived that part of her life once, she didn't need to live it again.

She was disoriented. She had no idea what was going on or where she was. Her vision swirled.

"Woah," she heard a voice, familiar, almost comforting, in her ear. "Slow your breathing down or you'll pass out again."

Tory listened. A surprise to both of them. She put her head between her knees and slowed her breathing.

"That's it," the voice said, her familiar sass a comfort. "That's it. Three counts in, one count out."

Once Tory settled her heart and could see straight she raised her head and looked around her. She was in a small shelter made of wood with a fire burning brightly in a rough stone fireplace in the corner. The smell of cooking meat filled the cabin. There was a small stool in front of the fireplace with a couple of pots hanging from the wall. She was on a small bed of blankets. Her bag was by a rickety door. Tory could hear the wind howling outside. The shack rattled in the wind but none entered the sturdy little wooden shelter.

The fire was burning brightly, so she figured she hadn't been alone for long. She noticed her clothes were hanging by the fire. She checked herself under the blankets.

"Yup, naked," Black Eyes said in her ear.

Tory couldn't bring herself to get up and do anything. She was so comfortable in the small bed. She lay back down and cozied up under the blankets. She hadn't been warm in a long time.

"What happened?" she asked Black Eyes.

"Well, you almost died," Black Eyes said. It sounded like she had settled on the floor beside Tory's bed. "You passed out. I told you to never stop moving, you know."

Tory nodded, "Yes, I know. Never been that tired though."

"Well it was fucking stupid," Black Eyes said sharply.

"Were you worried about me?"

Black Eyes stayed quiet.

"You were! Well I'm sorry I worried you."

"That seemed genuinely sincere," Black Eyes said. "What game are you playing?"

Tory sighed and cozied herself deeper into the blankets. She heard her stomach grumble with hunger but she didn't care. She was so comfortable. "No game," she said, "I must just be less miserable than usual as I'm in a comfortable bed. So after I passed out, what happened?"

"Well I saw what looked like a reflection of metal across the tundra so I went towards it as fast as I could."

"So you could leave me?" Tory asked quietly. It seems they hadn't figured out the rules of this phantasmal partnership at all.

"Think I could out of necessity," Black Eyes said.

"Something to test at some point," Tory said.

"Agreed. But can I finish my story?"

Tory nodded.

"Thanks. Anyways, I found a man hiking across the tundra towards you."

Tory smiled.

"I managed to yell at him and he followed my directions towards you. He found you and brought you here."

Tory's head was reeling. There were a lot of mysteries that she and Black Eyes would have to work out. But first, the most important thing.

"Thank you," Tory said.

"You sure you didn't hit your head?" Black Eyes asked incredulously.

Tory laughed, "No, I'm not. But I'm being sincere. Thank you for saving my life."

"Well," Black Eyes said hesitantly, "most of your life."

Tory looked at her confused.

"Left hand," Black Eyes said.

Tory hadn't noticed any pain or discomfort at all. When everything hurt, it was hard to distinguish what hurt most. But a burning was spreading throughout her hand that was worse than the aches and pains of the rest of her body.

She brought her hand above the covers. Her left hand was wrapped in cloth. She unwrapped it and sighed. She had lost her left pinky finger. It had been cut off right above the palm and cauterized. The rest of her fingers were bright red but she could move them.

"Shit," she breathed.

"Yea," Black Eyes said. "It was black. Your toes and the tips of your other fingers were cold but he said they were salvageable. That one, though, was frozen solid. He said he wanted to cut it while you were asleep so you didn't have to be awake for it thawing. He didn't have all his fingers so I thought he'd know best."

Tory sighed and wrapped her hand up again. It was done.

"How can he hear you?" Tory asked. "No one else but me and the Shaman have been able to hear you."

"Not sure," Black Eyes said. "I think maybe because I really needed him to."

Tory lay back in bed and sighed again. She had a lot to think about.

"Where is he?" she asked Black Eyes.

"I think he went out for food."

"Where is he getting food?"

"I'm not sure," Black Eyes said. "He brought you north to this shelter. I thought it was just ice and snow up here. I don't even know where he got the wood from."

"He hasn't been gone long though," Tory said, staring at the crackling fire.

"No, and he's back," Black Eyes said.

Tory nodded and the door of the shack burst open. A large, husky man stooped through the door. He was covered head to toe with a polar bear fur. He had seal mitts and a balaclava covering his face. Only his eyes were showing. Tory could see his breath coming out in icy puffs. The icy wind flowed through the shack and Tory huddled underneath the blankets. The man quickly closed the door.

The fire had been nearly extinguished by the gust of wind. The man took off his mitts and rushed forward, tending the fire back to life.

He ignored her presence entirely. He stripped off his outer layer of clothing and hung it by the fire to dry. He was dressed in layers and was left with a wool sweater and wool leggings. He kept his back towards her the entire time.

"Tea?" he grunted. Tory was immediately taken to the past. She hadn't heard her father's voice for a long time.

"Yes, please," Tory answered. She was suddenly nervous. She felt her palms get sweaty and tried to wipe them on her blankets. That hurt her hand so she stopped. She knew he didn't recognize her. At least she hoped he didn't. His complete and utter lack of… *anything* was gut wrenching. Either he didn't recognize his own daughter. *Or he doesn't care that you're here*, came the devastating thought.

Her father busied himself in front of the fireplace. Tory was suddenly embarrassed by her nakedness and kept herself hidden under her covers.

"I'm sorry I had to undress you," her father said, seemingly following her thoughts. "You would have died if you would have stayed in those wet clothes. I can assure you I used the utmost discretion."

He spoke softly but gruffly. Tory could tell he hadn't used his voice for a long time. But he also spoke eloquently, as he always had. Her father had always been an odd man out. He went to Carabesh shortly after she was born to study. Rarely did the Melanthios do this, their entire world was a simple one. But her father had wanted to expand his mind at a young age. When he had returned he spoke and thought differently than everyone else. Then her mom had died and everything had changed.

He turned towards her and handed her the cup of tea. She noticed that a chunk of his nose was missing, as well as the tips of three of his fingers. He kept his eyes averted as she took the cup. He turned around again and put his tea on the chair in front of the fire. He checked her clothes hanging in front of the fire.

"They are dry," he said. The shack rattled again in the wind. He folded them and placed them behind him, never looking back.

"I'm sorry but I can't leave the shelter," he said, staring into the fire. "There is quite a storm outside and I could get lost within fifteen feet of the door."

"That's ok," she stammered. She hurriedly grabbed the clothes and threw them on under the blankets. She instantly felt more comfortable. She was unnerved by her modesty. She had never been embarrassed about being naked. Her body was hers. If someone didn't like it, they didn't have to look. For her it was that simple. But this blast from the past, this hulking man, had thrown her completely off her game.

"Now then," he said, "I'm assuming that you are more comfortable. There is plenty of nourishment for us for the next few days. I have some holes in the ice flow outside but I won't be able to find and check them until this storm passes."

Tory didn't say anything. Black Eyes was mercifully silent.

"Now," her father said, "I am wondering what a young woman like yourself is doing this far north."

"I'm looking for someone," Tory replied hesitantly. He didn't know who she was. That simultaneously hurt her and was a relief. He didn't recognize her but he wasn't ignoring their bond.

He turned from the fire. "Drink your tea," he said to her. She had placed it beside the blankets while she was changing and it had been forgotten. She sat cross-legged at the end of the bed and drank deeply. The tea warmed her from the inside out. She hadn't realized how hungry she was.

Her father watched her drink the tea greedily. He rose and rummaged around beside the fire. He tossed her a bag of dried seal meat. She tore into it. She barely even managed a grunted "Thank you."

Her father smiled. "I'm sorry it took me so long to offer you food," he said. The beautiful greasy meat lined her mouth as she tore into it. "I'm not used to having visitors and my manners elude me sometimes. I have spent excessive time alone."

Tory began to slow. The meat was filling and she had gone a long time without being full to the top. She nodded and took a gulp of her tea. She felt younger, refreshed, and beautifully full and warm. The nervousness hadn't dissipated.

She wiped her face and stared at him. He was everything she remembered. Handsome, tall, wide shoulders. Soft face with dark brown eyes. A piece of his nose was missing and he was short on a few fingers but he was exactly the same. He hadn't changed in twenty years.

He stared at her, expectantly. Tory realized there wasn't even a hint of recognition. He had no idea. The last she had seen him she'd been five. Everything about her had changed. She realized he had never even been looking for her as an adult.

"So," he said, "now that you have been fed and watered, I have a few questions."

She must have blanched when she nodded because he said, hurriedly, "We have time to talk. Or not, it's up to you. We have at least a few days until this storm burns itself out."

Tory nodded again.

"I don't want to pry into your business but I have to say I am curious," he said. He flashed her a big smile, "How about I talk a little bit about myself first, get you more comfortable."

Tory nodded. "You're awfully quiet," Black Eyes whispered in her ear. Tory ignored her. She was engulfed in her father's face and eyes.

"Well," he said, "my name is Nirav."

Tory's stomach rumbled. It was him. She'd had no doubt but this confirmed it. Her "dead" father was standing in front of her talking to her.

"Maybe he is dead," Black Eyes whispered. "You hear me just fine."

I can't see you though, Tory thought. Black Eyes didn't have an answer. Tory focused on her father. She was engrossed.

"I am from a Melanthios village far to the south of here. I came here, in all honesty, because I was running away. From what, I will not discuss. I stay out here by myself for a few years at a time. Sometimes I venture south to the last northern village to visit with my friend Ira. We catch up, I learn of the things going on in Langundo." He paused to put on more tea.

"I have to admit," he said, fiddling with the kettle, "that you look a lot like women from my old village. Can I ask where you are from?"

"Ismat," Tory said. She was watching him for any recognition.

His body froze in front of the kettle for a moment then he went back to fiddling with the water.

"Well, what a small world," he said. "You are from my old village! What are the odds? Can I ask you your name?"

"Tory," she answered.

The change was immediate and violent. Her father turned and threw a tea cup across the room. It didn't break, but it clattered to the floor. He rose to his full height and yelled, "WHAT ARE YOU DOING HERE?"

The change and the violence caught her by surprise. She didn't rise to meet him. Her fear had her scurrying back across the bed.

"The Shaman…" She stammered.

"NO!" he yelled. He threw the stool across the room and it smashed against the wall. The shack rumbled in the wind. "I TOLD THE SHAMAN TO KEEP YOU AWAY!" he yelled.

"He sent me to find you," she said hurriedly. His anger was focused on inanimate objects. She hoped that's where it stayed.

"You're leaving," he said. His chest was heaving, his eyes were wild.

Shocked, "Why?" she asked. "You said it's instant death out there!"

"Then I'll leave," he said.

"No, I want to talk to you," she said. She reached for him, desperately. The same way she had reached for him all those years ago.

He shook his head violently and started throwing things into a pack.

"I came all this way to get away from you," he said roughly. "How dare he send you here?"

Tory didn't have anything to say. Tears started forming. "Fine," she yelled back at him. "Leave me again! I never asked to be your daughter."

"You don't understand," he said gruffly, "I'm out here to protect you." He was struggling to put on his layers overtop of his clothing.

"Protect me from what?" she asked desperately.

He stopped and looked at her, "Myself. You have to leave this place," his face was soft. He was pleading with her. "Please Tory. For me. Leave. I can't control it…"

He buried his head in his hands. "No," he pleaded, "not her.

Anyone but her." He sobbed and his massive shoulders wracked with grief.

"Something's happening," Black Eyes said. "He's changing."

"Clearly," Tory muttered. She wiped her tears. She wouldn't run from him, no matter how much he wanted her to.

His sobbing stopped instantly. His hands lowered in a jerking motion. He looked at her and Tory tried to step back but the wall stopped her. His eyes were white and milky. The beautiful dark brown was covered with a milky haze.

"I am desperately sorry about my outburst," he said, head jerking slightly. He got to his feet and picked up the cup from the ground. He wasn't moving fluidly anymore. It was deliberate, mechanical.

Tory was far more scared now than she had been when he had been angry.

"I will finish our tea," he said. He walked over to the kettle and busied himself.

"Not good," Black Eyes said.

Tory couldn't even nod. She just stood at the back of the bed, paralyzed.

Her father turned and walked her over a cup of tea. His head cocked awkwardly when he gave it to her and he smiled. The smile was too big and crooked.

"Drink this," he said, eyes white, "it will make you feel better."

Tory nodded and reached for the cup. "He fucking put something in it," Black Eyes said hurriedly. "Tory don't!"

"It's why I'm here," Tory said. She took the cup. It rattled in her hand a bit, like someone was trying to knock it out of her grip. She steeled herself and drained the contents, staring at her father over the rim the whole time.

The effect was instantaneous. The world swirled around her and blurred. The man in front of her, the one who used to be her father, smiled crookedly. She reached out for him. The cup dropped to the bed and she fell backwards. It all seemed to happen in slow motion.

She heard Black Eyes yell for her but she couldn't do anything about it. She fell backwards. Instead of landing in the bed, she fell into a black liquid. It swallowed her. She tried desperately to claw her way to the surface but she couldn't. Her lungs burned and she held her breath as long as she could. She clawed her way up to the light but something was pulling her down.

Finally, after ages, she couldn't resist anymore. Her lungs were going to explode. She breathed in, expecting the pain of water filling her lungs. Instead the world spun again and she was dropped onto a hard floor on one knee. Her hands slapped the ground hard. The spinning slowly stopped and she was standing right behind Eli.

He didn't see her, he was looking intently through a door in front of him. Tory rushed forward. She was so excited. She hadn't seen Eli in years.

"Eli!" she said and tried to grab his shoulder. She couldn't, her hand passed right through. Eli ignored her and kept staring. Tory couldn't see what he was looking at.

"ELI!" she yelled. The door burst inwards and Eli leapt backwards. He didn't have time to run. She could see the fear on his face. A hand grabbed him by the front of the throat and pulled him forwards. He flew off of his feet and inside the door. It slammed behind him.

"Eli," Tory said and fell to her knees. She fell through the floor again. The black water engulfed her. This time, instead of struggling, she relaxed and took a deep breath in.

She was thrown on to solid ground again. This time she was prepared for it and kept her feet. Her knees buckled with the force of the impact.

She was standing in the middle of a town of scared-looking people. There were Sun Gods with their weapons drawn. It was evening, but the wind coming from the west was warm. The people were looking through her to something behind her.

She turned and her heart fell when she saw Jules. He was on his knees. A Sun God was pushing him down so his chest was over a piece of wood. The Captain was standing beside him.

"This man is a traitor to the Sun Gods and your king," the Captain yelled. "He has been sentenced to death."

Tory rushed forward to help him. The Captain bent over Jules and whispered something to him. Jules' eyes went wide and he started struggling. "No!" he yelled desperately. The Captain raised her sword high.

"No!" Tory yelled, reaching for him. The sword started its downward arc. Suddenly, the Captain dropped her sword and sputtered. A feathered shaft stuck out of her neck. She grabbed at her throat. Chaos erupted in the people around her. She watched Jules stand up, confused. A large man who looked like a fisherman ran up to him.

The earth turned into black water again and swallowed Tory. She breathed. She landed with a little bit of a buckle in a prison made of sand. She saw Ujarak sitting in a prison, examining his finger nails. Her heart leapt and she reached for him. He looked up suddenly and stared at her. Eyes boring into her.

She stepped back quickly. No one else had been able to see her. No one else had known she was there. Their eyes locked. He smiled at her, the smile he saved just for her. He gave her a slight nod and returned to examining his nails.

The ground swallowed her again. She wanted desperately to stay with her love but she couldn't. She knew she couldn't. She landed with a thud in Ismat. She recognized it right away. It was dark out but a massive bonfire ahead of her lit up the Melanthios faces around her. She recognized the outlines of two people ahead of her staring at the fire. Her heart beat in her chest and she made her way carefully to them.

"It's only started," the Shaman said.

"I know," Senka replied.

Tory was shocked. She didn't know what to think. Senka was back? She wandered forward more and she saw Senka burning on the pyre. But she was standing right in front of her, talking to the Shaman.

"You will come back," the Shaman said.

"Haven't I earned rest?" Senka asked.

"While the evil lives, no one can rest."

The Shaman ended his cryptic note. He opened his mouth. His skin bubbled and boiled. Flames shot out of his mouth and eyes. The Shaman erupted into fire. The sparks flew so high that some landed on a thatched roof of a shack close to the bonfires. The house burst into flames. People screamed and the flames soon spread. Tory rushed to go grab water but she couldn't find any. She saw Ujarak run into a burning shack. The ground turned soft and she started to sink again.

"No!" she yelled. She pulled at the sinking black water. She watched the shack that Ujarak entered burn around him. The water was rising, pulling her in.

"No!" she yelled again. She started clawing at the hard ground around her. She needed to see what happened to Ujarak. She was desperate to see. There were screams all around her and people were running around. Then, after ages, she saw Ujarak burst through the door of the shack with Jules draped around his shoulders. She smiled and let go of the ground. She was pulled into the water without a sound.

She landed again. This time she was inside a dark hall. There were flickering lights above her head. She couldn't place them. They weren't fire and were too yellow for Pulse lights. The walls were thick, grey and smooth. She had never seen anything like them before. She heard the padding of feet behind her and she turned. Her stomach lurched. She saw Senka in clothes that she had never seen before. Beside her was a small wolf-like creature. But it was dressed in a vest. Senka was holding something in front of her, pointing it ahead. It was small and black. Her finger was on a sort of trigger on the bottom.

Tory watched them run by. Senka didn't see her. She turned the corner. Tory watched Senka aim the metal weapon and quickly pull the trigger three times. Three men down the hallway dropped dead. Tory had never seen such a weapon, her mouth gaped at how clean and easy the kills were. Senka aimed at the ceiling. A light down the hall from her exploded in sparks. Tory reached for her but she couldn't touch her. The floor melted away again.

This time Tory landed just in a black space.

"About time you showed up," the Shaman said to her. He was exactly as she remembered, hunched and grey, holding his staff.

"What the fuck is going on?" Tory asked sharply. Her voice was hoarse. She must have been yelling at some point. With all that she had just seen, she wasn't surprised. Her chest was heaving and she tried her best to steady her breathing. The stump on her hand was hurting and she had ripped out a fingernail clawing at the ground trying to get to Ujarak. She heard her blood hitting the ground in a slow drip. She had bled through her bandage.

"So much you don't know," he said. He stared at her and snapped his fingers. Senka's bow appeared on her back with her quiver of arrows. He smiled. He fiddled with his staff a bit and removed the large red crystal from the top.

"So why don't you tell me then," she snapped. She moved her shoulders. It felt good to have the bow back. "Is this real?" she asked more calmly.

"Past, present, future. All are real," he held the crystal out to her. "There is much for you to learn. We were never supposed to meet here. Cass's Remiel will show you the way," he nodded towards the ruby. Tory took it. It was the size of her fist. She put it in her pocket.

"You are about to face trials you can't possibly imagine," the Shaman said. "Don't make my mistake. Don't try to control. Just guide. I caused all of this because I tried to control. We have no more time. I died for this very moment, one that was never supposed to occur," the Shaman turned away.

"I don't understand!" Tory yelled.

"You aren't meant to," the Shaman said, almost desperately. "Fear not, dear child. Fear not."

Tory felt the floor go soft under her feet again. She wanted desperately to stay with the Shaman. She wanted answers. With a last look at his back, she was engulfed in the black water again.

Tory dropped again. This time she was in a chamber. It was decorated with gold and purple. A tribal symbol of a wasp was repeated throughout the room in patterns and painted on the wall. The earth moved slightly beneath her feet. There was a woman, gorgeous and blonde, sitting draped across a velvet chair. Her long body was covered in a sheer silver dress. She was adorned with rubies, from her head to her toes. She smiled at Tory when she dropped unceremoniously into her dinner chamber.

"My dear Roald," she called. Her voice was beautiful and silky. She stood up. She was easily six feet tall. Much taller than Tory. "Our visitor is here." Tory couldn't place the accent. It was as foreign as the woman in front of her.

Tory took a step back hesitantly. The woman was staring right at her. She had beautiful green eyes that stared at her, unblinking. Tory was afraid.

A man, Roald, stepped into the chamber. "Yes, dearest Malin?" he said to the woman. He was taller than the woman. Broad shouldered, with hair so blond it was white. He had short hair, almost shaved. He was dressed in furs. He walked up to the woman and kissed her hand. The woman, Malin, nodded as he did. He rose and she looked pointedly towards Tory.

"Ah!" Roald said smoothly. He opened his arms wide, "Welcome, dear stranger."

Tory took another step back. She wanted to ask so many questions. She was confused and terrified beyond anything before. The ground shifted under her feet again.

"You have no reason to be afraid," Roald said kindly. He smiled, but his brown eyes did not.

"You are an expected guest, Tory," Malin said. They were speaking to her softly, welcomingly.

"How do you know my name?" Tory asked. She glanced around. The chamber was large and she was trapped in the middle. There was a table and two chairs behind her with two large plush chairs in front of her. There was a lot of room to manoeuvre but there were only two doors in the chamber. Roald and Malin, as they called themselves, were between her and the doors.

"We've had our eyes on you for a long time," Malin said, sickly sweet.

"Since you were born, in fact," Roald added. "And please, sit and eat. I'm sorry, we forget ourselves as hosts sometimes."

"I'm good standing," Tory said curtly. "Back to the point, why have you been watching me since I was born?"

"Well that was not entirely true," Malin said. "Your father was gifted with the opportunity to prove himself to our cause. It seems he did not free you from your earthly bonds as he led us to believe twenty years ago."

Tory was confused, her head was reeling. "Wait, you wanted him to kill me twenty years ago?"

Malin opened her arms welcomingly. She looked hurt. "My dearest child. We offer salvation from the cruelty of this world. Your father was sent to free you from terrible decisions. That is our gift to you."

"Well I'm not in a receiving mood," Tory said. She was suddenly bone tired. She had just been hit with wave after wave of visions and information. "Why would you want to kill me in the first place? What am I to you? I've never heard of you, nor do we have a quarrel."

Roald sent Malin a warning glance, "It was not aimed at you, specifically, child. We merely wanted to test your father's allegiance."

"He's lying," Black Eyes' voice whispered, barely audible in her ear. Tory kept herself from jumping. She hadn't expected Black Eyes to be here.

Malin looked at her sadly, "If you're not with us, we will have to take that choice away from you."

"You can't take any choice away from me," Tory said. "You can kill me, but I make my own choices."

"Unfortunately, we can," Roald said lowly, eyes sad.

"It's for your own good," Malin said. "A small sacrifice of fear, then you won't have to make a decision again. We take away the burden."

Tory took another uneasy step back. She shrugged the bow off of her shoulder. Malin looked sad.

"It's for your own good, you know," Malin said, eyes downcast.

Roald snapped his fingers.

"Run!" Black Eyes yelled. But there was no time.

Sun Gods ran in to the chambers through the doors. There were at least six of them, all in full, glinting armour. Tory took the bow from her shoulder and fired an arrow into one's throat. He dropped. Others replaced him. She ducked a sword and stabbed one through the throat with an arrow then pulled back and fired it into another's eye.

An arrow whizzed over her shoulder. She couldn't believe that they were behind her already. She ducked and pivoted and fired all in one movement.

She saw it in slow motion again.

Black Eyes was standing behind her. Beautiful, tall, elegant Black Eyes. She had forgotten what she looked like. She had only been a voice in her head. Black Eyes coughed, Tory's arrow sticking out of her chest.

"No!" Tory yelled, sobbing. She ran forward and skidded towards Black Eyes on her knees. She cradled her head in her hands.

"Not again," Tory sobbed. "I'm sorry. I'm so sorry Black Eyes."

Tory noticed that even the whites of Black Eyes' eyes were black, instead of just the irises.

Something was wrong.

She heard Roald say behind her, "She's ready for you, my dear."

Black Eyes was staring at her, dead. Tory was trying to memorize her face again. Then Black Eyes winked. It was so subtle that Tory barely saw it, but it was there.

She turned fast but Malin was already directly behind her, staring at her in the eyes. Tory noticed that the Sun Gods, both dead and alive, were gone. It had just been a vision, a hallucination. The room was exactly as it had been.

"So noble," Malin said softly, gently. "Being most afraid of taking a friend's life." Her green eyes were calling to her. Tory couldn't look away. They were mesmerizing.

"If you join us, you never have to be afraid of that again," Malin said. She stroked her cheek. Her hands were warm, inviting.

Maybe that wouldn't be so bad, Tory thought, staring at the gentle green eyes, feeling the warm hand on her cheek. *Maybe not thinking about it would be good.*

She felt her body relax.

"That's it, child," Malin said, so softly, so sweetly that Tory didn't know why she had mistrusted her in the first place. "Just relax. Then you never have to be afraid again."

Tory nodded slowly, dumbly. It all made perfect sense, really. Just to be able to live with no regrets. She had no idea why she had wanted to escape. She felt a burning start in her right leg. It focused her a little, distracted her from Malin's eyes and sweet voice.

Malin's eyes focused a bit. "No, pay no attention to that," she said, a little harsher, "Focus on me. You are so close."

Tory tried to listen but the burning was growing in her thigh. She couldn't figure out why.

It's that stone, she thought, *the one the Shaman gave to you. The one he called the Remiel stone.*

The burning was getting unbearable. She fumbled around in her right pocket. She shook her head and took a step back from Malin.

She saw the gentle eyes turn to rage and Malin lifted her hand to slap her. Tory grabbed the stone, cool to the touch now, and lifted it in front of her face, trying to block the blow.

A force erupted from the ruby with a bright red light. Malin and

Roald were thrown back hard against the walls of the chamber. The table and chairs were thrown with such force that they shattered. It stopped as fast as it occurred. Malin and Roald slid down the walls. Tory figured they must have been knocked unconscious with the force.

"Holy shit!" Black Eyes said beside her.

Tory looked and saw her in all her Melanthios glory. She was standing tall, dressed as she had been the day she had died. She was spinning two daggers in her hands. Her eyes were still black as night.

Tory must have looked surprised because Black Eyes said, "You ok? You look like you've seen a ghost."

"I have," Tory said. "I can see you now. And I've killed you twice."

"Apparently it takes more than two arrows to the chest to get rid of me."

Tory saw Malin start to stir.

"Let's get out of here," Tory said.

"Right. Any ideas?"

"That's your job, dead one," Tory replied.

"Far as I can see we are hundreds of miles from your actual body," Black Eyes said. "No idea how we're going to get back to it."

Roald sprang up. He was bleeding a bit from the head. He yelled something and pulled a long sword from his hip. He held a hand outward towards the broken table and gestured it swiftly towards Tory. The table was thrown towards her with so much force that Tory barely dove out of the way. It crashed behind her and shattered into tiny pieces.

"Ok, so he can throw things with his mind," Tory yelled to Black Eyes over the crash.

"Fucking Zoya!" Black Eyes yelled back.

Roald charged Tory. Malin sprang up as well. She pulled a sword out of the rubble and followed Roald.

Tory barely managed to avoid Roald's swings. She didn't have a sword and was at a severe disadvantage with only a bow. She landed a kick to his chest and he stumbled backwards slightly.

Black Eyes threw herself between Malin and Tory, parrying her swing with her daggers. The ring of metal echoed on the walls. Tory saw Black Eyes smile hugely and she swung a dagger. It cut across Malin's cheek and blood started flowing from the perfect white face.

Tory was so wrapped up watching Black Eyes in disbelief that she didn't see Roald point his empty hand at her. She was flung back towards the wall. Pain erupted all over when she hit the wall and she crumpled into a heap on the floor.

Black Eyes saw and, with a final swing, disengaged herself from her fight with Malin. She rushed to Tory's side.

"I'm pretty sure if you die here we're both fucked," Black Eyes said quietly in her ear. Malin and Roald met in the center of the room. Roald wiped the blood gently from her cheek.

"They don't think we can get out of here," Tory grunted.

"The Remiel," Black Eyes said. "Just look into it and try it."

Tory shrugged. It was worth the shot. She didn't have any ideas. She was still holding the perfect ruby in her hand. She stared into it. She didn't see anything.

Malin and Roald noticed and started making their way towards her, side by side. Black Eyes stood and positioned herself between them and Tory.

"Hurry up," she said.

"It's not working," Tory said. All she saw was a ruby.

Black Eyes drifted forward, keeping low and light on the balls of her feet. Malin and Roald raised their swords. Black Eyes spun her daggers and steadied herself.

Panicked, Tory looked into the stone. She pictured herself in the tundra, in her father's shack. She saw the picture form. She saw herself in the ruby, face up on the floor of the shack. She focused hard.

She felt the Remiel heat up in her hand.

"Black Eyes!" she yelled.

Black Eyes disengaged and ran towards her. Malin on her heels. The Remiel flashed red again, knocking Malin back.

Tory was transported instantly to a vision of Malin sitting in front of a burning village house. She was holding a bundle in her arms. She was screaming and rocking back and forth. Roald was holding her by the shoulders, tears pouring down his face.

Tory broke herself from the vision and fell backwards into the black water that had formed around her, grabbing onto Black Eyes' arm. She heard Roald yell and they disappeared together into the black.

19 TORY

October 26, 210, 01:04
Location: North Langundo.

Tory came crashing back into her body. She was lying on her back, staring at the ceiling of the shack. She was sweating and gasping. Her father was wiping her face with a towel. He noticed that she was awake and pulled his hand back in surprise, but Tory was faster than he was. She wrenched his wrist around and sitting up swiftly put her other hand onto his straightened elbow, pushing down hard. The pain and surprise caused him to fall flat on his face with Tory putting a knee into his back and holding on to an arm-bar.

"What did you do?" she yelled fiercely.

"I'm sorry, I'm sorry, I'm sorry," he mumbled, sobbing into the floor.

"Look at me," she said sharply. He didn't react fast enough. "Now!" she commanded.

He turned his head sideways but he couldn't get his head all the way around.

"Black Eyes?" she asked sharply.

Black Eyes, whom she could still see, rushed to her side and looked at her father.

"He's clear," she said. "But probably not for long."

Tory nodded and released the pressure on his arm. Her father sobbed and Tory let him up. His eyes were back to their beautiful brown. They were pained, and Tory knew it wasn't because of the arm-bar.

"We don't have much time," she said. "I distracted them but they will be after you soon enough." She turned to start packing.

"Tory, wait," her father said. She ignored him. She started pulling her extra outside clothes off the hanger in front of the fireplace and was shoving them into her pack. "I said wait!" he said, loudly and with authority. Tory stopped what she was doing and stared at him. She had started crying softly.

"I need to tell you as much as I can before she comes back," he said.

She shook her head and wiped her eyes angrily. She hated crying. The weakness it showed.

"No, I'm saying it. Then I'm leaving. You're not."

"You said we'd die in the blizzard," she exclaimed.

"Yes, most likely. But I have more of a chance of surviving than you. Now shut up and listen."

Tory nodded swiftly. Her father started talking fast, years of guilt pouring out of him. "I left when you were a baby. I didn't go to Carabesh. I went west, over the sea."

She shook her head again, "No, don't lie. There's nothing over the sea. It's just us and Carabesh."

"You're wrong," he said. "There's a whole big world out there. Langundo and Carabesh are tiny compared to other countries across the sea. We don't know about them but they know about us. I went to a country called Anzen. There, I met a woman called Malin. She did things to my head. I think you know."

Tory nodded.

"She wanted me to kill you. Just you. It has to do with your mother and a woman called Cass. They didn't tell me and I didn't ask. I came back for you. They let me out of their sights for a time, to be sure. She got control again and told me to kill you. Your mother tried to stop me. I killed her in the forest. The grief allowed me to overpower Malin for a short time. I went to the nearest village and killed a young girl around your age."

They were both crying.

"I had to, or I would have killed you. I'm not as strong as you. I can't fight her. I killed the lovely little girl and I fled. She saw a young dead girl through my eyes and felt my guilt. She let me go and live freely. What she wanted was done."

Tory took a step back, "You're a monster," she said.

"I know. I did what I had to do. To protect you! I don't want your forgiveness," he said. "I don't deserve it."

He started blinking rapidly and his head jerked slightly to the side.

"Fight her!" Tory said, rushing towards him. "Dad I know you can do it. Fight her!"

He grabbed both her shoulders. "Go north," he said fervently. "I have food stashes set up under upright pieces of wood. There's another shack like this a week's walk. Keep going. Eventually the route will curve west then south. That is Anzen. You will have crossed an ice bridge to the other country."

He blinked and his eyes went white. He blinked again and they went back to brown. He was sweating. He was fighting to stay with her as long as he could.

"There is a monastery in the mountains there. They can answer your questions."

His head jerked again.

"No!" he yelled. "Get out!"

He let go of Tory's shoulders and started grabbing at his head. "I said get out!"

Black Eyes was suddenly standing by Tory. "You don't have a weapon," she said.

"I won't need one," Tory answered. She was crying again.

Her father was beating on his head. He was working his way towards the door.

"Fight her!" Tory said. "Fight her, then you can come with me!"

Her father looked up at her, eyes clear for one last time. "They feed on fear," he said. He mustered his strength and opened the door. The wind howled and the temperature inside the cabin dropped immediately. The fire was snuffed out.

"Don't fear," he said. And, without any outdoor clothing, he ran outside into the storm.

The cold air rushed inside the cabin. The storm blew snow

through the door. Tory stood still, shock and loss rocking her to her core. She watched the outline of her father disappear into the storm.

"Tory," Black Eyes yelled in her ear.

Tory ignored her. He'd killed her mother. He'd killed another girl. To save her. Tory didn't feel the cold air. She was too shocked to feel anything.

"Tory!" Black Eyes yelled again. Tory snapped out of it and realized she was freezing. She rushed forward and slammed the door closed. Her hands were already numb. She rushed back to the fireplace and hastily tried to relight the fire. She realized that her fingers were cut at the top and she was missing a fingernail. She managed to light the fire. The warmth was immediate. She held her hands close to warm them.

"So it was real," Black Eyes said, nodding towards her hands.

"I suppose so," Tory said softly. "I had all my fingernails. At least on the fingers I had left when I drank the tea." Black Eyes was still staring at her fingers, "And now I can see you. So that makes it worth it too. Though your eyes creep me out."

Black Eyes smiled sadly at her.

They sat in silence for a long time. Tory reached into her pocket and pulled out the Remiel.

"Any idea what this is?" she asked Black Eyes.

"None. I've never heard of Cass or this Remiel before in my life."

"Sounds like Cass is a person," Tory said. She looked into the stone and spun it around over and over. She didn't see anything inside. It just looked like a plain old ruby.

They sat in silence again. Legs folded, staring at the fire.

"Thanks for saving my ass back there," Tory said. The wind howled outside and Tory shuddered.

"Which time?"

Tory laughed, "Every time. All of it. Thank you."

"Well I'm stuck with you. And you're stuck with me. I think our fates are going to be intertwined for the time being."

Tory nodded, "I think you're right." Silence. But a comfortable one.

"Who do you want me to go to first?" Black Eyes asked.

Tory smiled. She should have expected that she would know the plan, "Ujarak. He doesn't have much time."

"And what should I tell him?"

Tory thought for a long time. Her father had said that Carabesh and Langundo weren't the only places on the earth. That was hard for her to fathom. All she knew about were those two countries. No one ever headed west. No one came from the west.

"Tell him to go east," Tory said finally, staring into the stone.

Black Eyes looked at her questioningly. "But the end of the world is east?"

"Maybe not," Tory answered quietly. "Maybe not."

"I don't know if I can get to your other friend," Black Eyes said. "It's crossing a plain. One that I don't know how to navigate."

Tory stared at the ruby. "Think of it like crossing an ocean," she said. "You can practice going to Carabesh. Cross the ocean to where Senka is."

Black Eyes nodded and stood up, "What should I tell her?"

They feed on fear, her father had said.

"Make her angry," Tory said. "Shouldn't be hard to do."

Black Eyes nodded and stepped away from the fire. She sank to her knees and started meditating, eyes closed, breathing deeply.

"Be safe," Tory said to her.

"Don't do something stupid like fall through the ice," Black Eyes muttered back, opening her eyes again to stare at Tory.

Tory laughed. Black Eyes winked and snapped her fingers, disappearing from the cabin.

20 HEAD OF HOUSING

October 29, 210, 17:55
Location: Solias, Langundo.

Helena, the Head of Housing, sat nervously in her chair at council. It was the day of the attack. Or it should be the day of the attack. After Mud had sent the raven to the rest of the Revolt they hadn't heard a response. There had also been no alarms ringing this afternoon, no word of an attack on the city. All was quiet, eerily so. She had a bad feeling about this.

It's nerves, she thought to herself, *you're expecting something to happen so the quiet is getting to you.*

She played with her long white braid waiting for the others to show up to council. She was alone in the council chamber. She'd been the Head of Housing in the city of Solias for thirty years. They had mostly been good years, especially when she worked with the Sol line and the late Queen. Queen Anita had always had the good of the people in mind over the good of the King, something that had been new and refreshing. Housing's eyes teared up just thinking about the demise of the Queen. She'd been a good woman.

Housing played with her hair, braiding it and re-braiding it. She was never usually the first one at council. And she didn't know where Justice and Goods were. She figured that they would be here early as well. They needed to keep the council meeting going as long as possible today to give the Revolt a fighting chance at getting as many people to safety as they possibly could.

She looked anxiously down at her meticulously written list of things to bring up at the council meeting today. She knew she'd make the King angry but that was the point.

The door burst open and Housing jumped in her chair. Her face reddened as Treasury walked in. She hated that man with every fibre of her being.

"Jumpy?" he asked gratingly.

"You surprised me," she replied tersely through a clenched jaw.

Treasury walked up to her and leaned over her shoulder. He was too close to her and she wanted to shy away from his foul smelling breath. He looked at her list sitting on the table.

"Not sure our dear King will want to go over that entire list tonight," he said lowly in her ear. He made her skin crawl. She was trying to keep her back straight and not lean away from him. She knew that he was trying to intimidate her.

"He needs to hear about this," she said weakly.

The door banged open and Goods walked in.

"Is there a problem here?" he asked loudly. Treasury slowly stood straight and put a hand on Housing's shoulder. It took everything in her power not to shrug off his hand. She was scared and felt violated but she kept her back straight. He didn't need to see any weakness.

"Not at all," Treasury said. Goods stared at him hard. "I was just going over the list of things to talk about at today's council, kindly provided by dear Housing here," he said.

"I think you've perused the list enough," Goods said sharply.

Treasury laughed and removed his hand from her shoulder. Housing suppressed a shudder as he walked away from her to the other side of the table and took his seat.

She avoided Goods' gaze. Treasury didn't need to know that they were a couple. Relationships between council members weren't exactly forbidden, but they were frowned upon. Goods sat in his chair completely avoiding eye contact. He took out his own notes and began to go over them. Housing kept watching him. They'd only found love and each other over the last year. She'd been alone before that, for sixty years she'd been content to throw herself into her work and serve the King and her city. But the King was insane, the city was floundering, and she was watching everything she'd worked so hard for go up in smoke. Goods had found her one day, and she'd found something to distract her from the city's demise. When the city started crumbling her life's work lost its meaning.

The door banged open and Housing jumped in her chair again, surprise tearing her from her thoughts. Intelligence came in, followed closely by Justice. Housing's heart sunk. Justice looked gaunt. He had bruising and swelling around one eye and he was looking around nervously.

Intelligence had caught Justice.

She was instantly afraid.

She searched Justice's face and he avoided her gaze, eyes shifting shamefully to the floor.

That gave her the answer.

Intelligence knew about the attack.

Meaning that the King knew about the attack.

Housing went to rise. She had to get in touch with the Revolt. Somehow, someway she had to call off the attack. The door burst open and the Mad King bounced in, smiling wickedly.

"Going somewhere?" he asked her happily.

"No, sir," she said hastily and sat down.

"I thought not," he said with a wicked grin.

He went and took his place on his throne, legs draped over the side. Housing waited tensely. The King's guards, who he customarily brought everywhere, didn't enter the chamber.

They sat in silence, the tension rising. The King sat draped across the chair, staring at each and every one of them. He had a manic smile on his face and he was daring anyone of them to speak.

Housing looked around. It seemed like Treasury and Intelligence were both starting to get as uncomfortable as she felt. That made her even more uneasy. If they didn't know what he was planning then she knew this wasn't good.

"Sir…" Intelligence said, breaking the silence.

The King held up a finger and Intelligence fell silent. They waited again in uncomfortable silence.

Housing looked around again. Justice had his head down and was averting his eyes. Goods looked as confused as she felt. The humor was lost out of Treasury's eyes and he was looking genuinely confused.

The door burst open and everyone jumped except the King. A large dark-skinned man walked through the door. He was bald, with gold and ruby earrings and jewellery. He was wearing dark purple robes lined with gold. He had patterns painted in gold across his head and face. He was joined by large soldiers. Their shining silver armour rang out as they ran into the room, surrounding the council at the table. They held crossbows out in front of them, a weapon rarely seen in Langundo.

Housing knew in one crushing instant that she wasn't getting out of this council room.

She had a sudden desperate feeling of regret. For her entire life. The city she had been devoted to was being destroyed. She'd never had a husband. She'd never had kids. She'd only focused on her work.

And now it all meant nothing.

"My dear council," King Sebastian said smoothly, "I'd like to introduce you to some friends that I've invited to our country. This is General Kapre of the Ampulex."

Kapre nodded and made his way around to the throne. He held out his hand and King Sebastian kissed his ring.

They were here. They had come early.

Housing was filled with desperation. She knew that she had to do something. Anything. She toyed with a dagger in her pocket. She'd never killed a man before. But she had brought it today just in case. Now she wasn't sure who was the bigger threat, the King or this General Kapre.

"Now," General Kapre said smoothly, "I am from an army called the Ampulex. We do not herald from any place but from all places. We go from country to country, inviting those living to join us in our quest for ultimate freedom."

"You do not offer freedom!" Treasury said loudly. Housing was shocked that he would say anything against his King. "You offer slavery. Don't think I haven't heard the whispers of your men. You ask for complete obedience. And if we don't kneel, you will make us."

The King's eyes flashed and he went to rise, but General Kapre held up his hand. "We do not deal in slavery," he said. "Everyone in the Ampulex army is given the choice to join us."

"We will never agree to follow you," Goods said strongly. Housing's heart leapt at the sound of his voice. "The people of Solias, of Langundo, are their own people. We do not need some foreigner to step in and rule us. We are doing just fine."

"Just fine?" Kapre asked. He started to chuckle. His men around him chuckled. "You call this fine?" Kapre said, gesturing around himself. The King's smile faded.

"Your people are starving. You have allowed this man," Kapre pointed aggressively towards the King, "to come in here and kill anyone and everyone he wants. You have allowed a mad man to rule your nation. And you're surprised that it didn't work out?"

The King rose angrily. An Ampulex guard rushed forward and pulled a sword out. He pointed it at King Sebastian's throat. The King raised his hands and slowly sat back down on his throne, face flush with embarrassment.

"Good dog," Kapre said with a venomous smile. "We will dispatch you of your King," he said to the council. "In return you must publicly announce your allegiance and bend a knee to our illustrious leaders, Lord Roald and Lady Malin. They will soon arrive to your mockery of a country."

"We will never bend a knee to someone who is not our King!" Goods said loudly.

Housing nodded weakly.

"Fine. No loss to us," General Kapre said with a shrug.

The Ampulex guards stepped forward and aimed their crossbows. Housing grasped for Justice's hand. She needed to feel someone, anyone. She desperately felt around for him. He found her hand and held it. His hand shook and she knew he was as scared as she was. They clasped hands tightly. She had flashes of her life. Her boring, lonely life. She had only worked for her country. For her city. She'd had no one. She knew Goods was only involved with her because she was the best of a bad situation. There was no love there. She had lived her life alone. Had lost herself in her work. Her now pointless work.

She would die as she lived. Completely and utterly alone.

"You tried," she muttered to herself. Tears started falling. Justice gripped her hand tighter. "You did your best."

She didn't believe herself. Her entire life had been a waste.

She let out a sob.

She heard a thunk.

She felt a tearing sensation through her back. She felt herself fall, but was dead before she hit the ground. Her dagger, brought to council so she could save her country, was left forgotten in her pocket.

21 ELI

October 29, 210, 19:07
Location: Solias, Langundo.

Eli watched the slaughter of the entire council slack-jawed.
He had come to kill the Mad King. That was his job and his alone.
The attack of the city had started. Eli didn't know how it was going.
He had left the Revolt early in the attack to find and kill the King.

Something was wrong, everyone felt it, but they were too busy trying to rescue the people of Solias to figure it out.

Eli had sneaked to the council chamber door. He had his daggers on him and a small bow. He had to kill the Mad King by any means necessary.

He had opened the door a crack, just in time to see a bald black man dressed in gold shrug his shoulders and five soldiers shoot their crossbows into the council members' backs.

"Now we're even," the man said to the King, completely ignoring the bodies of the council dead on the floor.

"Kapre, I didn't appreciate you ridiculing how I rule this nation," the King replied indignantly.

"Your rule is one to be ridiculed," Kapre fired back. "Your people hate you. They have nothing. There's no honor in what you have done here."

"I didn't invite you here to belittle me," the King snapped. "I invited you here to help me to establish *my* rule."

"And I've done what you asked of us," Kapre replied. He was pacing around the table towards the door, careful to avoid the blood pooling on the floor. Eli could see him coming in and out of his vision. He was dressed in gold and painted in a way Eli had never seen before. He had no idea where this man had come from. He wasn't from any Melanthios tribe that Eli knew.

Maybe Carabesh? Eli thought to himself. He didn't think so. Those from Carabesh didn't adorn themselves in gold and robes. They wore light clothing and their soldiers didn't wear full metal armour, preferring the lighter style of leather armour.

Eli was thoroughly confused as to where these people had come from.

West. The thought popped into his head.

Eli shook his head. There was nothing to the west, just water. He was sure of it.

What makes you so sure? he asked himself.

He didn't have an answer to his question.

"Where do we go from here?" the King asked Kapre. "I've kept my end of the bargain. You said you'd come here and help me if you were allowed to remove the council. Now it's your turn to help me gain control of these people."

Kapre was standing with his back towards Eli at the closest end of the table. He said something softly and Eli pushed his face closer to the gap in the doors to listen.

Suddenly, the doors burst open. Eli didn't have time to react, to turn, to run. He stood there dumbstruck as a hand grabbed him by the throat and pulled him violently into the room.

22 JULES

October 29, 210, 22:00
Location: Solias, Langundo.

Jules and Titus were exhausted and riding hard into the night. It was day five, the day of the attack, and they could see the glow of Solias in the distance.

It made him uneasy. The attack was well on its way if Solias was on fire.

Jules didn't think that he and Titus would be much use in battle. They hadn't slept much in the last five days. They only stopped to rest their horses when they could. He could tell his horse was fading beneath him. Jules knew this ride would probably kill his horse, but he couldn't stop. They couldn't rest. They had to make Solias to present Titus for when the King was killed. If they didn't make Solias in time it would be chaos.

"Come on," he said urgently to his horse. He could feel him struggling beneath him but he was trying to run as hard as he could. Jules heard Titus say something beside him and he knew he was encouraging his horse as well.

They had to make it, they just had to.

The broken wall of Solias crumbled in front of them. Jules reined in his horse and jumped off. His legs and hips were stiff and he struggled to be able to run or move fluidly. His teenage sidekick, however, seemed to jump off his horse and start running with ease.

By the time Jules caught up with Titus he was almost at the wall.

"Stay with the horses," Jules said when he caught up with him. "None of this works if you die."

"Then keep me alive," Titus said angrily, refusing to stop. "This is bigger than any of us."

Jules didn't have the energy to argue. They ran through the crumbling wall into the city. Jules hoped their horses found rest and water, they had earned it.

The city was on fire. Thick acrid smoke billowed through the air. People were coughing and sputtering, trying to find their way out of the city to fresh air. The people from here looked gaunt and poor. Jules could tell they hadn't eaten well in months. Bodies littered the ground. Blood stained the buildings. Men and women were screaming and crying, trying to drag their children and each other out of the smoke. It was complete and utter chaos.

"What happened?" Titus turned and asked him. His eyes were wide. The kid had never seen war. And he was much too young to see this. But Jules didn't know any other way. "I thought they were just here to sneak people out! They were never supposed to kill civilians!"

"We don't know if this was us," Jules yelled back. The black smoke coated his tongue as he yelled and it tasted horrible. "We need to find Vick!"

Titus nodded.

"Keep low and follow me!" Jules yelled. He stooped, lowering himself to where the air was clearer and they stumbled forward. The smoke made it hard to breathe. They managed to get past the house that was burning and causing most of the smoke. Once the air cleared Jules stood tall and looked around. He could see members of the Revolt yelling at the civilians, shouting directions to the crumbled part of the wall.

Jules ran up to one of them, Titus close behind. "Brother!" he said. He coughed slightly. The man turned and looked at him. "Where are Vick and Eli? I must speak with them."

"They went towards the center of the city and the castle," the man yelled back. He pointed. "That way. They are trying to evacuate as many people as possible."

Jules nodded, "Did we do this?" he asked, gesturing. A small girl of perhaps four or five was trying to drag her stunned mother out of the chaos, who was limping and disoriented.

The man ran over to help the child. He put his shoulder under the woman's armpit, "This was not us," he yelled, "the Sun Gods did this. There's someone else here as well! Whatever you do, don't engage!"

The man dragged the woman into the smoke with the young girl in tow.

"What did he mean there's someone else here?" Titus asked,

"Your guess is as good as mine," Jules said. "We're going to listen to him though. Don't engage with anyone if you can help it, we have no idea which of the Sun Gods are on our side or not."

Titus nodded. They ran the way the man had pointed, directly into the center of the city towards the castle.

Only a few of the houses were burned. Bodies littered the ground as they ran, both Sun Gods and Revolt alike. Jules ran to one of the bodies of a Sun God and pulled out an arrow embedded in the dead woman's chest.

"What are you doing?" Titus asked, shocked.

Jules looked at the arrow closely and held it out to Titus for inspection.

"You recognize this?" he asked.

Titus looked at it and shook his head. "Not one of ours," he said, referring to the Sun Gods. "Must be a Melanthios arrow."

Jules shook his head, "No," he said, "they use hawk feathers. This isn't a feather," he said, running his finger over the base of the arrow. It was paper thin and white, but Jules hadn't felt this type of texture before. "It's unlike any arrow I've ever seen."

Jules put the arrow back down. Jules drew his sword and, eyes wide but face determined, Titus followed suit.

"Just in case," he said. Titus nodded his agreement.

They made their way carefully down the street. The smoke was still there but thinner. Two soldiers materialized in the distance. They were standing perfectly still. They were dressed in bright silver armour and held crossbows in front of them. Jules had never seen anyone dressed like that before in his life. They were flanking the street. They must have seen them coming but they didn't move a muscle.

Jules noticed Titus shift his grip on his sword.

"No," he whispered. "He said don't engage."

He looked around them. There was no way to get to another street or up on the roofs to sneak by. And Jules was sure that these soldiers would have already seen them.

Jules shrugged and just walked up to them. He expected a shot to the heart at any point. He just kept his head high and walked towards them. The soldiers didn't move. Jules and Titus just walked past the soldiers and continued on their way down the street. Jules let out a breath that he didn't know he'd been holding.

"Ok, I'm weirded out now," Titus said shakily.

"Me too buddy," Jules said. "Let's find Vick or Eli."

Titus nodded. They sheathed their swords and ran forward a bit, exhaustion replaced by fear. They jogged through the city towards the moat and castle. There were other odd soldiers but they all acted the same. They just stood there and let them pass, unflinching.

They made it to the inner wall. Jules saw Vick, standing on a fallen bridge, barking orders. They ran up to him. Vick noticed them coming and his smile was huge. He took Jules into a big bear hug, squeezing the life out of him.

"I hoped you'd make it," he said. Vick turned to Titus and bowed. Titus just nodded curtly, still uncomfortable with the reverence.

"My King," Vick said.

"I am yet a Prince," Titus said. "My brother is the rightful King."

"Unfortunately there's been no word of your brother or the man we sent to find him. It has been quite some time since we've heard from Ujarak. We are assuming they are both dead. You will be my King in three years on your nameday."

Titus nodded but Jules could see a tear in his eye. He felt the loss as well. He'd loved Ujarak as a brother, hearing of his suspected demise was hard to swallow.

"Until my nameday I am still a Prince," Titus said. "And you will address me as such."

Vick smiled, "Yes, my Prince," he said. "You've done well, Jules."

"What's happening?" Jules asked. "Why the rush?"

"Well we were trying to get here before this other army arrived but it seems we were too late." Vick shrugged. "Notice anything unusual about them?"

"Besides the fact that they have had plenty of opportunity to kill us and they just stand like a statue?" Jules asked.

Vick smiled, "They seem to only engage when attacked directly. By the time we realized this we lost good men. Most of the Sun Gods have defected and fled the city. The other Sun Gods set about killing civilians until the Revolt and this unknown army stepped in. I have no idea if they are an ally. They killed plenty on both sides, they seemed to just be protecting civilians. I'm just overseeing the last of the exodus."

"Eli?" Jules asked.

Vick shook his head, "I have not heard. He went to kill the Mad King alone. He has not returned."

Jules' stomach did a back flip. Poor Eli. He was the youngest of all of them, with laughing eyes and his stupid face tattoo.

"I'm going to find out for sure," Jules said.

Vick nodded his agreement. "The Revolt pulls out in ten minutes. I can't leave anyone behind to make sure you get out. You'll be on your own. We've lost enough soldiers today."

Jules nodded. "He deserves it."

Vick hugged him again, "Good luck. I hope this mysterious army continues to be passive against us."

Jules disengaged from the hug and ran across the bridge. He noticed Titus follow him.

"No!" Jules said. "This is a suicide mission. I cannot allow you to come."

Titus rose up and his eyes flashed. Jules cowered a bit. The boy looked like a King. "I will go where I am needed," he said. "And tough shit, Jules, you need me. Now let's get your friend out of there and get us out of here. My lungs hurt." He shrank back down again and once again he looked like a teenager, like Titus.

Jules didn't argue. They ran across the bridge over the moat into the castle.

"Where do you think they will be?" Jules asked. They didn't meet any of the unnerving guards.

"I'm getting the feeling we need to go to the gallows," Titus said, "and main fountain. I'm not sure why."

"I will follow you," Jules said.

Titus took the lead. The castle was quiet, eerily so. No guards, no bodies. Nothing. No one.

They ran through open halls and roads to the center of the castle where it opened to the main gardens and fountain. Directly ahead was the main chambers where the council was held and where the personal chambers of the King and Queen were kept. A single gallows was set up right underneath the balcony of the council chamber. The noose was empty but fluttering ominously in the wind.

"Nice of you to join us!" a voice boomed loudly across the open terrace. Titus and Jules skidded to a stop. The voice was louder than anything they had ever heard or was humanly possible. It reverberated off the surrounding walls. Titus covered his ears with his hands.

"We've been waiting for you!" the voice boomed.

Jules pointed. There were three men on the outer balcony across the open field. Dark-skinned, skinny Eli was up there. Jules could recognize his posture anywhere. There was a large man beside him in robes of gold and purple. In the center was the Mad King. He wasn't hard to spot, with his black clothes and crown sitting stupidly on his head.

"Zoya," Jule mouthed. Titus nodded his agreement.

"You have a choice," the voice echoed around them. "You can join the majestic Ampulex. You can bow to me and to Lord Roald and Lady Malin. Or you can flee at your own risk. Your friend here has already made his choice."

Eli nodded and stood beside the large man, unflinching.

"Your King refused to kneel!" the man yelled. "He had made a deal and refuses to honor his part. Lady Malin does not allow this kind of insubordination."

The King lurched forward. His movements were jerky, unnatural. Like he was a puppet on strings. He put a noose around his own neck.

"She hates to do this, but a slight to my lady's honor is of the upmost treason!" the voice echoed so loudly it hurt Jules' ears. He covered them with his hands. He watched in horror as the King lurched his way to the edge of the balcony.

"Eli!" Jules yelled. His voice didn't carry. He watched as the King threw himself over the railing. He tumbled over the balcony. He was stopped right before the ground by the noose attached to the balcony snapping his neck. The crown fell from his head and landed with a thud on the ground beneath him.

Eli stayed beside the man with the booming voice, eyes staring straight forward, unmoving. Seemingly unaffected as the King killed himself.

Titus went to rush forward.

"No!" Jules said, grabbing his arm. "No! He's gone. Leave the crown. Titus we need to get out of here!"

Titus didn't struggle. He allowed Jules to pull him away from the grisly scene. They turned and fled, leaving Eli to his fate behind them.

The dead King swayed on the rope as a gust of wind blew by. Jules heard the creak of the rope as they fled.

23 UJARAK

October 30, 210, 13:45
Location: Artesia, Carabesh

Ujarak sat in the prison made of sandstone, picking his fingernails with a small piece of wood he had found.

He was inside a cage made of steel bars. They kept him in comfort, with a blanket and a place to relieve himself. They fed him three times a day and even allowed him to go outside and see the sun twice a day (under close supervision, of course).

Prison in Carabesh was a luxury compared to current Langundo living conditions.

He knew by the reaction of the President that his sacrifice had done its job. Prince Sol was now owed a life debt by the President of Carabesh. Ujarak just hoped that the kid didn't blow this golden opportunity.

He tried to keep his mind off the last time he saw her. When she was leaving him to go north, following the guidance of the Shaman. Ujarak had intercepted her on her attempt to flee the village without being seen. He saw the scene like it was happening in front of him, all over again. It was the day his life changed forever.

*   *   *

He hiked hard up the mountain, puffing. He was exhausted from the battle. Emotionally and physically. Watching Senka die was harder than any of his physical exhaustion. Watching how it broke Tory was worse. He would never forget her once bright eyes, sunken and ghostly as they stared at her dead friend on the battlefield.

Ujarak knew that the Shaman was sending her over the mountain alone. He'd heard their conversation in her house. He wanted to see her one last time.

He crashed straight upwards through the underbrush, completely avoiding the path. He needed to make his own path to cut her off.

He came upon the path. His chest was heaving and he stumbled slightly. He was more tired than he thought. He sat beside the path, slowing his breathing and his pounding heartbeat, settling himself.

He heard her coming, whispering away to someone. Ujarak's face fell. He was sure Tory had gone insane in the battle. She was talking to thin air.

She emerged from the darkness. The sun had set, the only light coming from the moon and the flickering of funeral pyres burning in their town below.

She stopped and stared at him. He stood and rushed to her, gathering her in his arms.

She sobbed something incomprehensible into his shoulder. He held her. He was taking note of the feeling of her body. He had held it so many times before but this time would be the last. He needed to remember everything about her. He breathed deeply, the floral smell of her hair assaulting his senses.

He held her until she pulled away.

"I have to go," Tory said, looking up at his face.

"I know," he said gruffly.

"I'm sorry," she said.

"Don't be. I know you need to do this."

"Be safe," Tory said. "Take care of them."

"Always. Take care of yourself, love. I will wait for you in this life."

"And the next," she whispered and pulled him into a kiss. Their words, their motto, muttered to each other in the darkest and lightest of times.

Ujarak lost himself in her kiss. Then, gently, always gently, he pushed her away. She was looking for an excuse to stay. He couldn't give it to her.

"Don't look back," he said gruffly, softly brushing her hair out of her face. "You don't do well when you look back."

Tory gave him a stiff nod. She squared her shoulders and continued up the path. North, over the mountain, into the unknown.

Ujarak watched her go. He made sure she turned the corner without looking back at him. He wasn't sure if he could let her go a second time. He waited for ages then turned away.

There, he saw his town, Ismat, glowing at the base of the mountain. Ismat was on fire! He ran down the mountain, crashing through the brush.

He'd made a promise to Tory to take care of their family. One he wouldn't break.

* * *

Ujarak pulled himself out of the memory. He didn't need to relive his mad dash to Ismat and pulling Jules from the burning building. The scars on his forearms from the burns were reminder enough.

He sat picking his fingernails when he felt her presence. He smelled the floral scent of her hair first. He was startled but he didn't want to look up, to ruin it in case it was his imagination. He couldn't fight the urge for long and he looked for her. Tory was standing just outside the bars of his prison, staring at him. His heart melted. He hoped this meant she was still alive, not dead and cursed to walk the world as a ghost. He flashed her a smile, one he saved for her. She took a step back. She obviously hadn't expected him to be able to see her. They locked eyes. *I hope you're alive, love*, he thought to her, *I hope you're happy and you've found what you are looking for.*

He broke eye contact and smiled, examining his fingernails. He decided to take the weird occurrence as a good sign. When he looked back up, Tory was gone, but another woman, a Melanthios, was staring at him intently,

Ujarak knew she was a ghost. He didn't know how he knew, he just did. She was tall and skinny and really quite beautiful. Her eyes were black. There were no whites, just wall to wall black.

"Can I help you?" he asked her.

"Tory sent me," she answered.

"I figured. I just saw her, you know."

"Time is a funny thing in this abyss," the woman said. "She saw you in a vision almost two days ago."

"So she's alive?"

The woman nodded, "My name is Black Eyes."

"Fitting."

The woman smiled, "I can see why she fell for you. You're very direct."

Ujarak shrugged.

The woman stepped forward and reached for the keys to his cell hanging on a hook. They were kept close to the cell, but far enough away that Ujarak would never be able to reach them. The woman's hand passed right through the keys but they jingled on their hook. She sighed, made a fist, and swung up hard. Her hand passed through the keys again but they jiggled enough that they were thrown off the hook. They landed just within Ujarak's reach.

"Go east," Black Eyes said.

"Over the end of the world?" Ujarak asked. He wasn't questioning Tory, he would do whatever she asked even if it meant certain death. He just didn't want to get it wrong.

"Yes, over the end of the world. Then keep going east."

"What am I looking for?"

Black Eyes smiled at him, "You'll know it when you find it." She winked at him, snapped her fingers and disappeared from the prison.

Ujarak shook his head. Go east, over the end of the world, then keep going east. And he will know what he was looking for when he found it.

His love was a complicated woman.

PART 3

"Now I am become Death, the destroyer of worlds." – Bhagavad Gita, spoken by J. Robert Oppenheimer after he was instrumental in creating the first atomic bomb.

24 SENKA

October 30, 2023, 06:29
Location: Toronto, Canada.

She walked through the morning fog, head down, carefully picking her way through the graves.

It was rude to step on the dead.

The stark yellow daisies unceremoniously held in her left hand contrasted heavily with the foggy morning.

Leo padded softly behind her through the graves, following her lead. He wouldn't step on the dead either.

The fog started to clear with the rise of the sun and she saw Carter's hulking frame kneeling in the distance. She would go to him later. He had different demons than she had. She shook her head. They had died so close together. It wasn't fair to Carter. Melanie first, then weeks later Tomo.

She stopped in front of the tombstone.

The old wilted daisies from the week before slouched towards the ground, dew dripping onto her friend's grave. Senka removed them and put the new ones in their spot. She needed Tomo's grave to have daisies. Tomo was always bright and sunny, just like daisies.

She looked at the headstone and had an immediate flashback to the day Tomo had died.

"Carter, call off the airstrike!" she yelled. She was on a stolen dirt bike, chasing the truck Tomo was in through the jungle. She was far behind. Branches tore at her face and arms. She needed to catch up. The truck disappeared in front of her over a ridge.

She vaguely heard Carter's reply through her earpiece, "I can't! There's a communication breakdown. Sen, get out of there!"

She launched the dirt bike over the ridge to see the truck hurled into the air in an explosion of flames and a cacophony of sound. She heard concussion of the CF-18 fighter jet flying overhead as she screamed.

Leo gently licked her hand and the flashback changed. She tried to stop it but she couldn't. She didn't want to remember. But she couldn't stop the spiral into her own subconscious.

*   *   *

Lizzie was crying alone in her recovery room. Her body was tiny and fragile. The four years she had spent in a coma had eaten her muscle away, leaving a skeleton wrapped in pale skin. She'd only been awake a week and she hated her life.

She knew it was worse because she had been so fit, so strong, in her dreams. She had told everyone about what she had seen in her dreams, but no one believed her. It had felt so real. But everyone said there was no way it could have happened. She had remained in a coma after the accident. Her name was Elizabeth Brighton, not Senka. She found herself ignoring people when they called her. She didn't know who she was anymore.

She heard a soft knock on her door and she quickly tried to wipe the tears away. Her nurse, Amanda, walked through the door and closed it softly behind her. She crossed the room and sat at the foot of Lizzie's hospital bed.

"Lizzie," Amanda said, "why are you so upset?"

"I'm weak," she replied. "I used to be strong but I'm so weak."

"That's not it."

Amanda waited patiently as she watched Lizzie struggle.

"No one believes me!" Lizzie finally exploded. "I don't even know if I believe me. I saw and did and went through incredible things! And no one believes me. I was tortured in prison! I went to war! I killed a false King! Then I wake up here and everyone is calling me a name I don't recognize. My body is weak! I used to train it daily. Now I can't even stand without help!" she was yelling, she couldn't help it. Amanda waited patiently. "Oh and by the way my tongue was cut out a year ago! A whole year! Why can I speak?"

Amanda shrugged, "I believe you," she said casually, examining a long red fingernail.

Lizzie gaped at her.

"You're not the only one. Zoya have been around for thousands of years."

Lizzie was too surprised to speak. Amanda held out a card. Lizzie took it and looked at it. It was cream, with a bright green symbol embossed on it. A world surrounded by a shield, with a sword and Z on the hilt.

Lizzie took it and looked at it stunned. She didn't know what to think.

"If you want in, the plane leaves Friday morning from the Winnipeg airport. Go to the Firstline Canadian Air counter at eight in the morning and show this card to Sandra. She will tell you what to do."

Amanda stood up and headed for the door, "Senka, you need to be discrete. Tell your family it's a special camp for physio. I'll corroborate. They won't ask any questions."

Senka balked at someone calling her by her real name. She was flipping the card over in her hand. The shiny green symbol kept drawing her in.

"What am I in for?" she asked and looked up. Amanda was nowhere to be seen. If she didn't have the card she would have sworn she was in another dream. But she did have the card. It was thick and tangible.

She didn't need to know what she was in for, she just knew that she was in.

The next few days flew by in a blur. She was nervous. The lie was a non-event with her family. Her mother and older brother believed her without question. Senka felt bad, but she kept reminding herself that she needed this. Amanda believed her. That's all that mattered.

With Amanda reminding her of her real name all traces of Lizzie disappeared for good. She was Senka. She would make herself strong again.

She made her way to the airport by herself. Her mother and brother wanted to come but Senka had said that she needed to do it alone. She was twenty, she needed to act like it.

She made her way slowly to the main terminal at the airport. She was out of breath by the time she made it to the Firstline Canadian Air counter. Her half empty backpack felt heavy. She shook a bit when she walked and limped heavily on her right leg. She felt like a mess.

She looked at her watch. It was seven thirty, she was early. There was no line and a lonely man guarded a computer behind the counter. Senka doubted this was Sandra. She looked around nervously and found a bench with a clear view of the ticket counter. She dropped her backpack, the only baggage she had, at her feet. She didn't know what to pack so she had packed a little of everything.

She sat and watched the line for a while and noticed a few other Firstline Canadian Air employees had filtered out to man the computers. When it was ten to eight, she rose and limped to the growing line. There must be a plane leaving soon.

She waited nervously, alternating between touching the embossed card in her pocket and grabbing for the ring on the chain around her neck. James had told her that a nurse must have put it in her hand when she was sick. She hoped he was wrong.

That's why she was in. She needed him to be wrong. She needed the ring around her neck, the golden lion with the ruby eye, to belong to Jules.

Senka limped her way to the front and a new Firstline Canadian Air employee appeared from the back.

"Next in line, please!" she called, booting up a computer at the end of the row.

Senka shuffled slowly towards the woman, glancing around nervously. Her palms were sweating and she wiped them on her jeans. Her clothes hung on her skeletal figure and she grew instantly self-conscious. She was very much aware of the pain in her body. It was everywhere and she was so tired.

She made her way to the desk, puffing hard. The woman's name tag screamed SANDRA at her in bold letters. She should bail, she should run. She didn't know what this was. She could just go home, do physio, and convince herself that it was all a dream.

But it wasn't.

Jules was real.

Tory was real.

Appollyon was real.

And she needed to prove it to herself.

She shakily took the card out of her pocket and slid it towards the woman. She smiled and reached down under the desk. She retrieved a Canadian passport and a boarding pass and slid them, along with the card, across the desk towards Senka.

"Flight boards at nine-fifteen through gate C," she said brightly with a smile. In a low voice, lips barely moving, she added, "Amanda instructed you to show me that card, not to give it to me. Do exactly as we say. This is your first lesson. Give the card to your flight attendant when the pilot announces the descent."

Senka strained to hear her. She tried to smile and nod and collected the passport, boarding pass and card and put them into the front pocket of her loose sweater. She shuffled away, looking for the sign to gate C. When she reached security she presented her passport and boarding pass on request. She was so nervous.

"Going to Quebec City, I see," the man in the blue uniform commented.

"Yes, sir," she said. Her voice hitched a little and her face reddened in embarrassment.

"Scared of flying?" he asked kindly.

She nodded, "First time." She was internally berating herself for not looking at the passport or boarding pass before security. She had been too distracted with how surreal this whole situation was. She was going to get caught and arrested. That wasn't being discrete. And she highly doubted that Amanda would get her out of that. She would rot in jail and never figure out what the symbol meant or if anything was real. Her mind was racing a mile a minute and she felt her chest constricting.

The Canadian Border and Security Agency agent smiled as he gave her back her passport and boarding pass, "Flying is the safest way to travel. Have a good trip east, Ms. Bennet."

Senka forced a smile and grabbed her documentation. She picked her bag out of the x-ray and limped her way towards Gate C. She was shaking violently and it took all her effort not to show anyone from security. She finally reached her gate, the brightly coloured television showing, "Quebec City, ON TIME," behind the gate.

She sat heavily, relishing the lack of pressure on her knees and muscles. She would never take walking for granted again.

She opened her passport and saw a recent picture of herself, looking stone faced, staring back at her. She didn't know when this picture had been taken. The name on the passport said, "Senka Bennet. DOB: April 30, 1999."

She smiled to herself. Same first name, same birthday. The only thing she had to remember was the last name Bennet. From her favourite book Pride and Prejudice. Amanda set it up so she couldn't fail.

She relaxed and her hand went directly to her ring around her neck. She missed her family. Jules, Tory, Ujarak, Eli. She missed them all. She hoped they survived the war.

She hadn't realized she had fallen asleep until she heard the boarding call for her flight. She hurriedly limped towards the gate, was through without hassle, and onto the plane quickly. Amanda had given her a window seat and no one ended up sitting beside her. She shoved her bag under her seat, did up her seatbelt and was asleep before the safety briefing began.

She slept the entire flight. Her body was always so fatigued.

She awoke confused and drowsy to the Captain's voice over the intercom, "Hello passengers. We've had a smooth flight and due to a tailwind have arrived ahead of schedule. Please put your trays up and your seats in the upright position. Flight attendants prepare for landing."

Senka sat upright and frantically dug through her pockets. The card was still there and she relaxed.

A flight attendant was coming around taking garbage and smiling. Senka hesitantly handed the cream embossed card to the flight attendant. She smiled and threw it in the garbage. Senka's heart fell. The flight attendant leaned over and said quietly, "I'd like to direct you to the magazine in front of you. The article on page thirty-seven is quite interesting."

Senka nodded, unable to find words to say. She had lived a long time alone without a voice. She often couldn't find the words to say in idle conversation. The flight attendant smiled at her and continued to move throughout the cabin. Senka excitedly flipped through the magazine until she found the proper page. A note was taped inside, reading, "Left through the main doors at the taxi stand. Go to Parkade D."

Senka folded the note and placed it in her pocket. With the card gone, it was the only tangible evidence that she had that all of this was real. *Well*, she thought, *real to me*.

The plane landed without incident. She flashed the flight attendant a smile as she left the plane. The flight attendant smiled back. Senka limped her way through the Quebec City terminal. She didn't understand French, but it was all very exciting. She was noticeably winded by the time she hit the main exit. Her attitude suddenly faltered. She had been wrapped up in the adventure and mystery of this trip. It was all very exciting, almost like a movie. She missed excitement. Physio wasn't exciting. Her dreams had been. She stopped outside the main entrance.

To her right were the taxis and the door to go back in the terminal. She had a credit card in her pocket linked to her brother's account. He had given it to her shortly after she woke up. She should go right back into the terminal, buy a ticket to Winnipeg and go home. Her brother would understand. She would finish physio and just live the life set out for her before the crash. But…

But.

The "but" was what drove her. She had a deep-seeded feeling that she was meant for more. She set her shoulders and drew her feeble form up. She turned left and limped her way away from the taxis.

She didn't look back.

It was a long way for her to walk. She followed the signs to Parkade D. It was a long ways away. The farthest parkade. She was hurting and sweating by the time she got there. Her hands shook violently as she tried to take off her backpack and place it at her feet. She didn't look around. She gasped, hands on her knees.

Once she recovered she tried to straighten herself up. She was listing dangerously to the left. Her chest was heaving. But her master had taught her to always face the future standing straight, and dammit she was going to try.

The parking lot was empty. Not a person or a car in sight. Her shoulders fell and her thoughts started racing faster than she could control them. She figured this was someone's cruel prank. She didn't know who. A tear fell from her eye and she wiped it away angrily. Who would promise a sick person the world then take it all away?

Suddenly a black SUV with black tinted windows skidded into the parking lot and sped towards her. Her arms instinctively rose and she sank into a defensive stance. Her muscles burned but she ignored them. She was laser focused.

The SUV screeched to a halt and four huge men in black suits jumped out. They had clear headphones in their left ears. She heard one say, "Contain the asset." The men, hearing their cue, bull-rushed her. All four came at her at the same time. Senka struck out at the leader and caught him in the face. She realized at the same time as he that she was fast. She was just as fast as in her dreams. Faster than anyone they'd ever seen.

Unfortunately for her this body tired quickly. She landed a few punches and a well-placed groin kick but they were too much for her. One managed to pull her arms behind her back and zip tie them together as another put a bag over her head. They quickly picked her up and tossed her into the back of the SUV. She knew not to struggle right now. She barely had any energy left. She had to save it. The SUV sped away. It was silent inside.

She calmed her breathing and started to devise a plan. Instinct was taking over. She needed to get out of here. Her flight or fight instincts were in full gear. She was so skinny she managed to slowly work her hands out of the zip ties. Happy with her success, she slowly pushed the bag off her head to look around. She was in the back of an SUV with carpet around her. She couldn't see out the windows or anything but the floor around her. She needed to bide her time.

The SUV pulled off the main highway. She could tell from the increase in the bumps and lurches in the back. It eventually came to a stop.

She forgot about being weak.

She forgot about feeling worthless.

She forgot about feeling like a liar.

She was strong. She was fast. She was Senka.

Her muscles tensed in anticipation and she crouched into a small ball. For the first time since she had awoken from the coma she smiled from ear to ear. The back of the SUV opened and Senka exploded outward, catching the man in the black suit by surprise right around the middle. They fell to the ground, Senka on top. She punched him in the face with all her might. She smiled when she felt his nose break.

She reared up to punch him again when she heard a familiar voice yell, "Senka! Stop!"

She stopped and looked up, frail lungs gasping for air. Amanda, dressed in a tailored suit and heels, was standing in front of her. She was smiling. The man Senka had tackled scrambled out from under her. He was holding his bleeding nose. Senka felt a stab of guilt.

"Glad you made it," Amanda said, "Sorry about all the theatrics. We just had to be sure you were ready."

Senka looked around. They were at a training ground. She could hear a shot fired in the distance and realized it was a firing range. A man ran by her in a sweater.

"This is the Zoya Task Force training headquarters," Amanda said. She gestured and walked away. Senka followed, mouth gaping. "You will be here until you are physically and mentally ready for combat. We work very closely with the Canadian Army and the United Nations, but you will report directly to the Queen."

Senka felt a bone crushing fatigue creep over her. Her head was reeling. She wasn't the only one. This was well established. It was real.

She was a Zoya. It had all been real.

"I'll take you to your room. You'll be living with your partner. The Zoya Task Force has always run with teams of two, one agent and one handler. You will be assigned a handler. The handler stays in Canada, you go out in the field. However, your physical and psychological profile has lined up perfectly to be paired with another woman who awoke from The Other Place a few months ago. She's been training alone but welcomes a partner. This is the first time the ZTF will have two agents with one handler."

Senka was trying to keep up, both mentally and physically. They were entering what looked like a barrack. The way Amanda said The Other Place made Senka think of it with capitals. It was a noun. They were talking about a real place.

Amanda stopped in front of a door and stepped aside. Senka took the cue and opened it.

Inside was a bright room with two beds and two desks. It looked to Senka like a university dorm room. A woman was sitting at a desk, long red hair tied up in a ponytail. She turned and flashed Senka a bright smile.

"Hello!" she said, rising. She was taller than Senka and was muscular. Senka pegged her as older than her, maybe mid-thirties. Senka saw that she was very beautiful. She moved gracefully through the room, almost gliding.

The woman held out her hand, "Tomo."

Senka shook it, "Umm, my name is Lizzie Brighton. But over there they called me Senka." She stuttered over her words. It felt so awkward to say.

Tomo smiled warmly, "It takes some getting used to, this whole double world thing. Over there I was called Tomo. I like to think that The Other Place gives us our real names. But my name here before my accident was Dr. Charlie Penner."

*   *   *

Senka came crashing back into reality as Taser probes entered her chest. Fifty thousand volts rocked through her body and she dropped to her knees. She had no senses other than pain. She managed to work her hand up and rip the prongs out of her chest.

She focused and saw that she was in the middle of an unknown park surrounded by police officers. All of them were pointing guns at her. She stayed on her knees and laced her hands behind her head. Leo's back was towards her and he was barking and snarling at the officer who was holding the Taser gun. She saw sweat drip into the cop's eyes but his hand was steady.

"Leo, come here," she said hoarsely. Her muscles were twitching but she managed to keep to her knees and keep her hands behind her head. The dew in the grass soaked her knees and the cold cleared her head. Leo turned, startled to hear her voice. He padded towards her and licked her face. His eyes showed deep-seeded concern. Senka realized what must have happened and her face reddened. "I'm good. Sit." Leo obliged and sat beside her.

"Sen, you good?" she heard Carter yell from somewhere behind her.

"Yeah, I'm good," she yelled hoarsely back. She didn't turn her head or move.

"Sergeant Bennet," one of the officers in plain clothes in front of her said loudly, "my name is Detective Weaver. There has been a disturbance of the peace here today."

"I kill anyone?" she asked. She was serious.

Detective Weaver's eyes softened, "No ma'am," he said. His gun stayed pointed at her head, "Your dog there noticed you weren't really acting right. He went to get your partner there behind you, Sergeant Green. When your partner couldn't rouse you and you took off, he called for backup. Unfortunately, you may have broken the nose of one of my officers when he tried to calm you down."

"I'm sorry about that," Senka said sincerely. "Carter, that true?"

"Yeah, Sen, it's true. Sorry. I haven't needed help like this for you in a long time."

Senka nodded. She didn't blame any of them.

"What time is it?" she asked the Detective.

"Well ma'am it's half past seven in the morning."

Senka twitched. She had been out for almost an hour. She didn't know where she was. No wonder Carter had called the cops. It was lucky she hadn't murdered anyone.

"Now, Sergeant, unfortunately I have to take you in. Just for routine. Your boss, Warrant-Officer Nguyen will meet us there. You're not getting arrested."

Senka nodded. Amanda would smooth everything over, much to Senka's embarrassment. "Yes, sir, I understand. I have a handgun as a sidearm under my jacket on the left side. I also have a knife in my left boot and one in my right pocket."

Detective Weaver nodded and holstered his gun. The officers surrounding her did not. He approached her slowly. Leo watched him closely. He gently removed the gun from her sidearm holster and made sure the safety was on. He left the knives.

"Ma'am, I'm sorry but I need to cuff you," he said.

She nodded. He went around her and gently took both hands from the top of her head and cuffed them behind her back. She let him and they both ignored the twitch in her muscles as he touched her.

Senka still didn't like being touched.

Leo kept a wary eye as Detective Weaver helped haul her to her feet. The officers lowered their guns. The Detective turned them and Senka saw Carter. He looked at her sadly. She kept her head up and gave him a curt nod, one he returned.

"I'm sorry, sir, but I'm quite out of sorts. I don't suppose you'd allow me to bring my dog with me?"

Detective Weaver stayed silent for a while, mulling it over while he walked her to his squad car. Leo padded along on the other side, making sure to watch and protect her.

"I suppose he can fit in the back of the squad car," he said finally. He opened the back door of his car and Leo jumped in without being told. Weaver snorted and Senka bent over and sat heavily in the car. She leaned her head back and closed her eyes. She had a ripping headache. Weaver got into the front seat and she smiled when she heard him roll down the back window so Leo had fresh air. Senka hated all of this. It would be so much easier just to go to sleep.

Weaver started the car and drove them away.

"I served in Afghanistan," he said. Senka's shoulders were hurting because of the cuffs but out of respect she didn't slip them. "I get what's going on with you. I saw it happen to my brother too. He served with me. We did two tours. Wasn't near the same when I got out. I know sometimes it's going to feel like you should just end it."

Senka's eyes opened and she saw Weaver studying her through the rear-view mirror.

"Don't," he said, "I know people will tell you it's the coward's way out but it's not. It's more that it sticks with the people you leave behind. My brother couldn't take it. Ate a bullet a few years out of the army. We pay for it. You may not have much family but that partner of yours, Sergeant Carter Green, he loves you. He's family. Stay for him. Stay for your pup."

Her eyes teared up and she nodded.

"And slip the cuffs," Weaver said gruffly, looking ahead again. "We both know you can and your dog needs a pet."

Senka smiled through the forming tears. She slipped the cuffs and handed them to the man in the front. Leo curled up beside her and put his head in her lap. She put her head back against the back of the seat and buried her hand in his fur.

She had such a headache. And something was nagging at her, but she couldn't figure out what it was.

25 DR. CHARLIE PENNER

October 30, 2023, 12:43
Location: Dorfen, Germany.

Charlie refused to sit on her bed. She didn't deserve it. She had been sitting on the floor since Kelly had died. The lights stayed on and she didn't have a watch so she had no idea how long she'd been in the cell. Food from hours before was untouched on a tray by the bars by the door. They always removed the old stuff and put out a new tray. She drank water only. It was too easy to die of thirst. She deserved much worse than that.

The cells in the compound were made of stone, with bars at the door. She couldn't see the child next to her, but she could hear him.

When they had dragged her in and tossed her in the cell she had been sobbing. The pain in her shoulder was bearable, but the pain in her heart was not. The boy next to her had been yelling and screaming about Kelly. They had ignored him and left. Charlie stayed on the floor in silence. Shortly after she was tossed in the cell, she had calmed down and she had popped her shoulder back into place. It was sore, but usable.

There had been silence since. Days of silence and monotony.

Suddenly, out of nowhere, she heard the kid in the cell beside her say quietly, "Kelly's not coming back, is she?"

Charlie almost jumped. She was so lost in her misery and she hadn't expected anyone to speak. Her ZTF training barely kept her in place.

"No," she said in a low voice, "she's not."

The kid sniffed a few times, "Is she dead?"

How do you explain Zoya to a teenager? How do you explain more than one world to a kid who has been kidnapped, who was lost and alone and who would probably share the same fate as his friend?

The answer was easy for Charlie. You didn't explain any of it. "Yes," she answered softly, "she's dead."

The kid sobbed quietly. Guards walked by and they kept silent. The kid waited until the guards left and said quietly, "How?"

"Don't do that to yourself," Charlie breathed. "It only makes it worse. What's your name, kid?"

"Isaac."

"Who's your father?"

This time a long pause. Charlie knew she had overstepped but she doubted she would ever see the outside of the compound. She needed to know. Those copper-flecked eyes. She knew them so well.

"Why do you care?" Isaac asked harshly. Charlie smiled. She had hit a nerve.

"Just wondering a little bit about you."

"You shouldn't care. You were working for these assholes," he muttered angrily. He was barely holding on to control. "What, you think I didn't notice?" soon he would be shouting. Charlie didn't need that. All was lost for her but if they played their cards right Isaac might have a shot of getting out of here.

"Keep your voice down. These people will kill you if you give them a reason to."

Guards walked by again and Isaac quieted. She welcomed it. She began to have a new goal in mind. Charlie only functioned well with goals. The question was always what drove her. She was a doctor in both Biology and Chemistry. She became obsessive over questions, often killing relationships in the process. That quality was one that she hated about herself. It meant that, even being held against her will, she was the type of person who would help the bad guys.

Not that she was scared of death. She would have rather been killed. But they had taken her and had posed a question. And instead of telling them to go fuck themselves, as her young and steadfast partner Senka would have, she had done exactly as they asked. Purely to answer a question that she thought was unanswerable. Where Senka was fast, Charlie was smart. She was smart before she had a skiing accident that left her in a coma damn near a decade. But once over there, she was called Tomo because she was a genius. *You know that's not your only name,* she chided herself silently.

She had always told Senka that the names from The Other Place were their true names and that, as Zoya, they earned them. Charlie had stopped thinking of herself as Tomo as soon as she accepted the challenge laid before her from her captors. Tomo was noble. Tomo was the most successful general in the history of Anzen, the country where she had awoken in The Other Place. Tomo had risen to the title of Empress, had led with an iron fist. Charlie was weak. Tomo would have killed these men long ago. Charlie had helped them.

She was disgusted with herself. She was the worst type of person.

But she would try to help this kid. Because she needed to. She hoped she would take a bullet in the process. Or that she pissed Alejandra off enough that she beat her to death. She deserved a long, painful death.

The guards finished their rounds. They opened her cell gate and silently took her last uneaten meal and dropped off a new one. She could hear Isaac sniffling next to her.

"You're right, I was working for them," Charlie said once the guards left.

"You should burn in hell," Isaac snapped.

Charlie smiled. He was right. It felt almost good to have someone hate her as much as she hated herself.

"You're right, I should. Is your father your real dad?"

Isaac neither answered, nor did he sniffle. Charlie had guessed it right, after all.

"How did you know?" Isaac asked softly.

"I know your real dad. Or I knew him. A long time ago."

Isaac didn't say anything for a long time. Charlie, sitting cold and stiff on the floor, didn't rush him. It was a lot for a teenager to take. And as of right now they weren't going anywhere anytime soon.

"My mom never told me who my dad was. My dad's my dad, you know? But my parents are white and I'm black. I always knew he wasn't the guy who got my mom pregnant. I've never met you. How do you know who my dad is?"

"You have his eyes," she said simply. "Do you want to know who he is?"

A long pause.

"No," Isaac said, voice firm. "My dad is the guy who raised me. He loves me. We go to football games and he picks me up from practice. Not that other guy."

Charlie nodded to herself. She needed to save Carter's son. Just for her own soul. She didn't know how but she had to get him out of here.

"You're only going to get one chance to get out of here," Charlie said. "You're going to have to do something bad though. Can you do it?"

"Like kill someone?" Isaac asked.

"Yes."

"Yeah. I could kill someone. They killed Kelly because she was a prostitute. That's not right. That wasn't her fault."

"You're going to have to live with it forever kid."

Isaac's voice was firm, "I know. But I'll do it for her."

They grew silent, both lost in their own thoughts. Her hand went to the dragon pendent under her shirt. The one with the ruby. The only thing she had from The Other Place.

She would get him out of here, then she would die. It was the only way.

26 SENKA

October 30, 2023, 09:30
Location: Toronto, Canada.

Senka was sitting in Amanda's office. Her gun was tucked safely in her holster. Amanda had met them at the station. She had smoothed everything over with the Police Chief. Carter had hacked into civilian cell phones and deleted footage. Media outlets had been contacted, threats had been made, and the whole morning ordeal had been effectively silenced by 08:45 AM.

She had locked the embarrassment away. Her boots were kicked up on the table. Her leather jacket was clean and she had on new jeans. Leo was tucked beside the legs of her chair, sleeping in a ball.

Amanda strode in past Senka to her desk. The morning wasn't mentioned. Nor would it ever be. Senka's psychiatrist would try to bring it up but she would, inevitably, shut him out like she always did. Jack Daniels would help her through.

Senka kept her eyes on the news broadcast that was playing on the TV. The President of the United States of America was delivering another hate-filled speech. This time it targeted Muslims.

"When are we taking this guy out?" Senka asked, eyes never leaving the screen.

Amanda didn't have to look to know who she was talking about. President MacDonald had been growing consistently more brazen in the international political spectrum over the last seven years.

"Orders are coming down shortly. The Queen is just reviewing." Amanda placed a thick file on her desk, and silently put something in the safe behind her. "It will most likely be yours after you're done with this human trafficking ring."

Senka nodded. "Gonna be hard not to cause a war though," she said, watching the crowd start to cheer on the man. "If it's obvious it's a hit they will go to war with anyone they want and use it as an excuse. They love him down there."

Amanda went around her desk and joined Senka at the table, sitting heavily in one of the chairs. "I know. The brass was thinking a crazed white supremacist."

Senka shook her head, "No, won't work. They will still twist it. Blame atheism or refugees. The NRA will go ape-shit over gun rights and it still won't be good. Civil war would probably happen."

Amanda nodded again, "I agree but it's all we have. Any sign of a cover up, even a suicide, and the United States will declare war on someone."

"Civil war is still war, even if it's contained."

Amanda knew her job and stayed silent. They watched the President rant and rave to a crowd of fans.

"What's Simone up to?" Senka finally asked.

Amanda's brow furrowed, she was confused on where Senka was going with this. "Currently she's on the red carpet. Her new movie comes out soon and she's advertising."

"What is she working on?"

"Classified."

Senka sighed. Zoya knew about each other but their missions were strictly need to know. Simone was one of the original members of the ZTF. She had been in a coma for a year or so back in the beginning of the new millennium. She had been a movie star before becoming a Zoya and the ZTF had snatched her right up after she had awoken. Simone didn't feel pain. At all. She was drop dead gorgeous and was still an A-list celebrity. She was invaluable to the ZTF. She ran with the elite and gave them access to people they would never dream of meeting otherwise.

"Why do you want Simone?" Amanda asked her.

"Domestic dispute," Senka said slowly.

Amanda shook her head but Senka cut her off, "No, listen to me. Anyone else kills him or he kills himself there's going to be war with someone. We don't want that."

"Clearly, but there's no other way."

"No, there is. Make America hate him. Then they won't care. Look, we put Simone in there, in one of his condos he owns. Carter fudges a clear history of a two year affair with her."

Amanda started to understand where Senka was heading.

"We leak something about the affair. Get paparazzi all over there and lure him in. Then we beat the living shit out of Simone. She won't feel it. We make sure cameras catch the shadow of a guy beating her up. She stabs him with a kitchen knife and she runs out bloody and screaming. The paparazzi will help her for sure."

"She claims battered-wife syndrome," Amanda said.

"Yah, that's the gist anyway. Have it recorded. The President beating the shit out of his mistress, and it's Simone Dubois nonetheless. People fucking love her. They will hate him. Shit, they would lynch him if he wasn't already dead. Carter fudges the medical records, have a history of abuse established."

"The cops will take it to trial," Amanda said. "And it will put her at risk. CIA and FBI will want to eliminate her."

"We can rig the jury. We honestly wouldn't even need to. Carter's good. His evidence would be airtight and on the right computers. Or, if she wants retirement like she's been saying for the last two years, she hangs herself due to the stress. Make that public, Simone gets to go retire in Bora Bora. Not the first staged suicide we've ever pulled off. And the CIA? Please. We can run circles around them."

Amanda nodded, convinced, "I like it," she said. "Simple enough to pull off. Simone won't stab him, though. She doesn't like to kill people."

"Well, I'll beat the shit out of her and stab him. Easy enough for me to do. Simone doesn't have to do much. Just take a beating she won't feel. She's won three Oscars, this is easy for her."

Amanda nodded again, "Once we get the green light from up top we will set it up. Simone can clean up her current assignment within the next few weeks. I expect the same from you." She looked at her watch. "Carter should be here shortly and we can debrief what he's found out. He's had a week, it better be good."

Senka didn't say anything. That nagging feeling was bothering her. She didn't have time to think about it, however, because Carter burst through the door. He was holding a bundle of papers and he looked crazy and triumphant.

"I got in!" he exclaimed as he dropped the papers and files onto the table.

"All of it?" Amanda asked incredulously. She looked shocked and a little confused.

"Not all of it. That Ampulex folder is going to take months. As far as I can tell only one account and one computer has access to read anything in that folder and it's locked tighter than the Pentagon. The fact that I even found the folder to begin with is a feat. But I got in to the rest of it."

"What did you find out?" Amanda asked.

"Sen was right. It's a human trafficking ring. And it's huge," Carter excitedly plugged a USB drive into his tablet. The image of the folders appeared on the screen.

"But you were right too, Amanda. It's drugs. These guys have been designing and distributing shit for years."

"Designing?" Amanda asked.

"Yes!" Carter brought up a file, it had a list of designer drugs on it. "All that fake shit that's been going around. Sure, MDMA was bad, but these guys designed that super version that killed all those kids in Amsterdam a few years ago." He brought up the file.

Senka stood and looked at the file Carter opened, "Fuckers were even keeping track of how many fatal overdoses there were."

"Not only of that stuff. The fake marijuana, the super mushrooms, all of that has been designed by these guys."

"Holy shit," Senka muttered.

"That's just the start," Carter said, bringing up another screen. "It looks like they have labs all over the world. Germany, Russia, Columbia, the States. Those are just the big ones. They have a bunch more."

"How are we supposed to shut all this down?" Senka asked.

"Sen that's not the worst part. The human trafficking is the worst part."

Carter brought up a different folder. In it he pulled up a spreadsheet. There were thousands of first names. It had ages and characteristics, along with the country the person was from and where they were headed.

"This is only one of the spreadsheets. There are more."

"Holy shit," Amanda muttered.

Senka's mouth was wide open.

"These guys are keeping track. They kidnap people. I saw an age as young as four. Then they sell them to the highest bidder. There are auctions. Some of the names are in red. I'm assuming they died. Others are just sent to the drug houses."

The room was silent with shock and disgust.

"Let me kill them all," Senka whispered. Her fists were shaking at her sides.

"Chop off the head of the snake," Amanda said under her breath. "Carter please tell me you found out who is in charge."

"It's that Freudman. He's in charge of it all. He is doing all this for profit. He's got to be the richest man in the world. But he hemorrhages money. Into what I don't know."

"What's this have to do with Zoya?" Senka asked. "Isn't that what this guy was in to?"

"I'm not sure," Carter said. "It must have something to do with that Ampulex folder. There's no mention of Zoya anywhere. Only the stuff we found before and I honestly think that stuff was just put into the wrong folder."

Distracted, Carter scrolled to the bottom of the spreadsheet. There were two names, Kelly and Isaac. Kelly's name was highlighted in blue. It was the only one on the spreadsheet like that. They both had country of origin as Canada. Senka instantly understood why he was so excited. He'd found his son.

"These two were the most recent entry. They're Canadian and they've been shipped to a lab in Germany. Amanda we need to get them out of there."

Amanda sighed and walked to her desk. "Senka, you're going in alone. You go in, look around, get out."

Senka and Carter exchanged sidelong glances.

"Amanda there are civilians. Probably more than just the two kids. I need evac. I need a team. I'm not putting kids in the line of fire," Senka said. She was confused. She didn't always agree with Amanda but Senka could usually see her side of it.

"Then don't fire," Amanda snapped. "You go in, look around, get out. That's the end of it. Wheels up in an hour."

Senka started to argue, anger burned. Leo had even hopped to his feet, feeling the distress of his master.

"I don't have time to explain the international political spectrum to you right now," Amanda said crisply from behind her desk. "You go in and look around. I will take this to my meeting this afternoon and try to get approval for an international team. You're dismissed." She looked pointedly at Carter, who was staring at her wide-eyed, "Both of you."

They turned and strode out without a word, stopping at Carter's desk. Senka was so angry she couldn't think straight. Carter had finally found his son and Amanda wouldn't give them the tools to get him out safely.

More to the point, if Senka fucked this up, Isaac would die.

"I'll get him out," Senka muttered to Carter. He was stone-faced, but Senka saw tears in his eyes.

"I know," Carter said quietly. He looked at her for a long time.

"It doesn't make sense," Senka said quietly. "Watch your back, buddy. Something doesn't feel right."

Carter just shook his head in dismissal. He started busying himself at his desk.

Senka and Leo strode away to get their things together. There was more to this than they knew right now. She could feel it.

The tingling in her spine was back and worse than ever.

27 SENKA

October 30, 2023, 23:24
Location: Munich, Germany.

The plane landed. It lurched slightly and Senka's stomach rolled. But it settled again and pulled away from the main terminal, just as it had in Winnipeg.

She and Leo debarked the plane. She shouldered her hockey bag and made her way to the car that was left for her on the tarmac. This time it was a new, black SUV. Amanda wasn't joking around anymore. This wasn't a laughing matter.

She tossed her bag into the back of the SUV and opened the driver's side door. Leo jumped in without a command and made his way to the passenger seat. Senka followed. She adjusted the seat and the mirror and they made their way silently out of the airport. They went east on the A94 and ventured the hour towards Dorfen. It was midnight and traffic was quiet.

Carter had discovered the exact GPS location of the Germany lab without much trouble after they had received orders from Amanda.

Senka was still angry. It hadn't dissipated with her time on the plane. She still didn't understand why Amanda wouldn't send backup. She slammed her palm against the steering wheel. Leo growled.

"It doesn't fucking make any sense, Leo."

He stared at her, brown eyes all knowing.

"I know, I know. Carter said it's because she trusts me to do the job. But why the hell wouldn't she have the evac sent?"

Leo huffed, gave her a side long glare then continued to stare out the window.

"Does she want me to take the hit and order it myself?" her fingers drummed as she weaved her way through the country side. "What kind of political pressure could she be facing to not order backup for a bunch of stolen kids?"

"Leo, this doesn't make any sense. Carter said there were at least fifteen kids on the spreadsheet at this German lab, from all over the world. Shouldn't they want to evac their own fucking children out?"

She pulled over, six kilometers northwest of Dorfen, on a grid road. There were a few scattered farms around and she found an old building to hide the SUV in.

Something told her that she wouldn't be the one who would retrieve it.

Leo trotted happily around, smelling absolutely everything he could get his nose into while Senka got ready. She opened the bag from the back of the SUV. She changed into black cargo pants and a light black t-shirt. She put on her Tantos criss-crossed behind her lower back. She rarely used them in this world. In all honesty she preferred how clean and easy it was to shoot someone. But she had an urge to take them today. She attached a small camera to her shirt. The video feed would go to Carter so he could keep an eye out for her. She threw on a black sweater overtop that had a camera already in it. It was past midnight and was getting chilly.

She strapped her side arm on her leg and slung her C14 Timberwolf sniper rifle across her back with its newly developed silencer, straight from the ZTF. Its shot was near silent. She re-tied her boots and made sure she had extra ammo in her pockets. She whistled softly.

Leo ran towards her, panting happily. She fit him with his brand new Kevlar vest. It was equipped with a small camera. Carter would be watching out for him as well.

"Ready?" she asked Leo. He sat beside her, happily panting away, tongue hanging from the side of his mouth.

She crouched in front of him and scratched his ears. He leaned in warmly, eyes closed, enjoying the moment.

"I have a funny feeling I'm not getting out of this one, buddy."

Leo growled softly.

"No, it's true. You need to watch your back in there, alright? I go down, you get out. You got that?"

He happily panted away and enjoyed the ear scratches. Senka shook her head. She didn't know who she was trying to convince.

She sighed, "Alright buddy, let's get going." He sprang to his feet. They jogged north in the direction of the compound. She had on her wrist unit. It was equipped with GPS tracking and the target was about three kilometers away.

"Perfect time of night for a jog, hey buddy?"

Leo bounded beside her. She always loved being with him. He was so happy to be alive. She wished she would have thought of owning a dog sooner. They had only been together a little over a week but Senka felt as though they were inseparable.

They jogged through fields and over fences, avoiding the roads. The cold air flooded her lungs. Senka's mind went to her prison break in The Other Place, running under the Northern Lights to freedom. There were no Northern Lights today and her heart was heavy. She didn't know why. She usually loved missions and adventure and she trusted herself enough to get out of every situation. Today should be a wonderful day because she and Leo got to do their first legitimate mission together.

But with a heavy heart she jogged north, Leo padding beside her. She needed to clear her head and get excited, or this wasn't going to go well. Might just turn out to be a self-fulfilling prophecy.

They covered the three kilometers quickly. The terrain was flat and easy and the moon guided them.

She whistled softly twice and Leo slowed down and crouched. There should be a bit of a ledge coming up, from it she should be able to see the compound. That's what the satellite imaging showed.

"Leo, clear the ridge," she whispered. He took off, the night hiding his body. She crouched and waited. He returned within a few minutes. He wagged his tail happily and started heading back up the hill.

"Alrighty, I guess that means we're good."

Leo led her to the top of the ridge. She crawled the last of it, slinking to the top on her stomach. Ahead, around five hundred meters away, a massive compound spread out in front of her. It had high walls built of concrete. There were no windows. She unslung her sniper rifle and put the sight to her eye.

It was heavily guarded with a massive chain link fence surrounding the entire compound, barbed wire curled on top. There were two guards on every gate as well as guards on the doors of the compound. They all carried assault rifles. There were guards on the roof as well.

She pulled her ear piece out of her pants and put it in, sticking a mic to her throat.

"Carter I'm in position," she said quietly. She lay motionless, watching the guards. They were well trained mercenaries. She could tell by the way they held themselves. They were decked out in the same way as the men in Russia had been. Big guns, cargo pants and matching black shirts.

"What do you see?" he asked.

"Right now my count is fifteen. Three on the roof, two gates with two each, two doors with two each and two roaming. I'm assuming more on the other side as well."

"Sounds like suicide, Sen."

She didn't move, she calmly watched through her sight. "No, not suicide. Just really fucking difficult."

"You don't have to do this. Amanda ordered you to go in, recon, and get out. You could leave now. We could get a team together within a few days. Far as I know Matty is close, somewhere in Germany."

Matty was another Zoya in the ZTF. He was fun to work with, but liked to blow absolutely everything up. Thinking about it, Senka decided that Matty would have been ideal for this situation.

"No, I promised you I would get him, Carter. And I don't break promises. Besides, I have Leo."

"You're breaking a direct order," he mumbled.

"No, not at all. She knows I'm going to go in. It's assumed. Also I *have* to go in to recon properly. You're the one who's going to break a direct order," she said. "It's half past one. I'm going to watch for a few hours. I'll make my move at four. I want an evac here for four forty-five."

When Carter didn't say anything she chuckled a little, "I should have known you'd have already ordered it."

"I know what you are going to do before you do it," Carter replied.

"Then you should know that if you come to work drunk again, I will kick the shit out of you."

A long silence followed. Senka was happy to wait, she had all the time in the world.

"I wasn't drunk."

"Carter, I find it insulting when you try to lie to me. I may not be nearly as smart as Tomo was, but I know the smell of liquor."

"Like you're one to talk," Carter snapped. "You're an alcoholic. A high-functioning one, I'll give you that. You are drunk pretty much constantly."

"Never at work," Senka replied calmly. She was following, watching the roving foot guard, timing the interval. "I've never drank before a mission. You're drifting back to the summer after Mel died, Carter. Drinking at work and shit."

"I have a son. He's most likely dead. What do you want from me? You gave me the bottle!"

"I wanted you to finish that bottle then fucking leave it," it was Senka's turn to get snippy. "You were drinking this morning, Carter. Calling the fucking cops on me? You haven't had to do that since your drinking days."

"So, you're telling me that your basis in deciding that I'm an active alcoholic again is how well I deal with your cracked and mangled psyche? Well that's a definite unit of measurement. You assault a cop and it's my fault. Classic."

That stung. Carter knew it would. Senka had known that this conversation was going to be a tough one. She needed Carter to be on the right track before she went in there. She stayed silent.

The silence killed Carter. Senka's breathing was rhythmic, relaxing. Almost as if she was sleeping. She was watching the guards move, biding her time.

"Look, Sen, I'm sorry. You're right. Of course you're right. I just had a little pick me up in my coffee this morning."

"I know," she said. Nothing had changed at the compound.

"That's why I brought it up now, not ten hours ago."

"Learning about Isaac just brought up a lot of stuff."

"I know." Time ticked away. The conversation, though awkward, was sufficiently wasting time. She was getting chilly but she wouldn't move. The silences had been longer than she thought. They had wasted hours.

"It's just, Melanie and I wanted kids so bad. She would have totally been cool with me having a kid from before. I just wished I had known about him."

"Melanie helped you stop drinking before. She'd be pissed if she knew you came to work buzzing."

"I know that. Look, I'll never drink again."

"Promise?" Senka asked.

Another long pause. "Yeah, yeah I promise."

Senka was satisfied. She had to move in thirty. She had one more thing to tackle. "Carter, you know it wasn't your fault, right?"

"I should have been watching the road," he said quietly. "I go over it a thousand times in my head every day. I should have been watching the road better. I would have been able to turn the car so my side hit the pole, not hers."

"Carter, Tomo told you the stats before. I don't remember them. She went over it, the physics and everything. No one could have made that turn."

"If I had been watching the road..."

"Carter shut up. You were. You probably glanced away for a second because you guys were probably arguing about getting a cat again. You're human. It happens."

"You would have made the turn."

Senka twitched. Her first movement that wasn't speaking since she lay down in her spot two hours ago. "Carter. I know it's easy for me to say. But trust me. You don't want this. Yeah, I'm fast. So fast that I'm probably the only person on the planet that could have made the turn in that rain. But you're human. The other seven billion humans on the planet wouldn't have been able to make the turn. Tomo wouldn't have made it. No one could have but me. And I don't count."

He stayed silent for a long time.

"I want to eat a bullet daily," she said finally. She had the feeling this was her last time for honesty. "I don't do it, but I want to. I've seen too much, I've done too much. I'm starting to like killing people. How fucked up is that? It's the only way I feel alive. Nothing seems important unless I'm on a mission with bullets flying. That's the only way I feel like a person."

"Don't you think I know that?" he sniffed. "That's why I deal with your drinking and the string of men that come into our apartment. At least then I know you'll wake up the next morning."

Senka sighed. She was such a burden to Carter. To everyone.

She needed to move soon. She started lining up the first shot. The three on the roof would go first.

"Look. I'll come with you to AA when I get back. And I'll actually listen to that shrink they make me see damn near daily at headquarters. Deal?" she said. She started slowing her breathing. The shot was relatively close, well within her range. But she needed three consecutive head shots.

"Deal," he replied. "Amanda is asleep in her office. If you're going to go, go now. Evac forty-six out."

Senka breathed out and fired. Head shot. The first man dropped. She quickly worked the bolt action and fired again. The second man on the roof dropped. Bolt action, breathe, fire. The third man dropped. She was far enough away that no one but Leo and Carter heard the muffled shots.

She worked the bolt action again. She fired two more head shots at the two guards near the closest door. She dropped her sniper rifle and with a low whistle ran fast and hard directly towards the gate, Leo loping easily beside her. She had a two minute window until the roving mercenaries came back towards the gate.

She was fast. It was four in the morning and the mercenaries were tired. They likely were there more to guard from people escaping instead of people trying to break in. She used it to her advantage.

She had a silencer attached to her Sig Sauer and she fired two shots on the run towards the gate. The guards went down in a heap. No one had sounded the alarm yet. She stole a key card from one of the guards on the way by and tucked it into her cargo pants. The fence was ten feet high, and lucky for them the gate had no barbed wire on the top.

She squatted and Leo ran at her, launched himself off her back and he went over the fence, landing easily on the other side. "Cover," she whispered to him. He crouched and ran straight ahead to the darkness of the door. The two dead guards weren't going to sound an alarm.

Senka scaled the fence easily and joined Leo beside the dead guards. She smiled when she saw the ladder a few feet away from the door. At least Carter's schematics had been accurate so far. Leo bounced happily when she squatted for him to jump on her shoulders.

"Yah, your fucking favorite," she grumbled. She quickly climbed the ladder to the roof, a happy eighty pound German Shepard draped across her shoulders and panting noisily in her ear.

Leo jumped off and cleared the roof while she scaled the last three rungs of the ladder. He pranced towards her and sat happily as both her boots touched the roof.

"No alarm," Carter said. "Well done. There should be a large air vent, there, on your right. Looks like it leads directly to a room. None of these rooms are labelled on the schematic so I'm not sure what it's for."

Senka was uneasy about wearing the body cam for the mission, but she couldn't protect Carter forever. And she had the feeling he would need the video evidence to go back and review at some point.

She jogged towards the air vent and looked at it.

"Pretty sure that's from a fume hood in a lab," Senka said. "Direct vacuum source to the outside. Should be straight down."

She stuck her wrist unit into the air being ejected from the vent. She was careful to keep her face out of the way. The unit beeped and a green light flashed on her wrist.

"Well guess I won't die from any chemicals today!" she exclaimed. The tingling in her spine returned in full force as she lowered herself by her fingertips into the vent. It was a black drop. Leo skittered a bit and nuzzled her fingers from the roof, big eyes staring.

"Stay here," she said to him, looking up from the black, ominous hole. He licked her fingertips gently. "If I don't call for you, bail. You got that?" he replied with a high pitched whine and thumped to a sit beyond her view.

With a deep breath, she dropped into the vent. She didn't fall long and landed with a crunch. She took a small flashlight off her belt and pressed the button on a side, emitting a small white LED light. She looked down and saw broken glassware around her feet and a clear liquid seeping underneath her boots. She shone the light around and noticed that she was, in fact, in a fume hood. Still holding her breath, she opened the sliding door and hopped out.

She quickly took off her sweater and laid it overtop the broken glass and leaking chemical. She stuck her head in the fume hood and gave a sharp whistle. A happy Leo launched himself down the fume hood vent. Senka managed to catch the hurling, panting form before he hit the bottom of the fume hood and heaved him onto the ground outside.

He shook himself and stared at her, tongue out the side of his mouth. Senka smiled at him and patted his head.

"Stand guard," she said. Leo immediately stood and ran to the door. He'd let her know if anyone was coming. This gave Senka some time to look around.

She was in a world-class laboratory. There were computers directly behind her. In front of her were huge vats of chemicals, unlabeled. Machinery and equipment had been pushed against the walls to make room for the huge tubs of chemicals. There were empty animal cages lining the walls.

"Before you get too far, give me a second to find the proper video feed," Carter said in her ear.

"Then I'll stay in the lab," she said, walking around the vats. She was curious as to what they were.

"I've hacked in to their security feed. I'm just looping the last two hours of video. Should give you enough time to get in and get out. But it means that I won't be able to use the video cameras to help you out. I'll just be able to watch your personal camera."

Senka shrugged, "Old school is fine." Her flashlight highlighted a table behind the vats. She made her way carefully to the table, gun held in front.

"Where's Isaac?" she asked Carter as she picked her way through the lab.

"They don't have a lot of security cameras," Carter's voice rumbled in her ear. "Just five or six. Isaac isn't on any of them."

"Probably want deniability if anyone ever got in here," Senka said quietly. "Plus I think they got cocky. That was a pretty easy perimeter to get into. They probably didn't think anyone had them on their radar."

Senka stopped in front of the table. On it were thousands of little Ziploc bags. "You getting this?" she asked, reaching for a bag.

"Clear as day," Carter said. He was tense, she could hear it in his voice.

She picked up a baggie. Inside were ten little pink pills with no markings or anything distinguishable.

"What do you think they are?" she asked.

"I have no idea."

Senka grabbed a few of the packages and put them into her right pants' pocket. She joined Leo, who was patiently sitting facing the only door.

"Any chance you can unlock the doors in the compound?" she asked. The little light was glowing red. Senka took out of her sweater the key card that she had stolen and tapped it to the lock. It stayed red.

Carter paused for a long time, "It's weird Sen. They are all already unlocked?"

Senka pulled the door. The red light remained on but she heard the clink of the lock and the door slid open inwards.

"Oh this is very bad," she said to Carter.

"Bail. Evac is," she heard him typing away at his computer. "Evac was turned around. That wasn't my order," his voice was rising with panic. "Sen I'll fix it I swear."

"Well I guess the only way to go is forward then," she said calmly. Carter was typing so fast it was annoying in her ear. "Any ideas which way?"

"The schematics aren't right," Carter said, almost frantically, "It's like they have been scrambled. My guess is that straight is to the kitchens, left is to the gym and right is to the unknown."

"Right it is then."

"Sen I'm so sorry. I don't know who gave the order for evac to turn around. Must be a communication line down." Carter was frantic. She needed to get him under control.

"Carter I know," she started having a suspicion in her gut, but she couldn't voice it right now. "This isn't the same as Tomo, and I never blamed you for that anyway.'

"I messed up," Carter said.

"We all did. You tried to call off the airstrike, communication broke down. Life is rife with communication break-downs." She stepped through the door and swept her gun and flashlight. The hallways were concrete and dark, lit only by yellow lights spaced far apart. There were no windows. There was a hallway straight ahead and one to the left and right. She turned right. Leo took point.

"I was drunk that day, Sen," Carter said quietly. "The day Tomo died. I came to work still drunk from the night before. I killed her."

Senka sighed. She wasn't supposed to be dealing with an emotional partner and people trying to kill her at the same time. It was a lot to focus on.

"I know," she said quietly. They were walking swiftly through the dark hall. "We all knew. You were going through shit. But Tomo didn't die because you were drunk. She died because the radios cut out at that moment. Nothing more, nothing less. A freak ten second communication error killed her."

When Carter didn't say anything, Senka continued, "Carter you're the best handler in the ZTF. You didn't even make a mistake. It was beyond your control which is why it's bothering you."

She heard him breathing and typing.

"I need you here with me."

"I'm here for you," Carter said. "Sorry I panicked. Evac said they must have gotten the wrong code. They are just over an hour out. We will get you out of there."

"I will get Isaac out with me," Senka said. "I promised."

28 ISAAC

October 31, 2023, 04:07
Location: Dorfen, Germany.

Isaac was sitting on the floor of his cell. His back was towards the wall shared with the strange woman. He was lightly hitting his head repetitively against the wall.

He wasn't sure what to believe or what to think. The woman had been out of the cells and it looked like she was being forced here against her will when they came and retrieved Kelly. But François hadn't balked at her presence. And she had admitted that she'd worked with these guys.

He wasn't sure what time it was or even what day. They left the lights on in the hallway all the time. He slept when he fell asleep, woke when he needed to.

He tapped his head, over and over.

Kelly was dead. The woman wanted to help him out and get him out of here. She said she knew his father. He didn't really believe her. Those seemed like slim odds, he'd never seen this woman in his life. He didn't know why she would even try to help him when she had been working for the bad guys. She must have made them mad because she was in prison, but he didn't really feel bad for her.

Suddenly, quietly, he asked, "What's your name?"

A long silence followed. Isaac started fearing the woman was dead or hurt. He didn't know if he'd get out of here without her help.

"Dr. Charlie Penner," she answered finally, to Isaac's relief.

The lights around the cells flickered slightly. Isaac stayed silent as a couple guards jogged lightly past his cell door.

"Your time is going to come soon," Charlie said cryptically when the guards were gone.

"How do you know?"

"Didn't you see the lights flicker?"

Isaac scoffed, "That could be anything."

"How long have you been down here?" Charlie asked. "Tell me, have the lights ever flickered?"

Isaac thought back and found that she was right. The lights had been steady until that point. "No, they haven't."

"Exactly," Charlie whispered, "something was activated. I'm going with a silent security system of some sort. You have to be aware of your surroundings, kid."

"I'm a fifteen year old kid from the suburbs," he whispered angrily. "How am I supposed to know any of that?"

"Stop worrying about yourself and worry about what's around you. If you would have done that in the first place I bet you we never would have met."

Isaac wanted to yell. He settled for kicking the bed in front of him. It was bolted to the floor and pain exploded through his foot. "You know nothing about me," he exclaimed angrily, gritting his teeth and grabbing his foot.

"I know you probably ran away and got caught by some asshole because you were angry. Probably at your parents. For being good parents and giving you shit because you deserved it," she said steadily through the wall.

Tears filled Isaac's eyes and this time he did yell, "It wasn't my fault!"

"Take responsibility for your actions, kid. Even if someone is holding a gun to your head, you decide how you act."

The anger grew. He wanted to punch something, anything. He realized he wasn't angry at her but at himself. She was right. He had stayed at the party too late. He had run away from his mother.

A hurried whisper, "Good. He's coming. You're only going to

get one shot at this. I'm sorry it has to be you and not me."

Isaac was confused, he didn't know what she was talking about. Suddenly he heard the hall door open and the smooth steps of polished shoes, not boots, in the concrete hall outside.

"What am I supposed to do?" Isaac whispered frantically. The ominous steps grew closer, clipping sharply down the hall. Charlie stayed silent. "Help me!" he whispered loudly.

François stopped in front of his cell door. He was in a tailored blue suit with brown leather shoes. Isaac didn't notice that his tie was slightly askew.

"What is all this yelling about?" François said smoothly in his French accent. Isaac stepped back in fear. He had a predatory look in his eyes and Isaac was instantly uncomfortable.

"Help me!" he said again. Silence from the cell next to him. Isaac had a sick feeling grow in his stomach. Charlie wasn't going to help him. Charlie wanted him dead, just like Kelly, and he had bought into her lies.

François smiled broadly and scanned his key card. Isaac's cell door opened and he stepped inside, leaving it open behind him.

"I am sorry I haven't been able to break your spirit," François said. "I have been exceptionally busy. I have found a buyer for you, however."

Isaac took another step back. He was filled with disgust and dread. Someone had bought him. His back hit the wall. He had nowhere to go.

François approached him slowly. "Unfortunately, due to a recent visitor to our compound, I need to move you earlier than expected. The buyer won't be ready for you for another week," François stopped in front of him. "He's an especially affluent man in Norway. I think you will do well." François slapped him across the face, hard. Shock and pain caused Isaac to stumble. He steadied himself and wiped his mouth. The blood on his fingertips mesmerised him.

"But, fortunately for me, this buyer does not care if I have a bit of a go at you before you're sold."

Isaac's stomach roiled. He began to figure out what he was talking about and he was so afraid.

François rushed forward towards him.

Isaac reacted purely from fear. He pushed François back, hard, using the wall as an anchor. François was surprised by the sudden movement. He stepped back and his shiny brown shoes slipped on the concrete. He fell backwards. Isaac held his arm out to catch him. François fell in slow motion. He hit his head on the steel bed frame. His eyes rolled up into his head. His arm twitched a little and then he was still. Dark red blood pooled slowly around his head.

Isaac was shaking. He stumbled back and fell over his own feet, hitting the ground hard. His stomach was turning. He was sick.

"Good job, kid," he heard Charlie say from behind the wall.

Isaac lost it. He tried to steady his shaking hands and stood up. "I JUST KLLED A MAN!" he yelled. He accidentally looked at François' dead body. It made him sick and he threw up.

"Calm down," Charlie said quietly.

"I killed him. He's dead. I just wanted him off me. He's dead!" Isaac rose from his knees.

"You did what you had to. The real world is a terrible place. You did what you had to do to survive."

"How can you be so calm?" Isaac yelled. His hands were shaking. He was trying to walk it off. But he couldn't. That guy was evil, sure, but who was he to take a life?

"Isaac," Charlie said, slow and steady, "I need you to deal with this later, ok? You need to focus on the problem. Slow your breathing."

Isaac listened. He tried to slow down his breathing. But the panic, the panic was rising. It was going to break the surface again.

"Isaac, you need to get his key card."

Isaac shook his head, "No, no! I'm not touching him."

"It's in the right pocket of his pants, on a leather lanyard. You just need to grab the lanyard and pull."

"No, no, no!"

"Isaac," Charlie spoke softly but firmly. Isaac was instantly reminded of his mother. His heart rate slowed a little and he listened. "Isaac, there are other kids here. These guys are going to sell them. They are going to sell you. You need to get the keys. You need to get us all out of here."

Isaac looked up. He saw a little girl, no more than six, looking at him from across the hall. She was dirty, her hair was mangy. She was pressing her face to her cell bars, staring at him. He was surprised, he had always thought that the cell across from him was empty. She must have always cowered in the back corner in the dark. She was staring at him blankly, willing him to get her out of there.

Isaac rose and approached the body. He was still shaking but he had to do this for the little girl.

He saw the lanyard. He focused entirely on it. He didn't look at François' face or the blood. He kicked the leather away from the body. He composed himself when he saw the body move. He leaned down and grabbed the lanyard and pulled. His pulse raced when it caught slightly in the pocket, but he was relieved when it came free.

"I have the key card," Isaac said.

"Good job," Charlie said kindly. "You need to hurry."

Isaac nodded to himself. François had left his cell door open and he ran out. He hoped that no guards would come. That would be his fault.

He went across the hall and scanned the card. The light popped green and he heard the lock disengage. He pulled the door open and the little girl scurried out.

"Wait here," he said. He ran to the end of the hall and began to unlock the doors as fast as he could. There were no older children left, Isaac was the last of them. They had all been taken over the last few days. There were a total of six other children, all under the age of ten. No one said a word. They were all in shock and emotionally shut down. But they were listening.

Isaac returned to Charlie's cell. He didn't know what he was expecting. He hadn't really taken a good look at her when she had been brought to his cell. He had been too busy trying to stop them from taking Kelly. He saw a beautiful woman, mid-thirties, red hair that was still tied back pristinely. She was sitting cross-legged beside her bed, back against the wall that she shared with Isaac's cell.

They stared at each other. Isaac was frozen. This woman had helped him, but she had helped kill Kelly. He was sure of it.

Charlie smiled at him. "I get it. Go left outside the main cell doors. Stay right down the hallway. All the way to the end. There's a kitchen, go through the back and out the loading bay. There shouldn't be any barbed wire on top of the fence with the gate. Climb over and run. Find a house, call for help." She smiled at him, a sad smile.

"You killed Kelly," Isaac said. "I don't trust you at all."

She nodded, "I don't blame you. You shouldn't trust me. But make your decision fast. I hope whatever the disturbance was that François was mentioning buys you enough time to get out. There will be a couple of guards on the door outside. They are still too scared of me. Catch them by surprise."

That surprised Isaac. If they were scared of her, maybe she wasn't all bad.

"The enemy of my enemy is my friend," he said and unlocked her cell door.

Charlie looked surprised, and as she stood she replied, "Until they stab you in the back."

29 DR. CHARLIE PENNER

October 31, 2023, 04:16
Location: Dorfen, Germany.

Charlie gathered the children behind her and led them to the door. She used the key card to tap the lock and, thankfully, the light turned green and she heard the latch unlock. She slowly opened the door inwards. There were two guards, heavily armed, standing on either side of the door.

Where Senka was fast, Charlie was balanced. Senka saw auras, Charlie was so smart she knew exactly how her opponent would move before they did. That meant that Senka and Charlie were pretty much equals in hand to hand, close range weapons and long range weapons. Senka, however, had embraced firearms more quickly than Charlie had. Charlie still liked using her hands and her sword. She was still a wicked shot, and Senka was unreal when she had her Tantos in hand, but it was preference. And luckily for Charlie, she preferred close quarters. Charlie shook off the memories of Senka. She was most likely dead. It was no good remembering the dead.

Charlie was worried. It had been a long time since she was in a fight. But she trusted her decade in The Other Place. She turned to Isaac and held up a finger. "Stay," she mouthed to him. White-faced, he nodded. She could tell the adrenaline from killing François was wearing off and fear was starting to creep in. She needed to move fast, get him moving again. If he froze she couldn't trust any of the younger kids to get them all out.

She took a deep breath and exploded through the door, catching the guards by surprise. Before they could raise their guns she elbowed the man to her left in the nose, crushing it in a spurt of blood. His head snapped back and hit the concrete wall hard. She turned quickly and kneed the second man between the legs. He made a loud "Oof" sound as he doubled over in extreme pain. She used his forward momentum to crush his face into her knee. He fell to the ground, unconscious. She turned and kicked the first man in the face.

Both men lay on the floor in unconscious heaps. And her elbow and knee were sore. She shook her hand out a little to stop it from tingling. It was going to be a long day.

"Woah," Isaac said softly behind her, "how do I learn how to do that?"

She chuckled softly, "Trust me, kid, you don't want to know." She moved her shoulder, it was already starting to stiffen up. She wasn't as young as she used to be. She looked around. There was no one else in the long, dark concrete hallway. The only light came from flickering florescent lights spaced far apart.

"Remember stick right. All the way through the compound. Stay in the shadows. If you see anyone coming just duck somewhere and hide."

Isaac was still staring at the unconscious men. Charlie noticed him making a fist. Charlie grabbed his shoulder, turning him towards her. "Don't be a hero," she said harshly. "You run, kid. You get everyone out. You have to go see your mom."

Isaac nodded and the fist relaxed. He had determination all over his face. "What about you?" he asked.

"I'm going this way," she said, gesturing down the dark concrete hallway. "I'm going to make as much noise and hassle as possible. I'll draw them my way."

"You'll die!" Isaac whispered.

She smiled at him and knelt beside the downed men. She grabbed a steel baton and held it out to him. "Takes a lot to kill me," she said. When he reached for it she added, "Aim for the head. Swing to kill."

Isaac paled but grabbed it from her. She was struck again by how young he was. And how much he looked like Carter.

"You'll be good," she falsely reassured him. "Remember what François said? There's something amiss, a disturbance. Use it to your advantage."

He nodded again. Charlie could tell he was trying to reassure himself. She wasn't convinced herself. She knew that it was a long shot that the kids got out. But a long shot was a still a shot. And the only one in the foreseeable future. Isaac gathered the six other kids around him. They all were terrified, but they stayed silent. Not even a sniffle. Charlie gave them a reassuring smile and handed Isaac François' key. Isaac took it and stared at her.

"Go," she said harshly. They had been in this long hallway way too long.

He stared her in the eyes and held out his hand. He looked so much like Carter in this moment Charlie took a visible step back. She gathered herself and took his hand, giving it a firm handshake.

"I hope to see you again," he said.

She smiled at him and nodded. "Get out of here."

Isaac turned with the children. He went a few steps then, looking back, he asked, "Who is my father?"

Charlie waited a moment. "Carter Green," she answered.

He nodded and ran down the dark concrete hallway, children in tow.

They would never see each other again.

Charlie turned away from their retreating shadows. She had a job to do. And hopefully she died doing it. She searched the fallen guards again. One started to stir and she elbowed him hard in the jaw. He fell back to the ground, unconscious, but her hand went numb again. She sighed and tried to ignore it. She took the other guard's baton. She contemplated taking his assault rifle but decided against it. If a shot rang out in the compound all the guards would come running. She wanted that, eventually, but she needed to distance herself from the kids first. She hoped that whatever the "disturbance" was, it was a long ways away from the kids as well. She stole his key card and she went down the hallway, the opposite way as Isaac, towards the room where Kelly died.

She had a rudimentary plan. She hated rudimentary plans. That was a Senka move. She felt a familiar pain in her chest when she thought about her dead partner. She hadn't thought of Senka in over a year. She'd been given a challenge and, after accepting it, all memories of Tomo and Senka had gone into a lock box in her mind. A lock box she didn't open.

But all of this change, all of this action, seeing Carter's son, had dredged up the key from the sludge of her mind and unlocked the door. Memories, thoughts, feelings that hadn't been dealt with flooded out into her mind. She didn't know for sure if Senka was actually dead. That's just what Alejandra had told her when she arrived at the compound. They had been lying to her about everything else, she hoped that they were lying about that too. She hoped Senka and Carter had finally gotten together and retired.

She slammed the door of her mental trap before the one person, her love, her everything, managed to escape. She couldn't think about her spouse right now, not when she was ready and willing to die. She absent-mindedly rubbed the empty ring finger on her left hand.

A door appeared on the left. She opened it with the key card and looked inside.

Broom closet. Damn.

She worked her way through rooms in the hallway. She found another janitor's closet, a bathroom and a small coffee room for guards.

No guards in sight.

Nothing of value.

Something was wrong here. She could feel it in her bones.

She reached another nondescript door and opened it with reckless abandon. She was getting tired of hunting for someone in this compound. She hadn't heard a sound in the compound since she ran away from the kids. Right now she didn't have a plan and that made her excessively uncomfortable. She needed enemies so she could make a plan.

Inside she found a beautiful office, red with gold highlights. It was smaller than the office that she was taken to where Kelly was killed, but it was more intimate and cozy. It had a beautiful oak desk and paintings on the walls.

Her eyes were immediately drawn to a display box behind the empty oak desk.

Those idiots had kept it here, in the same building as her.

They should have destroyed it.

She tilted her head back and laughed, a wicked smile coming to her face. She walked around the desk and looked at the glass box containing her katana. It was crafted especially for her by the master swordsmith Yoshindo Yoshihara. She had named it Makaze. Makaze was staring at her, beautiful. She had an untraditional black leather-wrapped hilt, a black scabbard and silver highlights. Makaze wasn't flashy. But she was so, so dangerous.

Makaze hadn't tasted blood in a long time. "I promise you that will change," she whispered to her sword.

She smashed the display box with the baton she had stolen then tossed it away. She didn't need it. She wasn't trying to be quiet. She wanted to draw a crowd. Glass fell around her feet.

Her hand hovered over the mounted sword for only a second. She slowly wrapped her fingers around the hilt and lifted the beautifully balanced blade from its prison.

She turned back to the desk and noticed a photo of Alejandra, arms wrapped around a young boy of perhaps five or six. In a fluid motion she unsheathed the fury of Makaze and cut the picture in half. It sliced it like butter, right across the middle. The picture stayed together for a moment, mother and son together. Then it fell apart and shattered.

Tomo lifted her head back and laughed again.

Kogo Tomo Hachiman, the Empress of Anzen, bloodthirsty defender of her people, was back.

And she was pissed off.

She heard the guards run down the hallway. Finally a battle. She walked to the middle of the room calmly. She kept Makaze unsheathed held out beside her. Makaze needed to draw blood before she was sheathed again. She stood motionless in the center of the room, waiting. The Empress of Death waited for them to come to her.

Three men burst through the door. They didn't have their guns raised, only batons out. They must still be on orders not to kill. She smiled at them. The amount of stupidity in the compound was absurd. They hesitated, batons at the ready.

"Jergen, Kurt," she said, nodding to the two familiar faces. She recognized the third man, but didn't know his name.

"Come quietly. We don't want to hurt you," Jergen said, German accent thick.

"Oh, my dear," she said with a wicked smile. "Don't you worry. You won't."

It was unfair, how easy it was. With swift movements, she kept her promise to Makaze. She didn't need to be as fast as Senka. Her movements were precise and deadly. Blood sprayed. The three men fell dead at her feet, throats cut. Makaze dripped blood onto the carpet from the tip. She wiped the blood from her eyes with the back of her hand.

She kept Makaze unsheathed.

She lightly stepped over the dead men and returned to the dim hallway. She continued moving lightly through the hallway but avoided running. She came to a T-junction, one she recognized from her trip to Freudman's office. She was getting closer to her goal.

Her only option was to fight until they killed her. She was happy that she would die feeling like Tomo.

She stopped in the middle of the T-junction and stayed there. She heard a low rumble down each of the three hallways.

Footsteps.

Lots of them.

Tomo didn't need to wait long. She positioned her back against the wall, facing the way she had just come. Guards came from all hallways, three across, guns raised. The hallway in front of her was led by Luc, her old lab assistant. Everyone here was some sort of ex-special agent from somewhere.

They stopped around six feet from her, nine in all, guns raised and pointed at her head.

"Nice of you to come for me personally," she said to Luc.

"Come quietly," Luc answered.

"No."

"Then you will die in this hallway. Our new orders are to kill you by any means necessary if you don't comply."

Tomo stayed still. She heard an odd sound coming from the

hallway to her left. It was a soft padding of feet, unlike any she had heard in this compound before.

"Should have destroyed the sword," Tomo said.

"Put it down and kneel," Luc said.

"You should probably just put a bullet in my head. I kneel to no one."

Tomo heard the muffled sound of a bullet being fired through a silencer. A man to her left slumped forward and fell flat on his face. She tried to supress the surprise. She heard two more silenced shots and the two other guards to her left fell forward. Luc finally caught on and yelled, "We're under attack! Defensive positions!" Another shot and the florescent light to her left exploded in a shower of sparks. The hallway to her left was smothered in complete darkness.

"Leo, go!" a woman yelled to her left.

Tomo was distracted and looked down the hallway, trying to make a figure out in the black. The slight distraction was enough time to allow Luc to rush behind her and hold his gun to her temple, using her as a shield.

"If you move I'll blow your fucking brains out," he whispered in her ear.

She wouldn't move. Burning curiosity fired through her, giving her something to live for.

Bullets started flying around her. The remaining men were shooting at a ghost just out of vision in the darkness of a hallway.

Two more fell beside her, shot in the head.

A man fell in a scream. A giant furry animal was hanging off his neck. The two others turned to fire at the animal and they both fell with bullets lodged in their heads.

"Call him off!" Luc yelled to the black hallway, the only one left alive. "Or I shoot her in the head." He was ducking behind her pressing his gun to the side of her head.

"Leo, come!" a voice, oh so familiar, yelled from the black. It couldn't be her. She must have misheard.

The giant furry creature, whom Tomo soon saw was a German Shepard, released the man he had mauled and ran back into the black hallway, blood dripping from his mouth.

"Show yourself!" Luc yelled from behind Tomo. She could feel the cool barrel pushing hard into the left side of her head. Her pulse was racing. She knew the voice. Acting on instinct, she suddenly moved her head to the right and a shot rang out. Tomo jumped and closed her eyes hard.

Luc fell dead behind her, bullet hole bleeding from the center of his forehead.

The woman strode into the light, dog by her side. She walked with a familiar cocky sway to her hips. She wore black cargo pants with a black shirt. She reloaded her sidearm and placed it back in her holster, piercing eyes never leaving Tomo's face. Tomo saw her whisper something, seemingly to no one.

Tomo was shocked. And by the look on Senka's face, she just as surprised. They stared at each other for ages. Both risen from the dead. It felt like an eternity.

Tomo was brought back to the last time she had seen her old partner's face. She was being dragged backward into the old truck in the middle of the jungle. Senka was on her knees in the dirt, eyes big as she watched Tomo being dragged away. Senka had been surrounded by armed men, guns raised. Tomo had been tossed in the back of the truck and that had been it.

They had told her that Senka was dead.

They stared at each other, eyes wide, mouths open. The dog stood beside Senka, tail wagging happily.

Finally, Senka smiled wide, ecstasy apparent all over her face. "You're getting slow in your old age!" she said loudly.

Tomo burst into tears.

30 SENKA

October 31, 2023, 04:28
Location: Dorfen, Germany.

Senka and Leo jogged quietly through the hallway. The only sounds were the light padding of Leo's feet and the buzzing of the fluorescent lights overhead. It was too quiet and Senka was on edge.

All the doors they encountered were unlocked. They appeared locked, with the red light glowing. But when any pressure was applied the lock unlatched and the door opened.

"I like your new trick," Senka said to Carter.

"Not me," he muttered back. "I can't access any of the security other than the cameras. It's weird, Sen. It's like they know all of my tricks and have firewalls pre-made to block them. Doing the best I can."

"I know you are," she said. She was in a maze of hallways. She decided to stay to the right. It all looked the same. The doors she opened were different rooms, mostly guard rooms, living quarters and offices. There was nothing that stood out. And there was no one around. Not a soul.

"Carter," she said carefully, "I think they might have known I was coming."

Silence.

"I have no idea how they would have. It was classified, like everything the ZTF runs." Carter said lowly. He was keeping his voice down.

"I know. But this is too easy," Senka said.

"Yah I hear you," Carter said. "But I refuse to believe there's a traitor in the ZTF." He was keeping his voice low in case someone was listening.

Senka shrugged, "Any chance you can inform Amanda without raising suspicion?"

"There's another explanation," Carter said fiercely. "There has to be. And Amanda is in her office sleeping. I'm going to leave her there considering your mission was recon only."

Senka was going to argue when Leo let out a low growl. Senka stopped moving as she heard it too. There was an L in the hallway to the left and around the corner she could hear voices down the hall. She couldn't make out what they were saying but she could hear them. They were muffled and sounded like an angry discussion between a man and a woman. She ran to the corner and peeked her head around. She could see the backs of three armed men running down the hall. They were dressed much like she was, with cargo pants and black sweaters. It was hard to see what they were running at, the florescent light in the hall didn't offer much help.

The men stopped and raised their guns. There were words and she could hear a woman reply.

She and Leo jogged softly down the hall. Senka raised her sidearm and quickly aimed and fired three shots in a row. All head shots, as always, and the men dropped like dominoes, guns clattering uselessly to the concrete floor. She fired at the florescent light and it exploded in a flurry of sparks. The hallway around her was plunged into total darkness. Only a woman with long red hair and six men, fully armed, were visible down the hallway. One was hiding behind the woman, holding a gun to her head.

"Leo, go!" she barked and without hesitation Leo took off towards the lone field light left in the hallway. Senka stood against the wall as a barrage of bullets were fired towards her. They weren't even close. She fired two more shots and two men dropped. Leo went for the throat of the third man. The other two guards started to raise their guns in the direction of her beloved German Shepard and she fired two more shots without thinking. Perfect head shots, and the men were dead before they hit the ground.

"Call him off!" the man holding a gun to the woman yelled. "Or I shoot her in the head!"

"Leo, come!" she yelled. Leo immediately peeled off the dead man and ran back towards her. She gave him a few pats on the head for doing a good job and lined up the shot. The man was hiding behind the woman but he was almost exposed. She just needed another inch.

The woman looked familiar, but Senka couldn't place her. She was obviously against these assholes, making her worth saving. *The enemy of my enemy is my friend*, Senka thought to herself, focusing her breathing and lining up the sight of her gun. *At least for now.* Carter stayed silent, watching through the tiny camera on her chest.

"Show yourself!" the man yelled. He was getting desperate. His dead comrades would be starting to bury into his psyche.

Senka smiled as she watched the man sweat. She was enjoying this. *Just an inch*, she thought to herself, *then I can kill that fucker.* The woman suddenly jerked to the right and Senka pulled the trigger. Perfect head shot. The man dropped like a stone.

She reloaded her gun and strode towards the woman. She must be in a Special Forces somewhere to know to move to clear the shot.

Senka saw her in better light and her heart dropped.

"Holy fucking shit. It's Tomo," she said lowly to Carter.

"What the hell you talking about?" Carter asked.

Senka's heart was beating so hard in her ears she could barely hear him. She should have known Tomo couldn't be killed that easily. A whole year and these assholes had her all along.

She immediately was brought back to the last time she had seen Tomo alive. In that wretched jungle. Senka was on her knees in the dirt, surrounded by gunmen. Tomo was being dragged viciously backwards towards the truck. Tomo was looking at her desperately, eyes pleading with her to do something. But Senka had no opening to move. They had tossed her roughly in the back of the truck and driven away. Taking Senka's partner, best friend, and heart with them.

Senka snapped back into the present and strode towards Tomo. It took everything in her power not to run. She saw Tomo recognize her and the shock that crossed her face.

"You're right!" Carter yelled in her ear. So loud she almost jumped. "Tomo's alive!" he yelled. "Someone tell Amanda! Tomo is alive!" she could hear other voices through the earpiece. There must be other handlers working this late as well.

She stopped and stared at her old partner. She looked terrible. She had on ripped jeans and a tattered blue sweater. Her hair was beautiful and long, contrasting her sunken eyes. Senka could never figure out how Tomo always kept her hair perfect. Tomo's sword was by her side, bloodied. Senka was surprised she still had it and knew it was a story for the bar later. Senka could see the gold chain Tomo never took off peeking out of the neckline of her sweater. Her skin was pale, like she hadn't seen the sun in years.

Senka didn't know what to say. She felt as though a piece of her soul had been missing. Now it was back, staring at her. Senka smiled broadly.

"You're getting slow in your old age!" she said loudly. She heard her voice crack a little and was surprisingly nervous.

She was shocked when Tomo burst into tears.

Senka rushed forward and drew Tomo into a bear hug. They weren't huggers. They tended to tease and laugh over things. Black humor was how they dealt. But Senka needed to touch her. Needed to know that she wasn't just a figment of her broken mind. She needed to know that Tomo was tangible. Was a real thing. And when she wrapped her in her arms and Tomo buried her head in her shoulder, she knew she was real.

They stood there for an eternity. Finally, Leo started licking Senka's hand and she gently released her friend. Tomo sniffled and wiped her eyes.

"Well that's embarrassing," Tomo said tensely.

"No, what's embarrassing is that you let yourself be surrounded by nine guys," Senka said with a laugh. Tomo punched her in the shoulder, hard enough that Senka took a step back. They both knew that Senka let her land the punch. "Ow!" Senka said. "Guess you haven't lost it all."

Tomo shot her an appreciative smile.

"Tell her I say hi!" Carter said in her ear excitedly.

Senka laughed. "Carter says hi."

Tomo smiled and looked Senka in the face, "Hi back, Carter."

"How?" Carter asked.

"Yah I'm curious too," she said. She could tell that Tomo looked jealous. Usually Carter would be talking to both of them. "Sorry, no backup earpiece." Tomo nodded. "How did you survive?" Senka asked. "We buried you."

"They tossed me in the back of a truck. You must have been chasing us, I never doubted that you got out of the situation I left you in," Tomo was talking fast. "At one point they took a hard right and I heard them shouting about a decoy. Then I heard an explosion. One of the guys hit me in the head after and I woke in a Sea Can headed here."

Senka put her head back and rubbed her face. She had lost the truck over a hill. They must have pulled a switch on the trucks. Tomo's truck went into the jungle, another drove out. Easy enough if you're organized.

"And who's this handsome man?" Tomo asked, bending down and covering Leo with pets. The dog panted and flipped on his back. Tomo laughed and rubbed his belly. "I suppose you deserve a belly rub after saving my life."

Senka shook her head. "You're pretty much a man whore, you know that, right Leo?" Leo looked towards her and let his tongue hang out of the side of his mouth in a happy, panting smile.

Senka rolled her eyes. "That's Leo. Just got him actually, but I love him."

Leo wiggled happily on his back. Tomo gave his belly a couple of pats before standing up again. Leo stayed on his back, looking at Tomo longingly.

"He's an idiot," Senka finished.

Leo sneezed and flipped himself back onto his stomach, giving Senka a sidelong glance and resting his head on his paws.

Tomo stood and stared at her. There was an awkwardness between them that had never been there before. So many emotions. So many heart aches. Nights spent crying alone, or drunk fucking a random guy. So many terrible nightmares. Because Tomo had been gone. And never coming back. Because she was dead and it was Senka's fault.

Now she was here, standing in front of her, with a tattered blue sweater and sunken eyes. But she was alive.

"You know I would have searched the world for you if I had known you were alive," Senka said softly.

Tomo nodded. "But didn't you? Why did you come here? You didn't get my message?"

Senka was suddenly confused. "What message?"

"I signed my research," Tomo said. She went beet red and said quietly, "I did terrible things, Sen." She hung her head. Senka saw a tear form and drop to the concrete floor.

"One step at a time. How did you sign your research?" Senka asked. Her heart went cold, her hands shook. The tingling, the bad feelings about the mission. It all started to make sense. She didn't want to believe it.

"C.B.Penn," Tomo answered, "my name, or most of it. It's how I always signed stuff in university." Senka took a full step back in shock. Tomo was confused. "Wait, that's not why you're here?"

"Carter, you didn't show anyone else?" Senka asked icily. She was staring at Tomo so coldly that it was her turn to take a step back.

"No," Carter said. She could hear the hurt in his voice. Senka's world was crashing around her. Leo sensed it and hopped to his feet, rushing to lick her hand. Trying desperately to help her find her center.

"Find Amanda!" Carter barked to someone else in the room.

Senka's heart slowed. It all seemed like slow motion. She had guessed there was a traitor but she didn't want to believe that it was Amanda. Amanda was her friend, her confidant. Her trainer. She was her idol, her role model. Senka loved her. She shook her head slowly, trying to make sense of it.

"Senka, what's wrong?" Tomo asked her.

"It seems your wife offered up a trade," Senka said quietly, venomously.

Shock crossed Tomo's face. "No," she said quietly, "no, Amanda wouldn't do that."

Senka was looking at Tomo with such hurt in her eyes that Tomo didn't know what to do.

"No," Tomo said forcefully. "Amanda wouldn't do that. Senka it has to be a mistake."

The world was rushing around her. Everyone had betrayed her. Her sheer exhilaration of seeing Tomo alive was wiped away with the pain of the betrayal. She shook her head, trying to clear it, but it didn't work. She shouldn't be surprised. Senka for Tomo. It made sense. She shook her head again but it didn't work.

"Senka!" Carter said loud enough to snap her out of it.

Senka looked at Tomo so coldly that Tomo took another step back.

"We can't find her," Carter said. "She's not in her office."

"Let's get you out of here," she said to Tomo coldly. "Your *wife* is waiting."

Senka jogged ahead, leaving Tomo behind her in a stunned silence. Leo nudged Tomo's hand. She gathered herself and chased after her old partner. Senka allowed her to catch up and they ran in silence, each trapped in their own heads.

They came to another T and Senka could hear them coming from one of the hallways.

"There are lots of them," Senka said to Tomo. "Take Leo," she said, gesturing to the German Shepard sitting loyally beside her. "There are some kids being kept here. I need you to find them. Take Leo and get out."

"No." Both Tomo and Carter at the same time.

"I already found them. They were headed towards the kitchens when I left them," Tomo said. "And yes, before you ask, Carter's son is alive. They have the same eyes. I figured it out pretty quickly." Realization crossed her face, "That's why you came?"

Senka heard a sigh of relief from Carter. Her eyes narrowed. "Why didn't you go with them?" completely avoiding the last question. "They are sitting ducks!"

Tomo shook her head. "I was making a distraction," she said. She averted her eyes and lowered her gaze. "I figured they would chase them harder if they knew I was with them."

That single look and blatant lie diffused all of Senka's anger. Tomo was proud. She had been an Empress of a country six times larger than Langundo in The Other Place. She averted her eyes to nothing. The humility rocked her to her core.

"You didn't want to make it out of here," Senka said softly.

Senka crouched to look Leo in the eyes. "Get out of here bud. Find a way out." Leo looked at her sadly and nudged her hand, whining. She gave him a good ear rub. "You're a good boy. The best. You did your job." Leo whined again and lay down, looking at her sadly. Big brown eyes staring with pure devotion.

She stood. She could hear the men running down the hallway. Tomo looked at her and nodded. They left the rest unspoken. Carter didn't need to know.

They went to leave and Leo sprang up, ready to follow. "Stay!" Senka said quietly. He huffed at her and sat on his butt. He let out a low cry.

"Why are you leaving Leo?" Carter asked.

"There's too many. He won't be of much use," Senka lied. She had one full clip and one in the chamber. Eleven bullets. Then the Tantos would be used. Tomo had kept Makaze unsheathed.

They nodded to each other, each lost in her own thoughts. Each had her own reasons to die. They turned and ran full speed down the hall to the T. The men were waiting to ambush on both sides. Senka couldn't count them all, they were wall to wall.

She fired all eleven shots as fast as she could as Tomo leapt into the middle of the fray, Makaze flashing. Blood spurted high in the air. Eight of the men dropped with head shots. She hit three in the chest. Tomo went high, Senka went low and they dove over each other. Senka dropped her gun and pulled her Tantos out mid roll. She came up swinging. She was enjoying it, being back with her partner. They moved in tandem, like the year gap had never happened.

Blood was spurting. Bodies were falling. Senka turned quickly and saw a guard raising his gun to Tomo's back, who was busy attacking three guards at once.

"Tomo!" she yelled and she pushed Tomo out of the way as the shot rang out.

Senka's left hand went dead. The Tanto dropped to the floor with a bang. Blood started pouring from a bullet hole in her bicep. She felt the warm sticky fluid flow down her arm and it started dripping off her hand. She saw the blood, then the pain exploded in her arm.

Tomo kept her feet after Senka pushed her. She spun quickly and caught the guard at the wrist. His hand was cut clear from his body. It fell, gun still in its grasp and clattered to the floor. The guard barely had time to register the shock at losing the limb. Tomo spun the other direction and cut his head off.

She looked at Senka worried. Senka saw her gaze shift to behind her and her look of surprise. Then Senka felt the barrel of a gun pressed to the back of her skull.

"Well, Dr. Penner, I think you know what we want you to do." A woman's voice behind her.

Tomo looked at Senka and smiled. She whispered something inaudible to Makaze and sheathed her, blood still on the blade.

"No! Tomo!' Senka said sharply. Nails dug into the bullet hole in her arm. Pain exploded and radiated upwards. She didn't scream, though she could have. Her knees went weak and she dropped to them. The gun stayed directly against her skull.

"No! You need to go see Amanda," Senka gasped. "You need to live happily ever after! You two deserve that."

The claws dug into her arm again. Senka almost blacked out with the pain and listed slightly to the left.

Tomo smiled sadly at Senka and held Makaze out in front of her. "We don't deserve happily ever after," she said quietly and dropped Makaze with a bang. "We haven't earned it." She raised her arms and two men approached and grabbed them. They wrenched them hard behind her back. Tomo was staring at Senka, eyes never leaving her face.

"I love you Amanda," Tomo said to the camera on Senka's chest. "I always have."

"How touching," the woman behind Senka said, bored. Senka felt the muzzle of the gun removed from the back of her head. Suddenly pain exploded in her head as the woman pistol whipped her skull. Stars erupted. She fell heavily to her right and landed on the cold concrete ground. She tried to keep conscious but the darkness drew her down. The last thing she saw was Tomo's concerned face as she struggled against the guards. Senka's head fell to the ground with a thump and darkness took hold.

31 SENKA

October 31, 2023, 04:42
Location: Dorfen, Germany.

Senka blinked herself awake but stayed motionless. Her head was killing her. She was laying on her side on a soft and comfortable red carpet. Her hands were tied behind her. Not shocking. She had no weapons. Also not shocking. As she focused she noticed two things that did surprise her.

The first thing was that Tomo was awake and alive and tied to a chair by her hands and ankles. Tomo hadn't noticed that she was awake. She was staring straight ahead, looking at something behind Senka.

The second was that, under the desk located in the corner of the office, two bright brown eyes stared at her.

Fucking dog never listens, she thought to herself. She wanted to be mad at him for disobeying her but she was so glad to see him. She had no idea how Leo had gotten into the room without being seen. Frankly she didn't care. Leo was here. That was all that mattered.

She waited to hear the crackle of Carter's voice in her ear but there was nothing. She moved slightly, announcing her consciousness. Her arm throbbed and she could feel the cool wet of blood as it dribbled slowly from the bullet hole.

"Ah! Our second guest has woken!" a man's voice said silkily from behind her. He had a distinct German accent. Senka guessed who it was. There was complete silence in her head and she realized that they must have taken her earpiece. She was on her own.

Not alone. She had been alone for the last year. Tomo was alive and Leo was here. She had all the help in the world.

She felt hands grab her roughly and pull her to her knees. Her arm screamed in protest and her head spun.

"Be nice to our guest, Alejandra," the man said behind them. "We don't want her to feel unwelcome."

The hands held her upright as she adjusted and let the world settle back into position. She felt nauseous. The back of her head was cool and she realized she must be bleeding from there as well. She was a mess.

Once she caught her bearings and was stable on her knees the hands let go. She was facing Tomo. Their eyes locked. Unspoken apologies were made.

"Now," the man said. He walked from behind Senka approaching Tomo. It was Freudman, red beard and all. A woman followed, dressed in a tailored suit. Senka was more than a little disappointed that she had gotten herself into a situation where a woman in a power suit and heels had pistol whipped her. *Something to laugh about later*, she thought.

"Let us have a discussion," Freudman continued.

"Get on with this," Senka said.

"We don't have all day," Tomo added.

Freudman looked surprised, "Somewhere better to be?" he stuttered slightly. Senka smiled. They had already thrown him off of his game.

"Should be a decent movie out," Senka offered.

"I was thinking coffee," Tomo said. "Been a while since my last Pumpkin Spice Latte."

"You and your Pumpkin Spice," Senka said.

"Better than drinking coffee black, you psychopath."

"Enough!" Freudman said loudly. This time Tomo smiled at Senka. They had gotten under his skin. Senka took the time to do a quick aura check. His was the darkest purple she had ever seen. So dark it looked almost like black ink. The woman's was red. "If you don't shut up, I will shut you up myself," Freudman continued.

"As long as you shut up with us," Senka muttered.

Alejandra stepped forward and stuck her thumb in the bullet hole in Senka's arm. She gritted her teeth as pain exploded up her arm again. It had almost clotted closed, but this had ripped it open again and blood poured over Alejandra's hand and down Senka's arm. Senka's head swam.

"Bitch!" Tomo yelled.

Senka was trying hard to keep conscious. She clenched her jaw and tried to breathe through her nose. Finally, after ages, Alejandra let her go. Senka nearly fell over but she kept to her knees. The world spun again and blood was flowing freely, dark red falling to the red carpet.

Alejandra stood and Freudman held out the handkerchief from his front pocket. She wiped her hands on it. Senka was impressed. Not a speck of blood had gotten on her suit.

"Now," Freudman said, "may we have our discussion?"

"Why?" Tomo asked, "We don't really care to be honest. We aren't making it out of here, you're smarter than us, blah blah blah. We have heard it all before and honestly it gets boring. Just do what you're going to do and let us get on with our day."

Freudman put his head back and laughed. "You will not get out of here to enjoy your day," he said. "I know you are used to escaping, but that stops here."

"Why is she here?" Senka asked suddenly. She needed some information and she hoped that by switching tactics she would catch him off guard. She still had the camera on, she could see it attached to her t-shirt, basically invisible to the naked eye. She also still had the microphone that was attached by a sticker to her neck. Carter should be able to see and hear everything even if he couldn't speak with her.

"What do you mean?" Freudman asked.

"Well I know that Amanda made a deal," Senka said. Tomo blanched and shook her head, but Senka continued. "My life for hers. Why is she still here?" Senka was buying time. She could tell by the feel on her wrists that they had bound her hands with zip-ties. She shifted her weight and did a quick assessment of her clothes. No guns or swords, but she felt the bulge of the pills in her right pocket and the small knife she kept tucked in the back of her jeans. She smiled to herself. The bitch in the power suit hadn't done her job.

Freudman laughed again. "My, my, you have already figured out my big reveal! Yes, Mrs. Nguyen traded your life for hers. But as you've killed many of my men, I believe our deal will be retracted."

Tomo paled even more.

"You basically let me in. You had to know I'd kill people when you made the deal. It was too easy. I knew it was a trap."

"Well maybe I changed my mind," Freudman said.

"So you're a liar," Senka said. She spat on the rich carpet. Freudman turned to her angrily. "Never trust a German," she said, staring him angrily in the eyes.

"I did not lie!" he exploded. "I had every intention of freeing her once we had you captured. But my employer wants both of you. I cannot deny my employer."

This caught Senka off guard. All the information they had gathered had pointed to Freudman as being the mastermind. Relief crossed Tomo's face.

"Don't get too cocky, my dear Zoya," he said to Senka. "You don't actually know much of what's going on here."

"Well then," Tomo piped up, finding her voice, "why don't you tell us?"

"What?" Freudman said to her. "No more plans for a Pumpkin Spice Latte?"

"We've rescheduled," Tomo said curtly.

"I think I would rather show her what you did," Freudman said looking at Tomo. This time Tomo paled from fear. Pure fear.

Senka was caught off guard. Tomo wasn't afraid of anything.

"How long has Amanda been in your pocket?" Senka asked. She had to know before they got too far off topic.

"Not long," Freudman said waving his hand. He walked towards his desk and grabbed something from the top. He didn't notice Leo lying patiently underneath, flattening himself as much as possible. "She approached me around a week ago offering the trade. Of course I took her offer. I had everything I needed from our dear Dr. Penner and I thought that my employer would enjoy your company." The way he said it made Senka's stomach roil but she felt a little better. Amanda hadn't been selling her out for long. A week. That's all. And after she discovered her wife was alive. It was a move of desperation, not malice. But Senka was still pissed off.

"I'm sorry," Tomo said to Senka.

"Not your fault," Senka said to her. "You didn't know about it. She's your wife, of course she's going to trade me for you."

"No," Tomo said. Senka could see that she was terrified and that scared her. They didn't deal in fear, but Tomo was showing it all over her face. "Not that," Tomo continued. "I'm sorry for everything else."

"What are you talking about?" Senka asked, confused.

"Oh do I sense dissention in the troops?" Freudman asked. "See this is why I love discussions. Before I tell you anything more I need you to answer a few questions."

Alejandra took a few steps toward Senka.

"No, not her," Freudman said. "She's been tortured before. She won't say anything." Alejandra nodded and made her way towards Tomo.

Senka was surprised. Her experiences in The Other Place were classified to the ZTF. And Amanda wouldn't have given that information out to anyone, even if she was a traitor.

"Probably won't be necessary," Senka spat. "I was set-up, remember? My boss traded me for that bitch. I'm feeling generous with my information at the moment." She must lie with everything she had.

Freudman nodded, "We will see how much information you're willing to give," he said. "Alejandra will be ready just in case. Now, tell me, how did you find our compound?"

"Broke into that asshole Viktor's compound a couple weeks back," Senka said. She didn't need to lie about that. "I hacked your servers."

Freudman nodded but he looked angry. "Funny, did Viktor ever tell you there was a break-in at his compound?" he asked Alejandra. She shook her head.

Senka smiled grimly. Turn these fuckers on each other.

"Why did you come to this compound?" Freudman asked.

"Tracked a couple of kids from Toronto," Senka said. "You don't come on to our turf and steal our kids. Not allowed."

Freudman shrugged. "People steal children all of the time. You caught me, but thousands of others are stolen and removed or subjected to worse in their own country."

Senka gritted her teeth, "Anyway, it got you caught."

"What about any other hidden folders on that server?" Freudman asked, "Did you gain access to those?"

Senka feigned confusion. "All we found were some files on this compound and a list of kids you've taken. I have no idea what you're talking about." She saw relief flood across his face. *Carter you genius*, she thought.

"Good," Freudman said, "that's all I need." He turned to Alejandra and nodded. She smiled and punched Tomo in the face.

"Hey! Fuck you man!" Senka yelled. "I didn't lie about anything!"

"I know," Freudman answered, smiling, "but Alejandra has wanted to do that for a long time." He turned towards Tomo. "Now it's your turn to be honest," he said.

Alejandra rose and went and stood beside Senka. This time she took a gun out and placed it to the side of her head.

"If you lie to her once," Freudman said, "Alejandra will make sure her brains stain my carpet. Is that clear?"

"Why are you doing this?" Tomo asked. Her voice was muffled from the blood that was coming from her nose.

"Call me old-fashioned," Freudman said, "but I would love to be the one who destroys this partnership. It will make me feel good. So many have tried, and I will succeed." He nodded towards Senka. "Tell her."

Tomo looked at Senka for a long time.

"I don't have all day," Freudman said impatiently. "I actually have plans. Tell her so that when she gets to The Other Place she can hate you as much as I do."

"I made a pill," Tomo said.

Senka waited patiently. She had managed to flip the knife open behind her and was maybe a quarter of the way through the zip-ties.

"Tell her what it does," Freudman said.

"It makes…" Tomo paused. She collected herself. "It makes Zoya."

Senka was so shocked she forgot to keep working on the zip-tie. "You made a pill that does what now?"

"It… It makes Zoya. It sends people to The Other Place."

Senka stared at her.

"But I don't actually know if it does," Tomo said hurriedly. "Yes, the brain wave pattern is the same but I don't know how we can confirm…" She trailed off.

"Yes, I can confirm," Freudman said. He looked quite pleased with himself. "They die here and wake up there," he said. "Quite fascinating. Never been documented."

"How?" Senka asked. Her head was reeling. "That's not possible. It's not even known why some people in comas get to The Other Place and others don't…" Senka trailed off, confusion muddling her thoughts.

"Well," Freudman said speaking up, "you get the smartest woman to figure it out." He smiled at Tomo. She hung her head. The blood from her face dripped slowly onto her knees.

"I don't believe you," Senka said firmly. "You die here you die over there. That's what happens. You can't just wake up in The Other Place and be dead here."

Freudman smiled. "Well, our dear Dr. Penner figured it out! And trust me when I say the Zoya over there are very much alive. We've sent," he looked at Alejandra, who shrugged. "Damn near ten people over so far. And I can attest that they are very much dead here and alive in The Other Place."

"There's no possible way that you could know if they were alive in The Other Place," Senka said.

Freudman laughed. "My dear, speed and intelligence are not the only Zoya tricks. And as we're all Zoya in this room I would say that there are quite a lot of hidden talents."

"What's yours?" Senka asked Alejandra. She was beyond being surprised anymore. She needed to keep one of these people alive to get answers, and she knew which one it would be.

"That's for me to know," she answered softly.

"Quite a rude and personal question, actually," Freudman said. "Now! I have had enough of our little chat. And quite frankly I have been dying to do this." He walked toward Tomo swiftly. "Think of this as retribution for what you've done." He forced her jaw open and pulled open the bottle of pills he had grabbed off the desk. He popped it open and poured it into her mouth. He then forced her mouth closed and held it.

Tomo looked terrified. She coughed and fought but she eventually swallowed.

"No!" Senka yelled. She tried to break the zip-tie but she hadn't cut through enough. She tried to spring to her feet but Alejandra was there, thumb in her bullet wound, forcing Senka back to the ground. Pain exploded but Senka didn't close her eyes. She needed to watch.

Tomo was struggling against the chair but it held her too tight. She was looking around white-faced. She knew what was going to happen.

Senka calmed herself through the pain. She stared at Tomo and tried to stay as calm as possible. She willed Tomo to look at her. When Tomo finally did they locked eyes. She saw Tomo calm immediately. They looked at each other with love. Pure, undying love. A few seconds later Tomo's eyes rolled back into her head and she started shaking violently, foaming at the mouth. Senka didn't look away. She just looked at her partner with soft eyes. Her heart broke as she watched her best friend die, again. She watched her chest stop moving. It seemed so unfair that they would be reunited just to be torn apart again.

"No!" Freudman yelled suddenly. He pulled Tomo's shirt to the side, exposing the dragon necklace that Tomo always wore. The gold one with the ruby. He struggled to pull it off but Tomo went limp. The necklace disappeared as Tomo died.

"No!" he yelled. He kicked at the chair. Turning violently to Alejandra he yelled, "Tell me she was afraid when she died!"

Alejandra shook her head. "She made eye contact and it changed from fear."

Freudman yelled, "You were supposed to search her! How did she even get the necklace into the compound in the first place?"

Alejandra shrugged.

Senka was confused. She was barely listening. The pain and emotional toll was starting to drag her down to the blessed release of darkness. The relief of finding Tomo, Amanda's betrayal, the loss of Tomo were too close together. The pain in her arm was taking over. She could hear Freudman ranting about something. She was numb to everything. She hadn't dealt with losing Tomo the first time, this was too much. She felt the weight of Jules' ring around her neck, as she always did when she was stressed. She missed him.

"No matter," Freudman said suddenly. "She has crossed, even if it is to the wrong location. I'll inform Roald of the change. He will be able to fix it." He walked swiftly towards the door at the back of the room. "Kill her."

Alejandra looked at him, confused. "But... Our orders?"

Freudman shook his head, "Kill her. The other one went to the wrong spot. We don't need two of them uncontrolled in The Other Place. I'll deal with Roald. I've had enough of your failings for one day. Don't follow me." He strode from the room.

Alejandra nodded, lips pursed, face white. She stepped back from Senka. She didn't want to get her suit dirty. She cocked the gun. Senka was calm. It would finally be over. She'd finally be able to sleep.

Leo exploded from beneath the desk. Senka was as surprised as Alejandra. In all the action she had forgotten he was there. He ran as hard as he could across the room.

"No!" Senka yelled.

Leo launched himself at Alejandra and a shot rang out. Alejandra screamed. They fell to the ground in a heap. Senka exploded upwards. In pure strength of will she broke the zip-tie that was holding her wrists and ran towards them.

"No, no, no!" she yelled. She pulled Leo off of Alejandra. He had gotten her in the neck. It was bleeding freely but Senka could tell it wasn't fatal. Alejandra was stunned, clutching her bleeding neck. The gun had been knocked from her hand. Senka was far more concerned about Leo. She fell to her knees and flipped him onto his side, laying his head on her lap.

"No, Leo," she started crying. He was breathing heavily. The shot had hit him right in the chest, missing the vest. "I told you to stay. I told you to get out." His big brown eyes looked at her with pure love. She rubbed his head. "You're a good boy," she said softly between tears. "You're such a good boy."

Leo licked her hand. His tail wagged against the floor, making a slow thump. Senka cuddled against his neck. She had flashes of them running together at the start of the mission. Of her waking up in the ZTF hospital and Leo being by her side. They had barely known each other then, but he had waited, knowing she would need a familiar face when she woke.

"I wish we had a lifetime together," she sobbed into his fur. She was trying to memorize his smell, the soft texture of his fur. One week together seemed so cruel. It was so much more than a week in her mind. He was her heart. He was her everything.

Leo's wagging tail slowed to a stop and rested against the floor. He licked her hand one last time, big brown eyes looking at her for her support. "I'm here buddy," she sobbed. "I'm not leaving you," her voice cracked. He let out a soft whine and his breathing slowed to a stop.

"Oh Leo," Senka sobbed, weeping freely. She buried her head in his fur and held him against her body, rocking and crying. The same way they would sit after her terrible nightmares. His head in her lap, comforting her through her worst times. Now he was gone, and Senka felt the last good in her soul go with him.

Senka gently laid Leo's head to the concrete beside her and rose. She gave him a last pet around the ears, just as he liked, and stood up. She wiped the tears from her face. Her heart turned to stone. She was pure anger. It filled her soul. She was calm, ice cold. She bent and picked up Alejandra's gun. Her left hand was still useless.

She knew she needed to keep Alejandra alive. They needed answers.

Senka didn't care.

She walked up to Alejandra, who was still lying on the ground, writhing in pain. She was holding a hand to her throat, trying to stop the bleeding.

Senka stepped on her throat. She relished the bulge of Alejandra's eyes as she leaned on her neck. Alejandra wrapped both hands around her boot and tried to push up. Fear. She was pure fear. Senka was loving every moment.

Senka leaned harder, putting more pressure. Alejandra was gasping for air, writhing against the ground. Alejandra tried to shake her head. She was pushing up on Senka's boot, trying to survive, desperately trying to get air in her lungs. Senka leaned harder and aimed the gun at her head, making sure the safety was off.

"I'll... Tell you... Everything," Alejandra gasped through sucking breaths.

"Fuck you," Senka said.

She pulled the trigger.

32 SENKA

October 31, 2023, 04:51
Location: Dorfen, Germany.

Senka's chest was heaving. She should feel guilty. It was the first time she had taken a life out of pure revenge. She should have kept her alive. They needed information.

She didn't feel guilty. She didn't feel anything.

Bitch had killed her dog.

Senka removed her boot from Alejandra's throat and frowned. She had brain matter on the bottom of her pants. She shook her leg a bit, trying to get the sticky grey substance off her pants but it was no use.

Senka didn't look at the carnage of the room. She didn't need to see her dead best friend again, head rolling, tied to a chair. She didn't need to see loyal, wonderful, beautiful Leo. She needed to remember them alive and vibrant. Not what this place had made them.

She squared her shoulders.

Time to kill the fucker that had caused it all.

She didn't even look for her earpiece. She knew she would be removed from the ZTF and most likely arrested if she got out of here. She had killed a very viable and valuable piece of information. She didn't care. She was going to finish this, then face the consequences later. If she even lived to face the consequences.

Her left arm was useless but the blood had stopped flowing.

She checked the clip of the gun she had stolen from Alejandra. Ten left. Plenty of bullets to get the job done.

Without a backwards glance, Senka strode through the door.

She heard the click of the trip wire.

"Fuck."

She started to turn away. An explosion rocked the hallway in front of her, blowing her back through the door.

She landed hard on her back. The remnants of the fireball dissipated overhead. There was pain everywhere. She could feel burns on her face and arms. She tried to breathe but her lungs were crushed from the explosion. The golden ring Jules had given her had burned into her chest. She could smell her own flesh burning. The sickly smell of meat burning on a bar-b-que.

She smiled to herself, gritting her teeth through the immeasurable pain.

The end was near.

"You can't give up that easily," a new voice piped up from in the room.

Confused, Senka painfully raised her head to look. The fire alarm was going off and there was a red light blinking in the room. Sprinklers were raining water down from the ceiling. The room was in shambles, destroyed by the explosion. Sitting cross-legged on the wreckage of the oak desk was a woman. Her eyes were totally black, no whites visible at all. She had dark skin and was dressed like a Melanthios.

A Melanthios in this world?

Senka chuckled to herself, *at least I'll die crazy*, she thought. She wouldn't have been able to speak if she wanted to, her face was too burnt.

The Melanthios woman smiled and snapped her fingers. Time slowed. Senka could tell by the sprinklers. The water started falling in slow motion.

"You're not crazy," the Melanthios woman said.

Senka couldn't speak. Not without her lungs.

"My name is Black Eyes," the woman said. "Tory sent me."

Senka was in too much pain to be surprised. *Black Eyes? What a weird name,* she thought.

Black Eyes laughed, "Not my original one, to be sure. I was given it after my death by the hands of your friend. I liked it so I kept it."

You're dead?

"Yes, I'm dead. But unfortunately still part of existence. Don't ask me how that works," Black Eyes shrugged. "But I've learned not to question this kind of thing."

How?

"Your friend Tory is becoming quite powerful," Black Eyes said. "She's the daughter of a Zoya. She's going to do amazing things. As to be expected, I'm sure."

I don't understand, Senka thought. *I just want to die.*

"Pussy," Black Eyes said. "I told Tory you'd be too scared to come back. But Tory sent me anyway."

I'm not afraid... I just...

"Don't want to deal with the hurt anymore," Black Eyes finished for her. "Listen, kid, it doesn't get any better. There's hurt everywhere. Apparently even after you die." Black Eyes shrugged. "But I've had a weird time in the afterlife. Not sure if being attached to Tory is normal."

Senka lowered her head. She just wanted to sleep. She didn't understand half of what Black Eyes was talking about and she didn't care.

"Look, kid," Black Eyes said. Senka was annoyed. Black Eyes looked to be around the same age as her.

Who you calling kid? she thought.

Black Eyes laughed, "There's the spunk Tory was talking about. I was starting to wonder. Anyways we need you back. If you don't come back, both worlds will burn."

How do I get back?

Black Eyes was starting to fade. "Seems to me that you guys over here have already answered that question." She snapped her fingers again. Time went back to normal. Water started raining around her. She heard Black Eyes' voice over the falling water, "Oh, and do me a favor. Die angry."

Senka raised her head again. She would be dead soon. She had to hurry. She fumbled in her pocket and pulled out a baggie of those

271

pills that Tomo had created. Thinking of Tomo made her angry. She pulled the bag open with her teeth. Her burnt hand wasn't working well. She poured the pills into her mouth and chewed.

They tasted chalky and acidic. She forced herself to finish chewing them and to swallow. They hurt going down her burnt airway. She thought of Tomo. She thought of Leo. She let anger flow through her. The icy, slow burning anger. She would destroy them all. Her world faded to black. It didn't hurt as much as she thought it would. She could feel her body convulsing against the floor. She felt her mouth foam. She faded.

A flash of white.

Then nothing.

33 CARTER

October 30, 2023, 23:48
Location: Toronto, Canada.

Carter barked the order to find Amanda then watched it all, slack-jawed. He was ecstatic when they found Tomo alive. The ecstasy switched to fear when he saw Senka take the bullet to the arm and get knocked out. He watched, through Senka's camera, Tomo die again. He was sitting there, useless, helpless. This time Tomo was really dead and there was no going back, no helping. He saw it with his own eyes.

The other handlers had started gathering around his desk, watching with him. News had travelled fast and everyone had woken and come to watch with him. Handlers stayed at the ZTF headquarters when their Zoya were on missions. Every Zoya was out right now so all the handlers were there with him, watching. Kevin, Simone's handler, put his hand on Carter's shoulder in reassurance as Tomo was force fed the pills.

"They have to be lying," Leslie said.

Carter shook his head slowly, "If Tomo designed them, they aren't lying."

"This will change everything," Kevin said.

They watched Tomo die.

"Any eyes on Amanda?" Kevin asked. Carter couldn't pull it

together. He saw the woman raise her gun to Senka's head. *This is it*, he thought, *I'm going to lose them both at the same time.* There was no answer from anyone. They only had eight Zoya in the task force if you included Tomo. The loss of one was devastating, the loss of two in one mission was unprecedented.

Carter's heart leapt when he saw Leo spring up from under the desk to attack Alejandra. There were gasps from the other handlers and Kevin squeezed his shoulder. Then they watched as Leo died. Carter could feel tears falling. Leslie, Matty's handler, was sniffling beside him.

Senka stood. Carter watched her stoop and grab the gun.

"Oh, shit," Kevin said breathlessly.

Carter knew that Senka didn't have the earpiece in, but he needed to try.

"No!" he yelled into the microphone. Senka wouldn't hear him. "Sen no! Put it down and walk a–" He was silenced when Senka pulled the trigger.

"Not good," Leslie said through sniffles.

"What's she doing?" Kevin asked.

Carter could only stare at the bullet hole in Alejandra's head, almost mesmerized. Senka had given it all up for revenge. He hoped, selfishly hoped, that she would take the camera off and disappear. That way he wouldn't have to arrest her for treason.

Senka walked through the door and was blown back by an explosion.

This time Leslie audibly screamed. The other handlers gasped.

Carter couldn't breathe. He couldn't think. He could only see from the small camera. He had no idea how hurt Senka was. He saw the camera move and lurch and knew that Senka was writhing in pain.

"Not both," he whispered. "Please, God, not both."

Kevin dug his hand into Carter's shoulder, but there was no comfort to be had.

He heard the words, "Die angry," drift to him from his speakers, so low that later, when he replayed the day over and over, he convinced himself he made it up. He watched Senka struggle with the pills in her pocket. Her burnt arm entered the camera and his heart broke. She was so hurt. He knew she must be in excruciating pain. He saw her raise the pills to her mouth. The camera bounced a little as she seized. Then they were left with a still picture of the ceiling.

Tomo was dead.

Leo was dead.

Senka was dead.

Carter sat there stunned. He was left without his team. His family. They were all gone.

"What do you want to do now, boss?" Kevin asked quietly. Carter didn't listen to him, he sat there, staring at Senka's camera feed.

"Boss?" Leslie asked. She put a hand gently on Carter's arm, snapping him out of it. Carter realized they were talking to him. Amanda had committed treason. He was the next in command. The Zoya Task Force was his.

He turned his chair. Kevin and Leslie were there, along with Pierre, Cathy, John and Ram. They were staring at him, faces as white as his was.

"Find me Amanda," he said angrily, pushing his way out of his chair. "Number one priority." He walked towards Amanda's glass office. *Your office now*, he thought to himself. He stopped for a second with his hand on the door. He steeled himself then pushed the door open.

The room was immaculately kept, as always. Steel meeting table in the middle, big enough to fit all sixteen of the ZTF. The couch to the side was untouched. Amanda hadn't slept here at all. She could have been gone for hours, sneaking out when Senka was watching the compound.

Before his life had changed forever.

He opened the blinds. The handlers were gone, combing the building for any signs of Amanda.

He doubted they would find any. She was gone for good.

The desk was clean. He looked around for her tablet but it was gone. The safe behind the desk was left open. There was a sticky note on the combination. Carter peeled it off and read:

8-1-6-4

That was it. Nothing else. Just the combination to the safe. No apology, no explanation. Just a cleaned out desk and a combination.

Carter kicked the chair angrily. He leaned on the desk, catching his breath.

Kevin burst into the office. "We found her," he said breathlessly.

"Where?" Carter asked, surprised.

"On the roof," Kevin said.

"Shit," Carter said. He ran to his desk and grabbed the sidearm he kept there. He wasn't out in the field often but he could still shoot relatively straight.

"Send backup," he called to Kevin, heading towards the staircase. "Clear the street below."

"What's her endgame?" Kevin shouted as Carter raced for the stairs.

"She doesn't have one!" Carter yelled back.

Carter's heart was racing as he ran up the stairs, two at a time. It was eight floors to the roof of the building. He barely felt the passage of time. He pounded up the steps to the roof access. The padlock that locked the roof access had been recently cut.

Carter kicked it open and pointed his gun. He was greeted with the sight of Amanda, facing him, sitting on the ledge of the building. The cool night air blew her hair across her face. All she had to do was lean back and she was gone. She was looking down at her tablet. Carter could see she had been crying.

"Amanda!" Carter barked. He trained his gun on her.

She looked up at him slowly. "Didn't think you'd make it here."

"Amanda, step forward from the ledge."

She smiled sadly at him and looked down at her tablet again. "I didn't want any of this."

"I know that," Carter said. He lowered his gun. This required delicacy. He was so on edge from watching his team die that he didn't know if he could do it.

"I just... I just saw her signature. I panicked," she said. She sobbed so hard it wracked her whole body. "I thought she was dead. And they had her." She looked at him again, tears falling fast. "I just wanted to get her back."

"You should have told us," Carter said angrily. He shouldn't be angry right now but he couldn't help it. It just bubbled over. "You should have told us!" he yelled. "We could have gotten her out together! All of us!" He was trying to yell and drift his way towards her. He needed to get closer.

Amanda shook her head, "No, no they would have killed all of us."

"They did!" Carter yelled. "They killed them both! Your deal didn't matter. You can't deal with the devil!"

Amanda sobbed again and looked at her tablet. "I know. I watched it. I watched her die Carter."

Carter shook his head angrily. He had no words.

"You would have done the same," Amanda said softly, "if it was Melanie. If it was her there, you would have done anything you could to see her again."

Carter shook his head. "No, Amanda. I would have trusted Senka. She never once let us down. You knew she'd go in for my son. Even if you told her only to recon you knew!" He was screaming again, he couldn't help himself. "She wanted to help me! You used it against her!"

Amanda smiled sadly. She leaned back.

"No!" Carter yelled. He ran forward as fast as he could, dropping his gun with a clatter to the ground. Amanda dropped the tablet to the roof and fell backwards. Carter launched himself as far over as he could as she fell. He stretched out and caught her wrist with his right hand and managed to keep his feet planted on the other side of the ledge. He grunted as he took the force of the building into his stomach, but he held firm. A shocked Amanda was clawing at his wrist, trying to make him let go.

"We lost the rest of our family," he grunted through the strain. Amanda stopped clawing and stared up at him. "I'm not losing you too," he said and he pulled with all of his might. His brute strength came through and he lifted Amanda over the ledge.

They dropped to the roof gasping. The military backup that Kevin had sent burst on to the roof.

"Arrest her," Carter said gasping from his back. The men, dressed in camouflage, ran up and flipped Amanda on to her stomach, handcuffing her. Another man came and helped Carter to his feet.

Amanda didn't struggle. She let them haul her to her feet. She was crying silently, keeping her eyes down.

"Wait," Carter said. He walked angrily towards Amanda. She

flinched back, expecting a blow. Instead, Carter wrapped her in a hug. "I'll visit you every day I can," he whispered in her ear.

Amanda sobbed into his shoulder.

Carter broke away and nodded to the men guarding her. They nodded back and marched her away.

Carter bent to pick up the tablet. On it was the picture of Amanda's and Tomo's wedding day. It was the four of them, Carter and Senka in jeans flanking Amanda and Tomo in wedding dresses. All four of them were beaming at the camera. Carter remembered that Melanie had been the one taking the picture. He sighed and pressed the power button on the side of the tablet. The picture flickered off and the tablet went black.

Carter made his way back down to the ZTF headquarters. The handlers had all returned from their man hunt. They waited nervously in Amanda's office. *My office*, Carter reminded himself. It would take some getting used to.

"Ok," Carter said loudly to the silent room as he walked through the door. He was ashamed that his voice was hoarse from yelling. He walked over and put the tablet on the desk. "I want all Zoya pulled out of their missions, quietly. No blown covers, no more deaths, understood?" All the handlers nodded. "Good. We will all be working together to take these guys down."

"Who are these guys?" Kevin asked.

"Good question. I have no idea. We had no confirmation anyone else knew about Zoya before thirty minutes ago. Leslie, is Matty still close to Munich?"

Leslie nodded. "Yah and he can pull out anytime. No worry on his cover."

"Good, send him to the compound. We need boots on the ground there as soon as possible."

Leslie nodded and started typing away on her tablet.

"We are going to assume that the pills actually sent the women back to The Other Place," Carter said. Leslie stopped typing and stared. Everyone looked shocked.

"No way," Kevin said. "That's impossible. They're dead, Carter. I mean I don't want to believe it either, but they're dead."

Carter nodded, "But Tomo was the one who made them. She's never been wrong before. So we're going to assume that they worked. So there is something big going on here between our world and The Other Place. We need to figure out why they want more Zoya. Hopefully the girls are safe there and are trying for the same thing. We will hit them from this side as hard as possible, making it easier for them to hit them there."

All the handlers nodded, lost for words.

"So I need everyone on research. I want to know everything about Zoya ever written. Ever," he said. "Every piece of research, every legend that might somewhat apply, from any culture ever. We also need access to the Ampulex folder on the server. That asshole Freudman was especially worried about it, making it high priority."

The handlers could only stare. The amount of work was daunting.

"Speaking of Freudman," Carter said, "I want everything on him from every country. I want to know where he shits, where he eats, how he blow-dries his hair, what brand of toothpaste he uses. Absolutely everything. And I want someone to go over the video from Senka's camera feed with a fine-toothed comb. I want to have my own discussion with that asshole."

"Sir!" Ram piped up. Carter looked at him, annoyed at the interruption. "The Joint Task Force 2 evac you sent are close to scene. They want you to have a look at this," Ram said quickly.

"Put it up on the screen," Carter barked.

Ram nodded and sent the helicopter feed to the main screen. The helicopter was hovering over a group of kids in the middle of a field.

"They are about a kilometer away from the compound," Ram said.

Carter stared silently at the screen. His son was waving his arms overhead to the helicopter. There were six other much younger children cowering behind him. But Isaac was standing, unafraid. They were dirty and looked hungry and exhausted but they were alive. They had made it out alive. Senka and Tomo had provided enough of a distraction that Isaac had found a way out.

"Evac them to the nearest military base," Carter said through a dry mouth.

"Let's get those kids home."

KATE SANDER

EPILOGUE - SENKA

The smell came first.

It was a wet smell, musty. It smelled of a forest after the rain. There was no human smell to it. No exhaust or plastic smell that permeated everything in her world.

The sensation of breathing through her nose came next. She was lying in something damp and warm. It felt like grass.

Senka opened her eyes. There was no sun above her, just towering trees. She sat up slowly. Her head swam. She breathed the musty air and looked around.

She was in a rainforest.

Trees surrounded her thickly with moss growing over their trunks. She could hear the buzz of insects around her.

She was confused. There was no forest like this in Langundo.

Realization hit her.

She remembered everything. From both worlds. She remembered her time in Langundo. She remembered her time in Canada.

She knew she was in The Other Place but she didn't know where she was.

She looked down. She was naked except for Jules' ring laced around her neck on a chain.

A deep, vibrating sound echoed in the forest. She sprang up. Her hand went directly to her side, where her sidearm usually sat. She was naked. There was no gun.

"Shit," she said out loud.

She was confused about why she could remember anything at all. The last time she'd woken in The Other Place she'd had no memories, just a blank slate. She didn't know where she was. She hadn't heard of a forest like this from any Zoya she'd ever met. And she was unarmed. Not a good combination.

The air was hot and sticky, she was sweating already.

The call sounded again, this time closer. It reverberated off the trees around her and sent fear into her stomach.

Something didn't like that she was here.

The smell of rotting flesh suddenly started assaulting her nose. She gagged and tried not to vomit. It was overwhelming.

She heard some grass rustle and spun around.

A huge animal stepped into the clearing. It was easily ten feet tall. It looked like an elk, except it was walking on its hind legs upright. It was muscular and its huge arms dragged against the ground, its arms ending in claws instead of hooves. Its head was a huge mess of matted fur and blood. Antlers protruded from its head at odd angles. It sniffed with his nose and blood dribbled out of its snout.

It fixed its eyes on Senka again. It roared, so loud it took everything for Senka not to cover her ears. Its body language changed and it lowered its shoulders. Senka knew it was going to charge. Her hand went automatically for her sidearm before she could stop it.

The thing roared and charged her angrily, dropping to all fours. It was faster than its hulking size and massive presence indicated.

As she dove out of the way of the massive animal, she had time to mutter one word.

"Shit."

KATE SANDER

ACKNOWLEDGMENTS

This book took plenty of rewrites, edits, tears and sleepless nights.

Big shout out again to Sharon for Beta reading and figuring out the prologue for me when I was so far off.

Alanna McIntyre for her detailed editing, even when she thought it would make me cry. Takes a true friend to call you out on hard truths.

Of course and always my mother, Mary, for the constant guidance and emotional support. Also her edits and the way she deletes commas. No one deletes commas with such vigor as my mother.

And finally my sister and father. My family always supports me and truly allows me to dream big.

ABOUT THE AUTHOR

Kate Sander is a Primary Care Paramedic and lives in her hometown of Prince Albert, Saskatchewan, Canada. She lives with her husband Aaron, their four-year old Labradoodle named Sammi and one-year old Goldendoodle named Pippin. She prides herself on being a geek and enjoys pizza and beer. If you want to talk books, movies, beer or anything and everything geeky, email Kate at katesander.author@gmail.com or talk to her on twitter @K_sander10. Check out **www.zoyabooks.com** for all your Zoya Chronicles updates and merchandise needs.

Made in the USA
Columbia, SC
02 July 2017